Gloriana; Or, the Revolution of 1900

Gloriana; Or, the Revolution of 1900

Lady Florence Dixie

MINT EDITIONS

Gloriana; Or, the Revolution of 1900 was first published in 1890.

This edition published by Mint Editions 2021.

ISBN 9781513299921 | E-ISBN 9781513223483

Published by Mint Editions®

MINT
EDITIONS

minteditionbooks.com

Publishing Director: Jennifer Newens
Design & Production: Rachel Lopez Metzger
Project Manager: Micaela Clark
Typesetting: Westchester Publishing Services

Contents

Preface

"Thus we were told in words Divine
That there were truths men could not bear
E'en from the lips of Christ to hear.
These have now slowly been unfurled,
But still to a reluctant world.

"Prophets will yet arise to teach
Truths which the schoolmen fail to reach,
Which priestly doctrine still would hide,
And worldly votaries deride,
And statesmen fain would set aside."

I make no apology for this preface. It may be unusual but then the book it deals with is unusual. There is but one object in "Gloriana." It is to speak of evils which Do exist, to study facts which it is a crime to neglect, to sketch an artificial position—the creation of laws false to Nature—unparalleled for injustice and hardship.

Many critics, like the rest of humanity, are apt to be unfair. They take up a book, and when they find that it does not accord with their sentiments, they attempt to wreck it by ridicule and petty, spiteful criticism. They forget to ask themselves, "Why is this book written?" They altogether omit to go to the root of the Author's purpose; and the result is, that false testimony is often borne against principles which, though drastic, are pure, which, though sharp as the surgeon's knife, are yet humane; for it is genuine sympathy with humanity that arouses them.

There is no romance worth reading, which has not the solid foundation of truth to support it; there is no excuse for the existence of romance, unless it fixes thought on that truth which underlies it. Gloriana may be a romance, a dream; but in the first instance, it is inextricably interwoven with truth, in the second instance, dreams the work of the brain are species of thought, and thought is an attribute of God. Therefore is it God's creation.

There may be some, who reading "Gloriana," will feel shocked, and be apt to misjudge the author. There are others who will understand, appreciate, and sympathise. There are yet others, who hating truth, will receive it with gibes and sneers; there are many, who delighting in the evil which it fain would banish, will resent it as an unpardonable attempt against their liberties. An onslaught on public opinion is very like leading a Forlorn Hope. The leader knows full well that death lies in the breach, yet that leader knows also, that great results may spring from the death which is therefore readily sought and faced. "Gloriana" pleads woman's cause, pleads for her freedom, for the just acknowledgment of her rights. It pleads that her equal humanity with man shall be recognised, and therefore that her claim to share what he has arrogated to himself, shall be considered. "Gloriana," pleads that in woman's degradation man shall no longer be debased, that in her elevation he shall be upraised and ennobled. The reader of its pages will observe the Author's conviction, everywhere expressed, that Nature ordains the close companionship not division of the sexes, and that it is opposition to Nature which produces jealousy, intrigue, and unhealthy rivalry.

"Gloriana" is written with no antagonism to man. Just the contrary. The Author's best and truest friends, with few exceptions, have been and are men. But the Author will never recognise man's glory and welfare in woman's degradation.

> *"And hark! a voice with accents clear*
> *Is raised, which all are forced to hear.*
> *'Tis woman's voice, for ages hushed,*
> *Pleading the cause of woman crushed;*
> *Pleading the cause of purity,*
> *Of freedom, honour, equity,*
> *Of all the lost and the forlorn,*
> *Of all for whom the Christ was born."*

If, therefore, the following story should help men to be generous and just, should awaken the sluggards amongst women to a sense of their Position, and should thus lead to a rapid Revolution it will not have been written in vain.

THE AUTHOR

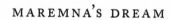

MAREMNA'S DREAM

Introduction to Gloriana; Or, A Dream of the Revolution of 1900

A rose-red sunset,
Mingling its radiance with the purple heath,
Flooding the silver lake with blushing light,
Dyeing the ocean grey a crimson hue,
Streaking the paling sky with rosy shafts;
Clinging to Nature with a ling'ring kiss,
Ere it shall vanish from a drowsy earth,
To rouse in new-deck'd cloak of shining gold
A waking world far o'er the ocean's wave.
Maremna sleeps,
Close cushion'd in the heather's warm embrace;
The rose-red sunset plays around her form—
A graceful, girlish figure, lithe and fair,
Small, slim, yet firmly knit with Nature's power—
Unfetter'd Nature! which will not be bound
By Fashion's prison rules and cultur'd laws.
Maremna sleeps.
One rosy cheek lies pillow'd on her hand,
And through her waving, wandering auburn curls
The zephyr cupids frolic merrily,
Tossing them to and fro upon her brow
In sportive play. It is a brow of thought,
Endow'd by God and Nature, though, alas!
Held in paralysis by selfish laws
Which strive to steal a fair inheritance,
And bid the woman bow the knee to man.
Maremna sleeps.
The white lids veil the large grey, lustrous eyes,
The auburn lashes sweep the sunlit cheeks,
Yet are they wet, and cling to the soft skin
Whereon the damp of tears is glazing fast.
Maremna's sleep is not the sleep of rest,
Forever and anon the blood-red lips
Unclose, and strive to speak, but yet remain
Silent and speechless, tied by some dread force

Which intervenes, denying to the brain
That comfort which the power of speech doth bring.
Who is Maremna?—
A noble's child, rear'd amidst Nature's scenes,
Her earliest friends! *They* guided her first steps,
Speaking of God and His stupendous works
Long ere Religion's dogma intervened.
Child of a chieftain o'er whose broad domains
She roamed, a happy, free, unfetter'd waif,
Loving the mountain crag and forest lone,
The straths and corries, rugged glens and haunts
Of the red deer and dove-like ptarmigan;
Loving the language of the torrent's roar,
Or the rough river's wild bespated rush;
Loving the dark pine woods, amidst whose glades
The timid roe hides from the gaze of man;
Loving the great grey ocean's varying face,
Now calm, now rugged, rising into storm,
Anon so peaceful, so serene, and still,
When passion's fury sinks beneath the wave.
Maremna sleeps
Amidst the scenes that rear'd her early years
Yet is Maremna now no more a child,
Nor guileless with the innocence of youth.
Hers it has been to roam God's mighty world,
And learn the ways and woful deeds of men,
And, weary with her world-wide pilgrimage,
Maremna's steps have sought her early haunts,
Hoping for rest where childhood once did play.
Rest for Maremna!
An idle thought; a foolish sentiment!
Unto the brain which God has bidden "Think"
No rest can come from Solitude's retreat;
For solitude breeds thought, and shapes its course
And bids it live within the form of speech,
Or bids the mighty pen proclaim its life,
And write its words upon the scrolls of men.
Thus with Maremna.
Rest she has sought, but sought it all in vain.

What God decrees no mortal hand can stay.
"Think." He ordains, and lo! the brain *must* think,
Nor close its eyes upon the mammoth truth.
Truth must prevail! Truth must be held aloft!
What matter if the cold world sneers or scoffs?
Sneering and scoffing is the work of man,
Truth, the almighty handiwork of God.
It may be dimm'd, it may be blurr'd from sight,
Yet must it triumph in the end, and win;
For is not truth a sun which cannot die,
Though unbelief may cloud it for a time?
Maremna sleeps;
Sleeps where in childhood oft she lay and dream'd,
Dream'd of fantastic worlds and fairy realms.
And now, in sleep, Maremna dreams again,
But dreams no more of elves and laughing sprites.
Hers, though a dream, is stern reality,
Mingled with visions of a future day;
Hers is a dream of hideous, living wrong,
Among which 'tis woman's duty to proclaim
And man's to right, and right right speedily,
Or crush the form of justice underfoot.
Maremna sleeps.
And in her sleep a vision fills her brain.
This is Maremna's Dream.

BOOK I

I

"I am tired, mother."

"Tired, child! And why?"

"Mother, I have been spouting to the wild sea waves."

"And what have you been saying to them, Gloria?"

"Ah, mother! ever so much."

Let us look at the speakers, a mother and child, the former as she stands leaning against a stone balustrade, which overlooks a small Italian garden, upon which the sun is shining brightly. Far out beyond is the gleaming sea, and on its sparkling, silvery sheen the woman's eyes are absently fixed as she hearkens to the complaining prattle of the child by her side. She is a beautiful woman is Speranza de Lara, one upon whom Dame Nature has showered her favours freely. As the stranger, looking upon her for the first time, would deem her but a girl in years, and exclaim admiringly at her beauty, it would be difficult to convince him that her age is thirty-five, as in effect it is.

Speranza's eyes are blue, with the turquoise shade lighting up their clear depths, and a fringe of silky auburn eyelashes confining them within bounds. Her magnificent hair is of a slightly lighter hue, and as the sun plays on the heavy coil that is twisted gracefully upon her noble head, the golden sparks dance merrily around it, like an aureole of gold.

And the child? We must look nearer still at her, for she not only is beautiful, but there is writ upon her face the glowing sign of genius. Like her mother, Gloriana; or, as we shall prefer to call her, Gloria, has blue eyes, but they are the blue of the sapphire, deep in contradistinction to the turquoise shade, which characterises those of Speranza. Auburn eyelashes, too, fringe the child's wonderful eyes, but again these are many shades darker than the mother's, while masses of auburn curls play negligently and unconfined, covering the girl's back like a veil of old-gold. Such is Gloriana de Lara at the age of twelve.

"Won't Gloria tell mother what that '*ever so much*' was?"

She puts the question gently, does Speranza. She has never moved from the position in which we first found her, and her eyes are still dreamily searching the waste of blue waters beyond. But as she speaks the child puts her arm caressingly through that of the mother's, and lays her golden head against that mother's shoulder.

"Ah! yes, mother, of course I will tell *you*."

"Then tell me, Gloria."

"I was imagining the foam flakelets to be girls, mother, and I looked upon them as my audience. I told them, mother darling, of all the wrongs that girls and women have to suffer, and then I bade them rise as one to right these wrongs. I told them all I could think of to show them how to do so, and then I told them that I would be their leader, and lead them to victory or die. And the wavelets shouted, mother. I seemed to hear them cheer me on, I seemed to see them rising into storm, the wind uprose them, and their white foam rushed towards me, and I seemed to see in this sudden change the elements of a great revolution."

"Like a dream, Gloria."

"A living dream, mother; at least it was so to me. It brought a feeling to my heart, mother, which I know will never leave it more, until, until—"

The girl pauses, and the great tears rise to her eyes. Speranza raises herself suddenly, and, confronting the child, lays both hands upon her shoulders.

"Until what, child?"

"Until I've won, mother," cries Gloria, as she raises her glorious eyes, in which the tears still tremble, to her mother's face.

"Ah, Gloria! the odds are against you, my darling."

"Don't I know that, mother; don't I know that well? But I am not afraid. I made a vow, mother, today, I made it to those waves; and something tells me that I shall keep that vow and win, though in doing so I may die."

"Hush, Gloria, hush, child; don't talk like that."

"And don't you want me to win, mother? After all you have suffered, after all you have taught me, would you have your child turn back from the path she has set herself to follow, because perhaps at that path's end lies death?"

"Child, it is a cause I would gladly lay down my life for, but how can I bring myself to wish you to sacrifice yourself?"

"What is sacrifice in a great cause, mother? I fear no sacrifice, no pain, no consequence, so long as victory crowns me in the end."

The mother's arms are round her child's neck now, her head is bending down and the bright gold of Speranza's lovely hair is close beside the glossy, wandering dark gold curls of Gloria. In the heart of the former a new-born hope is rising, vague, undefinable, yet still there, and which fills it with a happiness she has not known for many and many a day.

"My child," she exclaims softly, "can it åbe, that after all these years of weary, lonely suffering, I am awaking to find in you, you, the offspring of a forbidden love, the messenger that shall awake the world to woman's wrongs, and make suffering such as I have endured *no longer possible?*"

"Yes, mother, I feel it," answers Gloria earnestly; "and that is why I have made my plans today. Everything must have a beginning you know, mother, and therefore I must begin, and begin at once. You must help me, mother darling. I can do nothing without your co-operation."

"Tell me your plans, Gloria, and mother will help you if she can."

"My plans are many, but the first must have a premier consideration. Mother, I must go to school."

"To school, child! I thought you always have begged me not to send you to school."

"It must be to a boy's school, mother. You must send me to Eton."

"To Eton?"

"Yes, mother; don't you understand?"

HERE A RETROSPECT IS NECESSARY to enable the reader to comprehend the above conversation.

Thirty-five years previously there had been born to a young widow in the Midland Counties of England a posthumous child and daughter, to whom the name of Speranza had been given. The widow, Mrs. de Lara by name, was left badly off. Her husband, who had been an officer in the British service, had sold out, and accepted an estate agency from a rich relative, upon whose property he lived in a tiny but snug cottage, which nestled amidst some pine and oak woods on the shores of as beautiful a lake as was to be seen all the country round. Captain and Mrs. de Lara were a very happy pair. Theirs had been a love match; and she never regretted the rich offers of marriage which she had rejected for the sake of the handsome, dashing but well-nigh penniless young officer. Her father, furious at what he considered a *mésalliance*, had cut her off with a shilling; and thus it was that the two had had a hard struggle to make ends meet on the little possessed by the captain. What mattered it? They were happy.

Grief, however, soon came to cloud that home of peace and contentment. An accidental discharge of his gun inflicted on Captain de Lara a mortal wound. He died in the arms of his heart-broken wife, who lived just long enough to give birth to the little Speranza, dying a fortnight later, and leaving, penniless and friendless, two little boys and the baby girl referred to. The captain's rich relative adopted them. He was a kind-hearted man, and felt that he could not turn them adrift on the world, but his wife, a hard-hearted and scheming woman, resented the adoption bitterly, and led the children a sad and unhappy life. She had a son and daughter of her own, aged respectively five and six years, and upon these she lavished a false and mistaken affection, spoiling them in every possible way, and bringing them up to be anything but pleasant to those around them.

When old enough Speranza's brothers were sent to school, and given to understand by their adopted father that they might choose their own professions. The eldest selected the army, the youngest the navy, and each made a start in his respective line of life. But Speranza, being a girl, had no chances thrown out to her. She was a very beautiful girl, strong, healthy, and clever; but of what use were any of these attributes to her?

"If I were only a boy," she would bitterly moan to herself, "I could make my way in the world. I could work for my living, and be free instead of being what I am, the butt of my adopted mother."

It is necessary to explain that Speranza's adopted parents were the Earl and Countess of Westray, and that their two children were Bertrand Viscount Altai and Lady Lucy Maree. Dordington Court was the family seat, and it was here that Speranza spent the first sixteen years of her life.

There were great doings at Dordington Court when Lord Altai came of age. A large party was invited to take part in the week's festivities, and duly assembled for the occasion. Many beautiful women were there, but none could compare in beauty with Speranza de Lara. She was only seventeen years of age at the time, but already the promise of exquisite loveliness could not but be apparent to everyone. It captivated many, but none more so than young Altai himself.

He was not a good man was the young viscount. Injudicious indulgence as a child had laid the seeds of selfishness and indifference to the feelings of others. He had been so accustomed to have all he wanted, that such a word as "refusal" was hardly known to him. He had grown up in the belief that what Altai asked for must be granted as a matter of course. And now, in pursuit of his passions, he chose to think himself, or imagined himself, in love with Speranza, and had determined to make her his wife.

He chose his opportunity for asking her. It was the night of a great ball given at Dordington Court during the week's festivities. Speranza had been dancing with him, and when the dance was over he led her away into one of the beautiful conservatories that opened from one of the reception-rooms, and was lighted up with softly subdued pink fairy lamps. He thought he had never seen her look more beautiful, and his passion hungered to make her his own more than ever.

He put the usual question, a question which—no reason has yet been given why—a man arrogates to himself *alone* to put. He never dreamed that she, the penniless Speranza de Lara, the adopted orphan of his father and mother, would refuse *him*. He took it as of course for granted that she would jump at his offer. Were there not girls— and plenty too—in the house who would have given their eyes for such a proposal? He put the question therefore confidently, nay, even negligently, and awaited the answer without a doubt in his mind as to what it would be.

He started. She was speaking in reply. Could he believe his ears, and was that answer No? And yet there was no mistaking it, for the voice, though low, was clear and very distinct. It decidedly said him Nay. Yes, Speranza had refused him. It was the first rebuff he had ever received in his life, the first denial that had ever been made to request of his. It staggered him, filled him with blind, almost ungovernable, fury. More than ever he coveted the girl who had rejected him, more than ever he determined to make her, what the law told him she should be if he married her, his own.

He left her suddenly, anger and rage at heart, and she, with a sad and weary restlessness upon her, wandered out into the clear moonlit night, and stood gazing over the beautiful lake at her feet, and at the tiny cottage at the far end where her father and mother had died, and where she had been born.

What was it that stood in Speranza's eyes? Tears, large and clear as crystals, were falling from them, and sobs shook her graceful upright frame, as she stood with her hands clasped to her forehead in an agony of grief. Only seventeen, poor child, and yet so miserable! It was a cruel sight for anyone to see. But no one saw it save the pale moon and twinkling stars that looked down calmly and sweetly on the sobbing girl.

A harsh voice sounded suddenly at her elbow, a rough grasp was laid upon her arm. With a cry in which loathing and horror were mixed

Speranza turned round, only to confront the contemptuous, haughty woman, who had never said a kind or nice word to her in all her life.

"How dare you, girl, behave like this?" had cried the countess furiously. "How dare you so answer my darling boy, who has thus condescended to honour you with his love?"

In vain the miserable child had striven to explain to the infuriated woman that she did not care for Lord Altai. Such an explanation had only aggravated the countess's anger, who, after many and various threats, had declared that unless Speranza consented to gratify her darling boy's passion, she would induce the earl to deprive Speranza's two brothers of their allowances, and therefore of their professions, which, in other words, meant ruin to them.

She was a clever woman was Lady Westray. She knew exactly where to strike to gain her end. The threat which she threw out about Speranza's two brothers she knew pretty well would take effect; for did she not also know that out to them the poor child's whole heart had gone? Rather than injure them, the girl determined to sacrifice herself.

A month later a great wedding took place. Envied of all who saw her, Speranza de Lara became Viscountess Altai, and the wife of the man whom she detested and loathed. Sold by the law which declares that however brutally a man may treat his wife, so that he does not strike her, she has no power to free herself from him; sold by the law which declares her to be that man's slave, this woman, bright with the glory of a high intellect, perfect in Nature's health and strength, was committed to the keeping of a man whom Fashion courted and patted on the back, whilst declaring him at the same time to be the veriest *roué* in London. *He* could go and do as *he* pleased; indulge in brutal excess, pander to every hideous passion of his heart, poison with his vile touch the beautiful creature whom he looked down upon as "only a woman"; but *she*, if *she* dared to overstep the line of propriety, and openly declare her love for another, she would be doomed to social ostracism, shunned and despised as a wanton, and out of the pale of decent society.

She did so dare! For six long years she bore with his brutal excess and depraved passions; for six long years she suffered the torture which only those who have so suffered can understand. Then she succumbed.

It was a dark November evening when she met her fate. The Altais were in Scotland, entertaining a party of friends for the covert shooting in Lord Westray's splendid Wigtownshire preserves. The guests had all arrived but one, and he put in an appearance when the remainder of the party had gone upstairs to dress for dinner. Lady Altai had waited for him, as he was momentarily expected, and on his arrival he had been ushered into the drawing-room. His name was Harry Kintore, a captain in a smart marching regiment. As she entered the drawing-room he was standing with his back to the fire, and their eyes met. Right through her ran a thrill, she knew not why or wherefore, while he, transfixed by her beauty, could not remove his eyes. There have been such cases before of love at first sight. This was a case about which there could be no dispute; both felt it was so, both knew it to be beyond recall.

How she struggled against her fate none can tell. With her husband's increased brutality the gentleness and devotion of young Kintore was all the more *en evidence*. And when at length he bade her fly with him beyond the reach of so much misery and cruelty, was it a wonder that she succumbed, and flew in the face of law that bound her to the contrary?

She left him, that cruel brute, who had made her life a desert and a hell. She left him for one who to her was chivalrous and tender, loving and sympathetic. The world cried shame upon her, and spoke of Lord Altai as an injured man; the world ostracised her while it courted anew the fiend who had so grievously wronged her. And when, in the hunger of his baffled passion, this pampered *roué* followed the two who had fled from him, and with cold-blooded cruelty shot dead young Harry Kintore, the world declared it could not blame him, and that it served Lady Altai right.

Good-Morning, my dear," exclaims Lady Manderton, as she enters the cosy boudoir of her bosom friend and confidante, Mrs. de Lacy Trevor, as this latter, in a neat *peignoir*, lies stretched out, novel in hand, on an easy couch overlooking the fast-filling street of Piccadilly about eleven o'clock on the morning of the 5th June, 1890.

"Ciel! my dear, what brings you here, and dressed, too, at this unearthly hour?"

"Chute, Vivi, don't talk so loud. A mere rencontre, that's all. Arthur and I have arranged a little lark, and I told him to meet me here. I knew you wouldn't mind."

"He, he!" giggles Vivi; "but what have you done with Man?"

"Oh! he's safe enough, my dear. Gone off to his club. Thinks I've gone to get a gown tried on. He, he! What fools men are!"

"Think themselves deuced clever, nevertheless, Dodo," laughs Vivi. "It's not an hour since Trebby was raving at me, laying down the law at the way I go on with Captain Kilmarnock. Of course I pretended to be awfully cut up, rubbed my eyes, got up a few tears and sniffs, got rid of him with a kiss or two, packed him off to his club, and at twelve o'clock Kil and I are off to Maidenhead together."

This announcement creates the greatest amusement between the two ladies, judging by the peals of laughter that follow it.

"By-the-bye, Dodo, where were you yesterday?" inquires Vivi Trevor, after the laughter has subsided.

"I, my dear? Why, I was with H.R.H.'s party for the 4th of June. You can't think what a jolly day we had, Vivi. Some of the recitations were quite delightful, and there was a boy called Hector D'Estrange, who was simply too lovely for words. We all fell in love with him, I can tell you. I never saw such eyes in my life. Won't he break some of our hearts some day!"

"Hector D'Estrange; but who is he?"

"That's just what everyone was asking, but no one seemed to know. It appears he has taken the school by storm. Does everything tiptop. Splendid batsman, bowler, oarsman, wonderful at racquets, undefeatable at books—in fact, my dear, beautiful as an Adonis, and clever past expression."

"Oh, Dodo! I must see this Adonis. I love pretty boys."

"And plucky ones, too," laughs Vivi. "I was speaking to young Estcourt, who is his chum, and he told me that when Hector D'Estrange first came to Eton, a good many attempts were made to bully him, but he soon settled his tormentors, and gave one of them, a big overgrown monster, such a drubbing, that he never molested him more. What fun, Dodo, it would have been to see my Adonis punching the overgrown bully! I did laugh when Estcourt told me. I do so hate overgrown boys. Don't you, Dodo?"

"Of course I do, Vivi. Detest them!"

There is a ring at the door bell. Vivi jumps up and looks out of the window.

"It's Arthur!" is all she exclaims.

"Well, ta ta, Vivi! won't bother you with him," laughs Lady Manderton, as she stoops to kiss her friend. "See you tonight, I suppose, at Ferdey's—eh? Love to Kil. Don't let Trebby catch you, and a pleasant outing to you both"; saying which she is off out of the room, and running downstairs to meet her friend Sir Arthur Muster-Day, a smart young guardsman, whom it has pleased her for the time being to think that she likes better than anyone else in the world.

They are off together, happy in each other's company. Sir Arthur is not married, and he thinks it just the thing to be seen about as much as possible in the company of one of London's newest belles. Lady Manderton doesn't care a rap for her husband, and is considerably bored that her husband evinces a certain amount of affection for her; she only married him for his money and position, and did not at all bargain for the affection part of the affair.

As for Vivi, after her friend is gone, she jumps up and rings for her maid. That important individual having made her appearance, she and Vivi are soon engrossed with the all-paramount question of the moment—dress. Half-a-dozen gowns are pulled out, put on, pulled off and discarded, until at length one appears to please more than the others.

"How do you think I look in this, Marie?" she inquires a little anxiously. "Is it becoming?"

"Mais, madame, c'est tout-à-fait charmante," replies the well-drilled maid with an expression of admiration.

Vivi is satisfied. The gown remains on her person, and in a short time she is dressed and ready for her day's outing. Twelve o'clock strikes. A neat brougham dashes up to the door. In less time almost than it takes to tell it, Vivi has taken her seat in the carriage, and is being whirled through the busy streets of London, *en route* to Captain Kilmarnock's rooms. There she will pick him up, and together they will proceed to Maidenhead, what to do God knows. We had better leave them.

A few minutes later, and there is another ring at the door, and the footman opens it to Mr. de Lacy Trevor. As he does so, the latter inquires—

"Is Mrs. Trevor in?"

"No, sir, just gone out," answers the servant.

"Do you know where to, James?" again asks Mr. Trevor.

"I do not, sir, but perhaps Mademoiselle Marie will know."

Marie is called, and arrives all smiles and bows. "Really, she thinks madame has gone out for a drive with her friend Lady Manderton, and to lunch with her afterwards. *C'est tout.*"

Mr. Trevor sighs.

"There will be no lunch wanted, James," he observes quietly. "I shall lunch at the club."

He wanders down the street in the direction of St. James's. He wonders if Vivi has forgotten the promise she made him that morning to lunch at home, and go for a ride with him afterwards. He so rarely sees her now, and when he does it is seldom alone. She never seems to have anytime to give to him, and yet he is not brutal to her, or neglectful, or wrapped up in someone else, as many other men are. He loves her so dearly, and would do anything to make her happy; but he can quite see how she shuns him, and how much happier she looks when in Captain Kilmarnock's company. And then, with a shudder, he starts and stares eagerly across the street, for there she is—yes, actually there she is, in Captain Kilmarnock's brougham, with the captain beside her, driving rapidly in the direction of Piccadilly.

Mr. Trevor has a strange lump in his throat as he ascends the steps of the Conservative and enters that roomy club.

"Waiter!" he calls out, and his voice is somewhat husky.

"Yes, sir."

"Bring me a stiff brandy-and-soda, waiter, and mind it *is* stiff," continues Mr. Trevor, as he throws himself wearily into a chair. The soda with its stiff complement of brandy arrives. It is mixed carefully by the waiter, and handed to the sad-hearted man. He drinks it eagerly. He has not a strong head, and knows that he cannot take much, but he feels that oblivion must in this instance be sought, if possible, no matter how, so long as it is attained.

The brandy, in a measure, has the desired effect. He feels it perforating through his body and mounting to his brain. Things don't look quite so gloomy to him now, and the loneliness of his position is less acutely felt. Two men are talking to each other close by him. He knows one of them. It is Sir Ralph Vereton, and he holds in his hand a copy of the June number of the *Free Review*.

"It is a wonderful article for a boy to write, and an Eton boy, too," he hears the baronet exclaiming. "Have you read it, Critchley?"

"Well, no, I can't say that I have, but I will, old chap, when I get home. I'm afraid I haven't time to just now."

"What's that, Vereton?" inquires Mr. Trevor, leaning forward in his chair, "anything particularly clever?"

"Hulloa, Trevor! you there? Didn't see you, old man. What! you haven't read an Eton boy's 'Essay on Woman's Position'? Everyone is talking about it. It's deuced clever and original, whatever one may think of the opinions, and is clearly written by a lad who will make his mark in the world."

"Let's have a look at it, Vereton, if you don't want it, there's a good chap. I want something to read," exclaims Mr. Trevor eagerly, reaching out his hand for the periodical, which the baronet passes to him good-naturedly. It is open at the page of honour, the first page in the book, and as Mr. Trevor scans the heading he reads it as follows: "Woman's Position in this World. By Hector D'Estrange, an Eton boy." He starts reading it, languidly at first, as if the remarks of a boy on such a subject cannot possibly be worth reading, but he is soon absorbed in the article, and never budges in his chair until he has read it through and through.

And there are some parts to which he turns again and again, as though he would burn their truths into his brain, and keep them there never to be forgotten. One in especial rivets his attention, so much so that he commits it to memory.

"When a girl is born," it ran, "no especial difference is made in the care of her by doctor or nurse. Up to a certain age the treatment which she and her brother receive is exactly the same. Why, I ask, should there be ever any change in this treatment? Why should such a marked contrast be drawn later on between the sexes? Is it for the good of either that the girl should be both physically and mentally stunted, both in her intellect and body,—that she should be held back while the boy is pressed forward? Can it be argued with any show of reason that her capacity for study is less, and her power of observation naturally dwarfed in comparison with that of the boy? Certainly not. I confidently assert that where a girl has fair play, and is given equal opportunities with the boy, she not only equals him in mental capacity, but far outruns him in such; and I also confidently assert, that given the physical opportunities afforded to the boy, to develop and expand, and strengthen the body by what are called 'manly exercises,' the girl would prove herself every inch his equal in physical strength. There are those, I know, who will sneer at these opinions, but in the words of Lord Beaconsfield, I can only asseverate that 'the time will come,' when those who sneer will be forced to acknowledge the truth of this assertion.

"Well then, granting, for the sake of argument, that what I have stated is correct, why, I ask, should all that men look forward to and hold most dear, be denied to women? Why should the professions which men have arrogated to themselves be entirely monopolised by their sex, to the exclusion of women? I see no manner of reason why, if women received the same moral, mental, and physical training that men do, they should not be as fit—nay, infinitely more fit—to undertake the same duties and responsibilities as men. I do not see that we should be a wit less badly governed if we had a woman Prime Minister or a mixed Cabinet, or if women occupied seats in the Houses of Parliament or on the bench in the Courts of Justice.

"Of course woman's fitness to undertake these duties depends entirely on the manner in which she is educated. If you stunt the intellect, tell her nothing, and refuse to exercise the physical powers which Nature has given her, you must expect little from such an unfortunate creature. Put man in the same position in which you put woman, and he would be in a very short time just as mentally and physically stunted as she is.

"All very well to declare that it is a woman's business to bear children, to bring them up, to attend to household matters, and to leave the rest to men. A high-spirited girl or woman will not, in every instance, accept this definition of her duties by man as correct. That such a definition is clearly man's, it is not difficult to see, for woman would never have voluntarily condemned herself to a life of such inert and ambitionless duties as these. But so long as this definition of woman's duty and position be observed and accepted by Society, so long will this latter be a prey to all the evils and horrors that afflict it, and which are a result of woman's subjection and degradation.

"Think you, you who read these words, that hundreds of women now unhappily married would ever have contracted that terrible tie had they been aware of what they were doing, or had they had the smallest hope of advancement and prospects of success in life without? Certainly not. Marriage is contracted in ninety-nine cases out of a hundred by women desirous of making for themselves a home, and because in no other quarter can they adopt agreeable and pleasant professions and occupations like men. Were it possible, they would either not have married, or at least have waited until, with the knowledge of man which they *should* possess—but which, unfortunately, nowadays comes to them only with marriage—they could select for themselves, with their eyes open, a partner suited to them in every respect. As it is, what does one see? Women, especially in the higher grades of society, marry only to escape in many instances the prim restraints of home. Others marry for money and position, because they know that the portals, through which men may pass to try for these, are closed to them. The cruel laws by which men have shut women out from every hope of winning name and fame, are responsible for hundreds of wretched marriages, which have seared the world with their griefs. If, in the narrow sphere within which she moves, a woman errs, let not the man blame her, but rather look to the abolition of unnatural laws which have brought about her degradation."

MR. TREVOR SITS VERY STILL IN his chair. A flood of thoughts have come to fill his brain. They keep him very busy and occupied. The revelations thrown upon woman's position by the straightforward, truth-breathing article of Hector D'Estrange, have taken him by storm, and have completely revolutionised his ideas. He has hitherto been so accustomed to look upon and treat women with the self-satisfied, conscious feeling of superiority assumed by men, that such ideas as these before him are startlingly strange and extraordinary. His position with Vivi, and hers in regard to him, presents itself now to his mind in a totally different light to that in which he has hitherto been accustomed to regard it. He remembers how he first met her hardly a year ago, a beautiful, lively, healthy girl, whose scheming mother, knowing no better, had thrust her into the busy mart, willing to sell her to the highest bidder. He remembers how passionately he fell in love with this girl, how he never paused to ask himself if his love were returned. He recalls full well the bitter look that had crossed her face when he had asked her to be his wife, and the cold, matter-of-fact way in which she had accepted him. Then his thoughts fly back to his wedding day, and a shudder runs through Launcelot Trevor as he recalls the utter absence of love on her part towards him. And, remembering all this, he cannot but feel that Hector D'Estrange is right. If, in the narrow sphere within which poor Vivi had moved, she had, according to the notions of propriety laid down by Mrs. Grundy, erred, Launcelot Trevor feels that the blame must rest not so much with her, as with the cruel laws that had left that beautiful girl no other option but to sell herself for gold; for be it remembered, she had been educated up to no higher level, been imbued with no better aim. She had been taught that the only opening for a girl is to get herself well married, that while men could go forth into the world with a score of professions to choose from, she must forever regard herself as shut out from that world of enterprise, daring, and fame, created, so says man, solely for himself.

He sits on in his chair, his thoughts still busy with the new problem that has presented itself so startlingly to his mind. The luncheon hour is far past, much of the afternoon has slipped away, still Launcelot Trevor remains where he had seated himself many hours before. Men keep coming in and out; friends and acquaintances nod to him as they pass. He scarcely heeds them, or pays attention to what they say. His mind is absorbed by the truths which he has faced for the first time.

Suddenly he starts; the clock is striking seven. He remembers that at eight o'clock he and Vivi are engaged to dine out. He jumps up, bids the hall porter hail a hansom, and in a few minutes is being driven towards Piccadilly.

"Has Mrs. Trevor returned yet?" he again inquires of the servant who opens the door to him.

"Yes, sir, she is in the drawing-room with Captain Kilmarnock."

He walks slowly upstairs. All is very silent in the room mentioned. He stands on the threshold, hardly daring to open the door. He can hear a rustling inside, and, yes, unmistakably the sound of a kiss. He coughs audibly as he lays his hand on the door's handle. He can hear a scuffling of feet, and on entering perceives Vivi sitting bolt upright on the sofa, and Captain Kilmarnock apparently warming his hands over the fireplace. Unfortunately there is no fire!

She looks at him as he comes in, and for a moment their eyes meet. A bright flush rises to Vivi's cheeks. She expects to see him furious, as

LADY FLORENCE DIXIE

he had been that morning, and is surprised, nay, even awed by the sad expression on his face.

"Vivi," he says very quietly, "I think we ought to be dressing for dinner. Good-evening to you, Kilmarnock. Are you to be at Ferdey's tonight?"

"No, Trevor," stammers the captain, visibly uncomfortable. "I have another engagement."

"Oh, well, shall see you again, I suppose, soon? Goodnight, old chap. Must go and dress. Vivi dear, don't be late."

He goes out as he speaks, and closes the door behind him. Hector D'Estrange's words are still next his heart.

"Poor Vivi," he mutters to himself. "It is not her fault. Poor Vivi."

He is hardly out of the room, when she looks up at Captain Kilmarnock. The scared expression is still in her face.

"Kil," she whispers, "that *was* a near squeak. You had better be off, old man. Didn't hear the front door bell ring, did you?"

"No," he answers in a rather sulky tone. "Hang him! he's always where he's not wanted. But you are right. I'd better be off. Tomorrow at three. Don't forget."

"All right," she answers, with a smile.

III

Always busy and astir, the little town of Melton Mowbray presents a more than usually busy aspect on the morning of the 15th April, 1894. It is early yet, nevertheless the streets ring with the sound of trotting and cantering hacks, as well as the more sober paces of the strings of horses returning from exercise to their respective stables.

People are coming and going at a rapid rate. They nearly all seem to know each other, judging by the little nods, and "good-mornings," and suchlike familiar greetings with which friends meet, and in which these afore-mentioned personages indulge, as they hurry by each other.

A party of horsemen and horsewomen are just riding out of the stables belonging to The Limes. They are laughing and talking merrily. We have seen two of the women before, and their names are Mrs. de Lacy Trevor and Lady Manderton. Close in attendance upon them are two smart good-looking men, whom we must introduce to the reader as Lord Charles Dartrey and the Earl of Westray. The former appears to be entirely taken up with the first-named lady, the latter—already introduced to the reader in a former chapter as Lord Altai—with the last-named one.

There is yet another pair in that cheery group that we must particularly notice. They are a man and woman, both young, both good-looking, and both unmistakably at home in the saddle. If one can judge from appearances, the woman must be about twenty-two years of age, the man perhaps five or six years her senior. Both are mounted on grey horses, and both look every inch what they are, splendid equestrians. The woman is well known in Society's world, as also in the tiny hunting world of Melton. She is Lady Flora Desmond, and the man is handsome Captain "Jack" Delamere.

They trot through the streets at a merry pace, down past the Harborough Hotel, over the railway, away on by Wicklow Lodge, towards Burton Lazarus. It is a beautiful morning, and the sun is shining brightly on the flats that lie below. Dalby Hall, nestling amidst its woods on the far hillside, stands out distinct and clear, with the same bright sun gleaming on its gables and windows.

"What a glorious morning, Jack!" exclaims Lady Flora enthusiastically. "Why, it's like summer, is it not?"

The others are a little on ahead, and these two have fallen in the rear. Jack looks at the speaker with a smile.

"It is a grand day, Florrie, and it suits you, too. I never saw you looking better in my life."

She flushes up. Florrie Desmond does not care about compliments,— she values them at their worth,—but she and Jack are fast friends, and she is not quite averse to them from him. She answers, however.

"Shut up, you goose, and don't talk nonsense."

She is a clever woman is Flora Desmond, cleverer far than some people take her to be. Her bringing up has not been exactly like other women's, and she has always kicked against the restraints and restrictions put upon her sex. She is the daughter of the Marquis and Marchioness of Douglasdale, and an orphan, having lost her father at an early age. Lady Douglasdale was, in her day, a very beautiful woman, a *persona grata* at Court, where her husband exercised the duties of Comptroller of the Household, and was a favourite with his sovereign; but after the marquis's death she took greatly to travelling, and thus it was that Flora Ruglen, in conjunction with her twin brother Archie, saw most of the great world of Europe before she was ten years of age.

Travelling expands the mind, and brightens the senses. It had this effect upon the girl, forming much of her character before its time. At that early age she exhibited peculiar characteristics. No one could get her to settle down to study under a governess; she loathed the sight of school books, and led her unfortunate preceptors a sad life; yet, in strange contradiction to so much wilfulness and apparent indolence, she was seldom without the companionship of a book in her play hours, and when not otherwise engaged with her brother, would invariably be found poring over these books, thirstily seeking knowledge, or committing to paper, in powerful language for one so young, the impressions of her youthful brain.

She had dreams had Flora Ruglen—dreams of a bright future, an adventurous career. The time had not arrived when the road which she and her twin brother had been pursuing, would branch off in different directions, his leading forth to opportunities of power, fame, and glory, hers along a lane, narrow and cramped, and with nothing to seek at the end, save that against which her bright independent spirit rebelled and revolted. But it came at last, when the companion of her happy childhood's days was taken from her, when Archie was sent to school, and she was left alone. It came upon her with a suddenness which she found difficult to realise, and the blow was terrible. To describe what she suffered would be well-nigh impossible. Only those who by experience have learnt it, could be brought to understand the horror of her position. But Flora Ruglen, having faced it, brought all the courage of her nature to support it, though from that moment she became utterly changed. She had no one in whom to confide; neither her mother nor anyone else would have understood her. With girls of her own age she had nothing in common, and they looked on her with awe as a proud, stuck-up being. None could guess at the warm heart that beat beneath Flora Ruglen's apparently cold and reserved demeanour—except one, and that one was a boy of about her own age.

She had made his acquaintance during the holidays, when Archie, home from school, had invited his "best pal" to spend them at Ruglen Manor, the beautiful dower property of Lady Douglasdale. It was with young Lord Estcourt that Archie Douglasdale had struck up so keen a friendship. The lads had been "new boys" at Eton together, and in the first strangeness of introduction to that boy's world had been thrown into each other's company a good deal, being in the same house, and, as in Flora's case, much of the same age.

When Estcourt came to Ruglen Manor Flora Ruglen was about seventeen years of age. She was interested in her brother's friend, inasmuch as he had lately lost his mother, and was an orphan. It did not take long for a firm friendship to spring up between the boy and girl. Nigel Estcourt was an only child, had never known what it was to have brothers and sisters, and was ready to look upon Flora in that light gladly enough. He and she were a great deal in each other's company, and for the first time in her life she unloosed the cords of her heart, and told him of the trouble that had descended upon her life.

He sympathised with her did young Nigel. How could he help it, being, as he was, the friend of Hector D'Estrange? That extraordinary boy had risen to be head of the school. None could equal him at Eton, and his name had gone forth beyond the portals of the college as the coming man of his day. The article in the *Free Review*, which had first brought his name into prominence in the year 1890, had created a good deal of discussion in many circles. Of course it had been vigorously attacked. What great stroke aimed at Justice and Freedom but has ever been so opposed, hounded down, and decried? But truth is like a bright sun which no mortal power can dim. It may be clouded for a time, but it must shine forth and ultimately prevail.

He had left Eton, gone to Oxford, and had there taken high honours. He no sooner made his appearance in the world of fashion, politics, and letters, than he was received and courted everywhere. Never before had a youth risen so rapidly in the scale of success. He was undoubtedly the idol of his day, and in 1894 only twenty-one. It was extraordinary. Hector D'Estrange would marvel often at it himself. He had gone out into the world in what was mere childhood, prepared to combat with the many difficulties which he knew must beset his path. He was over modest was this boy. He had not sufficiently estimated his great and surpassing genius, but it had shone forth, been recognised and approved of, because he was a man.

To return to Flora Ruglen. At the age of eighteen she lost her mother, and the guardianship of the girl devolved on her aunt, a giddy, worldly woman, the late marquis's sister, and Countess of Dunderfield. No two women could have been more diametrically opposite then these two, no two characters more unlike. Briefly, and to cut the matter short, Lady Dunderfield insisted on taking Flora into Society, and set herself to bring about a match between the high-souled, high-spirited girl, and the Duke of Dovetail, a rich old monstrosity, whose rent-roll was nigh on a million, and whose body was afflicted by almost every disease under the sun.

Had the girl been in a position to map out her own line of life, what a different tale might now be told! She was not. The law denied her the right to choose her future; it curtailed her line of action within certain bounds. What could she do? The odds were against her, and she sought refuge through the first outlet that presented itself.

This outlet was in the shape of a young baronet, a youth of twenty-one. He thought himself very much in love with Lady Flora Ruglen. He proposed, and she accepted him. Lady Dunderfield forbade Sir Reginald Desmond the house. The young people took French leave of her, fled to Scotland, and were married, and Lady Dunderfield, green with disappointment and rage, had to accept the fact. This is how Flora Ruglen became Lady Flora Desmond. Had she erred in the step she took? Perhaps so. What other alternative had she? Had the law permitted her to go out into the world and adopt the profession of her choice, there is little doubt that ere this Flora Ruglen would have made a great name for good.

HE PRETENDS TO BE OFFENDED at her remark does Jack Delamere, and pulls his horse a little away from her own. She notices the movement, and laughs lightly, as she urges her animal alongside him, and taps him gently on the shoulder with her whip.

"Look there, Jack!" she exclaims at the same time; "we are not the first on the course after all. Look at those two riding over the fence alongside the brook. Who are they, I wonder? The woman *can* ride, it is easy enough to see that."

They are just turning to the left through the gate leading to the Steeplechase Course on the Burton Flats, and as Jack Delamere's eyes follow the direction indicated by Flora Desmond, he at once perceives two mounted figures, galloping up the course in the direction of the grand stand. One is a man, the other a woman.

As Flora Desmond has declared, the woman *can* ride. She sits her horse straight as a dart. He is pulling a bit, but she has him well in hand, and he is not likely to get away with her.

"Hector D'Estrange, by all that's holy! and with a woman, too," laughs Jack Delamere. "Look, Florrie! Is the world coming to an end, or am I dreaming?"

"That you are certainly not," she answers quickly; "there is no mistake about it. But who is she?"

They have joined the others now, and find them equally exercised over the female apparition.

It may be explained that this is the morning of the Melton Hunt Steeplechases, and that this party has ridden over early to the course to go round the fences, and inspect them severally. They had bargained on being the first in the field, but now perceive that they have been forestalled by Hector D'Estrange and his companion.

"Let's go and have a look," suggests Lord Westray. He is an admirer of women, and it is easy to perceive, even at the distance which separates the party from the stranger, that she is a fine one.

They all gallop down to the stand, riding along in a row towards Hector and his friend. He sees them coming, and says something to her, and Flora notices that she brings her horse closer to his side. Mrs. Trevor and Lady Manderton are all eyes and stare as they pass the two. Hector has raised his hat politely, and wished them a good-morning. His face is flushed with the exercise of riding, his rich auburn hair shines out like gold in the sunlight, his glorious eyes, dark in their sapphire-blue, look particularly winning and beautiful. But it is with his companion that the eyes of the others are busy. They are all struck by her extreme loveliness, and are loud in wonder as to who she is. Only Lord Westray is silent; white as a sheet, too. It is years since he set eyes on Lady Altai, and now he sees again, after a long lapse of time, the woman whom he so grievously wronged more than twenty-two years before—his divorced wife, Speranza de Lara.

"Come on," he exclaims, just a shade roughly to Lady Manderton. He has of late been, by the way, making up to her. She has got tired of Sir Arthur Muster-Day, and has shelved him for the "wicked earl," by which name Lord Westray is known in Society circles. Mrs. Trevor, too, though she still sticks to Kil, and makes him believe that she is as devoted to him as ever, has managed to hook on to herself several other devoted swains, to all of whom in turn she expresses a mint of devotion, while really feeling not the slightest affection for any of them. She has played her part well, however, for they each severally believe themselves to be "*the* favoured man" in her good graces.

They gallop forward in the wake of Lord Westray, and Flora Desmond and Jack Delamere are once more alone.

"What a lovely woman!" she bursts out, as soon as they have passed Hector D'Estrange and Speranza. "Jack, did you ever see such eyes? I never saw lovelier, unless perhaps Hector D'Estrange's. What a handsome pair the two make!"

"Well, yes, Florrie, she is certainly a lovely woman. Cunning dog, young Hector, to have kept her out of sight so long. Now we can understand why he is so cold to women. Of course that's where his heart is, without doubt," answers Jack Delamere, with a smile.

"The Melton Hunt Steeplechases of 1894 are over. The meeting will long be remembered by the unparalleled success of Mr. Hector D'Estrange, who, riding in the six races printed on the card for competition, came in first, the winner of everyone of them. This success is all the more remarkable, inasmuch as four of the winners were non-favourites, so that the wins must be ascribed to the splendid horsemanship of their jockey. The feat is unparalleled, the nearest approach to it being when Captain 'Doggie' Smith in 1880 carried off all the races on the card except one, being defeated in a match which closed the day's proceedings between Lord Hastings' Memory, and Lord James Douglas' The General. In this match 'Doggie' Smith rode Lord Hastings' mare, and Lord James Douglas his own horse, The General."

Such is the announcement chronicled in a well-known weekly sporting paper a few days after the Melton Hunt Steeplechases of 1894, scoring yet another triumph on the path of thoroughness for Hector D'Estrange.

IV

S o you will not?"

"A thousand times, no!"

They are standing facing each other are the speakers—one a beautiful, tall, graceful woman, with masses of rich gold hair coiled upon her noble head, and eyes whose light is like the turquoise gem, the other a middle-sized, handsome, good-looking man, whose dark eyes gleam with fury and disappointed passion.

We have seen them both before, this man and woman, seen them on more than one occasion; for it is not difficult to recognise in that evil-featured man the person of Lord Westray, or in that beautiful woman that of Speranza de Lara.

He has come here for no good purpose has the "wicked earl." Ever since, on the Burton Flats, he had fallen across the lovely woman whose life he had made a desert, Lord Westray had been a prey to a consuming passion to regain that which he had lost. Twice in her life Speranza had defied him, and on each occasion he had had his revenge. The first was when, as a girl of seventeen, she had refused him, and he, through the instrumentality of his cruel mother, who had played on her love for her brothers, had forced her to become his wife. The second was when, in defiance of man's laws, she had fled from his vile brutality and hateful presence, with the first and last love of her young life, poor Harry Kintore; and he, following up those two to the sunny land where they had sought a refuge, and where they asked for no other boon but to be allowed to live with and for each other, had shot down in her very presence the man to save whom she would have given a thousand lives of her own.

And now he is here, oblivious of all his past brutality, to insult her with yet another proposal, one more hideous than any he has ever made before. Consumed with passion for this woman, who had defied him, he has actually come to propose that she shall forget the past and re-marry him!

Forget the past! Is it likely? Will the memory of her suffering childhood ever pass away? Will the recollection of her wedding day fade from her mind? Will the six years of torture as his wedded wife disappear like a dream? Above all, can she ever forget her first meeting with Harry Kintore, the heart's awakening that came with it, or the terrible moment when, struck down at her feet, his dear eyes looked their love for the last time? Impossible.

He grinds his teeth with rage does Lord Westray as her clear, sad voice distinctly gives him his answer. He is racking his brain for a means of overcoming her, and forcing her once more to obey his will. The fact that she defies him, hates him, loathes him, has refused him, only arouses in him more madly than ever the desire to become possessed of her once again. Lord Westray possesses, in a heightened degree, in an aggravated form, the characteristic peculiar to all men, of desiring that which is either hard to get, or which denies itself to them, and which, if once obtained, fades in value in their eyes. It is Speranza's resistance to his wishes that fires him with the fury of a wild animal to regain her.

"You shall repent this!" he mutters angrily. "Speranza, you should know better than to defy *me*. Have I not been a match for you twice? and, by God I if you do not do as I ask now I will be again."

She shudders with horror as she hears his cold-blooded words, triumphing at his past deeds of brutality and crime. She pulls herself together, however. She is alone with him, and must keep him at bay. Speranza is no coward.

"I do not fear you," she answers haughtily; "you cannot do me more evil than you have already. I am beyond the reach of your vengeance now. Nothing you can do can harm *me*."

"I don't know so much about that," he replies savagely. "How about Hector D'Estrange?"

She starts, and the rich blood flushes to her face as she eyes him with evident terror. Can it be that he knows? that he will unveil the secret before—but no, it is impossible; she has it safe enough.

He notes the start, the crimson blush, and the look of terror, and he congratulates himself on having, by a chance shot, hit on the right point to cow her.

"You're a fine person to play the prude and the proper," he says, with a sneer. "They used to tell me that you were inconsolable over that ass Kintore, but the beauty of Hector D'Estrange appears to have effected a sudden cure. I congratulate you on your new conquest. You have aimed high. He is the rising man of his day, and you have thrown your net well to catch the golden fish. Are you not ashamed of yourself, however, woman,— you who are over the forties, to take up with a boy of twenty-one?"

She flushes again. Then he does not know? Thank God for that! How young she looks as she stands there in her unfading beauty, with a look in her blue eyes of contemptuous loathing. She will let him believe what he likes, so that he does not know the truth; that is all she desires to hide from him.

In pursuance of this desire she answers:

"Hector D'Estrange and I *are* friends. I am not ashamed to own it. Neither he nor I require your advice, however, as to how our friendship is to be conducted. And now I bid you leave me. I order you from my house, which I inhabit not by your charity."

"No, but by the charity of Harry Kintore, you wanton!" he answers with an oath. "You knew pretty well what you were about when you got the fool to settle all his estates and money on you, which you now lavish on Hector D'Estrange, but—"

"Peace, devil! fiend in human shape!" she cries furiously, as she clenches her hands, and brings the right one down with a crash on the table beside her. He notices a flash on one of the fingers. All the others are ringless but this one, and on it sparkles two splendid diamonds and sapphires set deep in their broad thick band of gold. He knows this ring of old. He saw it long ago, when she held the dying head of Harry Kintore in her hands, and he knows that it was the young man's gift to her. That she should wear it, now that she has taken up with Hector D'Estrange, mystifies him.

He is about to reply, when the door of the room they are in opens, and Lord Westray finds himself face to face with Hector. He is a head and shoulders taller than the earl is this young man, and as he advances into the room the latter's face falls slightly, and his fingers move nervously by his side. Like all bullies, Lord Westray is a coward, and doesn't half fancy his position.

But there is no angry look in Hector D'Estrange's eyes; only from their sapphire depths looks out a cold, calm expression of contempt.

"Lord Westray," he remarks, in a voice impressive because of its very quietness, "for what reason have we the honour of your presence here? Allow me to inform you that this honour is not desired by Mrs. de Lara. Your brougham is at the door. I must request you to seek it."

He says no more, but stands with the handle of the door in his hand, waiting for the earl to obey. This latter looks at him fiercely, the eyes of the two meet. Those of the bully and depraved coward cannot face the calm, disdainful look of Hector D'Estrange; they fall before it, and in another moment the earl is gone.

They listen to the wheels of the departing brougham as it rattles through the streets in the direction of South Kensington. As its echoes die away the young man turns to Speranza.

"Mother," he exclaims, "has he been here to insult you? Ah, mother! God only knows the strain I put upon myself, or I would have shot him down where he stood, the brute, the fiend! I nearly lost control of myself, but I heard your last words, and understood what you were striving to hide from him. Thank God I did, or in a hasty moment I might have laid bare our secret."

"And I, too, say thank God, Gloria. At one moment I fancied he was in possession of it, but I quickly found out that he was on another tack. Horrible as the idea was, it was better to let him foster it, than to give him a chance of learning the truth. Ah, Gloria dearest! if once the secret is in his hands, we need look for no mercy in that quarter."

"I know it, mother," answers Gloria, in other words Hector D'Estrange; for the reader must have had no difficulty in recognising in this latter, the beautiful girl who had made her vow to the wild sea waves, ten years previously on the sunny shores of the Adriatic, and who now, as Hector D'Estrange, is working out the accomplishment of that vow.

And she has worked well has Gloria de Lara, patiently and perseveringly, never losing an opportunity, never casting a chance aside. Her beauty and her genius have gone straight to the hearts of men, and she uses these gifts given her by God, not for vain glory and fleeting popularity, but in pursuit of justice and in furtherance of the one great aim of her life.

"Let us change the subject, my darling," exclaims Speranza, with a shudder; "let us drive from our minds the thought of one so horrible and contemptible. Tell me, my precious child," she continues, laying her hand on Gloria's shoulder, and kissing her gently on the forehead, "how have you got on with the clubs today?"

"Excellently, mother. I came to tell you all about them, or I should not have been here until tomorrow," answers Gloria, as she seats herself on a low stool at her mother's feet.

It is the middle of May, the sun is shining brightly, and the sparrows are hopping and chirping merrily about in the square outside. The early green on the trees is as yet unclouded by the dust of London's busy season, and all is fair, and soft, and young to look upon.

The large fortune and noble estates left to Speranza de Lara by young Harry Kintore have been well and wisely wielded by the woman, in whose heart the memory of her darling still shines as brightly as on the day he died. She has never misspent a farthing of the vast wealth that he confided to her care. It has been used in carrying out philanthropic works, alleviating suffering, and helping on the accomplishment of their child's design, his child and hers.

They are busy over a new one just now. With her mother's money at her command, Gloria, under the name of Hector D'Estrange, is establishing throughout London, and in the different large towns of Great Britain and Ireland, institutions where women and girls can meet each other, and for a mere nominal fee learn to ride, to shoot with gun and rifle, to swim, to run, and to indulge in the invigorating influences of gymnastics and other exercises, calculated to strengthen and improve the physique of those taking part therein. Classes, too, technical and otherwise, for the education of girls and women on an equality with boys and men, as well as free libraries, form part of these institutions, each of which, as it is founded, becomes crowded to overflowing.

In connection with these institutions Gloria has lately set on foot clubs, the members of which she is forming into volunteer companies, who are drilled by the hand of discipline into smartness and efficiency. The movement has been enthusiastically taken up by the women of Great Britain and Ireland, thousands of whom have been enrolled in these volunteer forces. Of course Hector D'Estrange has his enemies. The jealous and the narrow-minded; the old fogies who would have a great wrong continue forever, rather than fly in the face of prejudice to right it; the women who love their degradation and hug their chains; the men who think the world must be coming to an end if women are to be acknowledged as their equals, have all fought tooth and nail against the splendid idea and the practical conception of Hector D'Estrange. Ridicule, abuse, calumny, false testimony, have been hurled against his giant work. They have each and all failed to disturb or harm it, for its foundation is built on the rock of justice, of right, and of nature.

"Well, mother," continues the girl, "we have had a great consultation today. All the details for a big review have been discussed. We shall want two good years more to get everything efficiently arranged, when I calculate that Hector D'Estrange will be able to bring into the field quite 100,000 well-drilled troops. But I am in no hurry yet; there is still much to be done. And now I have some more news to give you, mother. I have been invited to stand by the Douglasdale division of Dumfriesshire for

Parliament, and to contest the seat when Mr. Reform resigns. I saw Archie Douglasdale today; he has promised to give me all his support. And what do you think, mother? Why, his sister, Lady Flora Desmond, has joined our new club. It is to be called the Desmond Lodge, and I have put her in command of it."

"She will be' a great help to you, Gloria," answers Speranza. "From all you have told me of her, she is the right sort in the right place."

"She is indeed, mother. Although I have many a good and true lieutenant thoroughly in touch with my ideas in our volunteer force, there is not one that can come up to Lady Flora. She will be a mountain of help to me, and I know I can trust her. I could trust her even with *our* secret."

"Oh! never divulge *that*, Gloria."

"Not I, mother! It was only an allegory, to give you an idea of my high opinion of her. But, till the right time comes, our secret will be with me as silent as the grave."

They talk on, busy with their plans, hopeful of the future, and what it is to bring, do these two women. The afternoon flits by, the chirp of the sparrows grows dull, the sun is sinking aslant the roofs of the opposite houses, the evening is creeping on apace. Gloria de Lara rises from her seat, and throws her arms around Speranza's neck.

"I must go now, mother," she says gently. "I wish I could stay, but I have an engagement. Goodnight, my precious mother. Kiss Gloria before she goes."

"God bless you, my child," answers the mother, as she presses the girl to her heart; "God bless you, and keep you prospering in your work, my valiant young Hector D'Estrange."

And the girl passes out from her mother's presence into the silent square. She is echoing Speranza's prayer, and is pulling herself together, for out of that mother's presence she has her part to play. She is no longer Gloria de Lara, but popular, successful Hector D'Estrange.

THERE IS YET ANOTHER SCENE at which we must glance before this chapter closes. Let us enter Lord Westray's house in Grosvenor Square. He is in the drawing-room pacing up and down, his face dark with anger and passion. A footman enters, bearing on a massive silver salver a tiny scented bijou note. He hands the missive respectfully to his lordship, who takes it impatiently.

"The bearer is to wait for an answer, my lord."

"Answer be d—d!" begins Lord Westray; but suddenly recollecting himself, he continues, "Very well, Walter, come up when I ring."

"Yes, my lord."

The servant retires. His face is very grave, but it relaxes into a leer as he closes the door.

"'Spec's the old un's rather tired of her by now. Gives her another week before they sez good-morning to each other," he soliloquises to himself as he goes downstairs. As he does so. Lord Westray opens the note. It is from Lady Manderton, and runs as follows:—

> DEAREST OLD POTSIE,
>
> Have got a ripping little supper on tonight. Man's away, and we will have some fun. Have asked several kindred spirits. Shall look for you at ten.
>
> Your ever-devoted 'DODO'

"I can't go," he mutters. "Hang the woman, I'm sick of her! She was all very well a little while ago, but nothing will satisfy me but Speranza now. I *will* have her or nobody; and if I don't have her, I will have what's next best, revenge."

He writes a note hastily. It is to excuse himself. He has an awful headache, and cannot come.

Lady Manderton gets the note a quarter of an hour later, and bites her lip as she reads it. "Never mind," she says quietly, "he sha'n't have another chance. My next man is Spicer. He's rich, he's good-looking, he's awfully in love, and he'll be very useful. He'll do."

She sits down and writes another note. It is addressed to the Hon. Amias Spicer, Grenadier Guards. She sends him the same sort of Invitation which she sent to Lord Westray.

It is not long before an answer comes back. Amias Spicer is in the seventh heaven. He will be sure to come.

And at ten o'clock he comes punctually. Poor young fool!

V

Montragee house is decked out at its brightest. The noble owner, Evelyn, Duke of Ravensdale, is giving a ball this night, to which all the pearl of London society has been bidden. Flocks of royalties have been also invited, and nearly all have signified their intention of being present. It is a wonderful sight as one drives up to the entrance gates of the great mansion, which is ablaze with light. Every window is neatly framed in soft green moss, from out of which fairy lamps peep and sparkle like thousands of glow-worms. Festoons of roses twine around the porch pillars of the great front door, and the scene that greets the eye on entry almost baffles description. Floating throughout the corridors and vestibules come the soft sounds of dreamy music, the atmosphere is redolent with the sweet scent of rare and lovely flowers, the place is a wilderness of beautiful sights, as up and down the broad flights of the magnificent staircase well-known men and women come and go.

A burst of martial music ever and anon heralds the approach of royalty. As each successive arrival takes place, the brilliant crowd sways to and fro to catch a sight of the gods which it adores. Above, the sound of lively strains announces that dancing has begun, and everyone hurries to take part in the measure of the light fantastic toe.

The dance music has suddenly ceased. Everyone has turned to ascertain the cause. The noble host is observed to be making for the centre of the magnificent suite of rooms where everyone is enjoying his or herself. He carries in his hand a telegram, and with the other hand slightly raised, appears to be enjoining silence. Very striking to look at is Evelyn, Duke of Ravensdale. His age may be between twenty-five and twenty-six. He is very tall and broad-shouldered, his hair, dark as the raven's wing, close curls about his forehead, which is high, and white, and intellectual. His eyes are also very dark, with a soft, dreamy look in them, his mouth firm set and well made, is sheltered by a long silken moustache.

Silence has sunk on all around. One might hear a pin drop so intense has it become. Everyone is on a tiptoe of expectation. The sight of that telegram has set every heart beating.

"Ladies and gentlemen," calls out the duke, raising it on high, "I have good news for you all. This is a telegram from my dear friend, Hector

D'Estrange. He has beaten his opponent by 2,330 votes, and is now member for the Douglasdale division of Dumfriesshire."

What a shout goes up! Men and women cheer again and again. It is felt that the pinnacle of fame on which that young man rests has gone up higher in the scale of merited success. Even his enemies cannot help feeling glad, for Hector D'Estrange is a name to conjure by.

"He'll be Prime Minister before another year or two are gone," exclaims Sir Randolph Fisticuffs, just a little jealously to a lady by his side. She looks at him earnestly as she replies,

"God bless the day when he is! We shall get justice then."

"Oh!" he answers pettishly, "that's just it. He has set all you women discontented with your lot; he has lit a fire which won't be readily extinguished. Mark my words, he'll burn his fingers over it yet, if he don't take care."

"Not he," she answers stoutly; "Hector D'Estrange knows what he is about. He has won the devoted, undying love of hundreds, nay, thousands and tens of thousands of women, for his brave, chivalrous exposure of their wrongs, and defence of their rights."

Sir Randolph Fisticuffs laughs.

"You ought to join the Woman's Volunteer Corps," he observes sarcastically.

"Ought I?" She opens her grey eyes wide. "As it happens, I joined it a year ago."

"The devil you did!" he exclaims in a surprised tone. "So you are a Hector D'Estrangeite, eh?"

"I am," she answers proudly.

The music has recommenced; a dreamy waltz is sounding through the room; everyone has begun dancing again. Only the dowagers are at rest. Not a man appears unoccupied. Yes, one is, though. It is the young Duke of Ravensdale himself.

He is leaning against a bank of moss and roses apparently watching the busy throng. There is a far-away look in his eyes, however, which tells that his thoughts have flown beyond the giddy pastime of the hour. He is thinking of his friend's latest triumph, and what will be the outcome of it all. For Evelyn Ravensdale's heart has gone out to Hector D'Estrange, and he loves him with that devoted, admiring love which some men have been known to inspire in others.

"Just look at the duke," whispers Lady Tabbycat to her friend Mrs. Moreton Savage; "one would think there wasn't a pretty girl in the room, or a heart aching for him, by the way he stands there doing nothing and saying nothing. I can't think what makes him so shy and reserved. He was all fire just now when he was telling us of Hector D'Estrange's triumph! and now just look at him, my dear."

Mrs. Moreton Savage does look at him, but she is just as far from making him out as her friend Lady Tabbycat is. Mrs. Moreton Savage is a dame whose mind has never soared beyond the fitting on of a dress, the making of matches, and the desirability of knowing all the best people in society. She has worked assiduously with those aims in view, and has the satisfaction of knowing that she has been more or less successful. Such a thought as the condition of society, and the people in the past, present, and future, has never entered her brain. She is quite content that things should go on exactly as they are, that there should be immense riches on one side, intense misery and poverty on the other. Such problems as the relation of man and woman in this world, and the terrible evils arising out of the false position of the sexes, has never troubled her. She has no wish to see mankind perfected, or to place Society on a higher level and basis than it is. There is just this difference, therefore, between herself and the man whom she and Lady Tabbycat are discussing, and that is that *he does*. Often and often have the young duke and Hector D'Estrange discussed these problems together in their early morning rides or cosy after-dinner chats. It is Hector D'Estrange who has converted him to his present way of thinking. He had come into his property a sufficiently self-conceited, spoilt young man; with the world at his feet, men and women angling for his favours, as many will do to the highborn and the rich. He had never paused to wonder what he should do with his money, and position, and power. He was preparing himself to enjoy life in the only way which up till then he had viewed as possible, when a fateful chance threw him in the path of Hector D'Estrange.

Men wondered at the change in the young Duke of Ravensdale. It was such a sudden one; they could not make it out; it mystified them altogether. Some put it down to love, and wondered who was the lucky one.

He has roused himself from his dreams with a shake and a start, and is standing upright now. A boy is passing close by him, a boy with pretty curling brown hair and large hazel eyes, a boy in whose face laughter and happiness are shining brightly, a boy whose life so far has been sunshine perpetual, without the storm and the hurricane. It would hardly be possible to find two brothers more extremely unlike than Evelyn, Duke of Ravensdale, and his younger and only brother, Lord Bernard Fontenoy. No one looking at the two standing together would take them to be related, certainly not so closely as they are.

"Bernie," calls the duke, as the boy passes along, and in an instant this latter is at his side.

"Yes, Evie," he asks inquiringly, looking up into his brother's face. "Anything you want me to do?"

"Yes, dear," answers the duke. "I want you to take my place for an hour or two. I have business that calls me away. Now, do you think, Bernie, that I can trust your giddy head to see to everything in my absence?"

"Giddy head!" pouts the boy, pretending to look seriously offended. "If you did well-nigh eight months' hard study out of twelve, you would like to enjoy yourself in the few hours snatched from toil and mental struggle."

"Poor boy! you look hard-worked and suffering, laughs the duke, as he eyes the bright, healthy, handsome face of the youthful complainant; "but seriously, Bernie, can I trust you to overlook everything for me?"

"Of course you can, Evie," replies Bernard, with a look of importance. "I promise you I will see to everything tiptop. I suppose if you're away I shall have to take in the Princess to supper, sha'n't I? Do you think Her Royal Highness will put up with a jackanapes like me?"

"I think so, Bernie. Anyhow, you must do your best. Go and make my excuses to the Prince—A sudden business calls me away; I will be back as quickly as possible. Meanwhile, my boy, do your best to take my place. I am sure I can trust you."

He lays his hand gently on the boy's shoulder as he turns to go. Bernie Fontenoy idolises his brother, but he feels at this moment as if there is nothing in the wide world he would not do for him, if it were in his power.

Evie Ravensdale passes quickly down the beautiful grand staircase towards the front door. Pompous servants are hurrying to and fro. A big portly butler, with a magnificent white waistcoat and ponderously heavy gold chain, is giving his orders in a voice the importance of which can only be measured by the value he puts upon himself. As he sees the duke descending, however, he moderates his tone, and is all obsequiousness in a moment.

"Repton, give me my cloak and hat, please," commands the duke in a quiet, civil voice, and the magnificent functionary hastens to obey. He is wondering all the time, however, what it can be that takes his Grace out at such a time.

"A hansom, Repton, please."

Repton turns to a crimson-plushed, knee-breeched, white-silk-stockinged subordinate.

"Call a hansom, John," he says loftily. It would be quite impossible for himself, the great Mr. Repton, to perform such a menial office; no one could expect it of *him*. The whistle rings through Whitehall. Rumbling wheels answer the summons. In a few minutes a hansom dashes up. The great Mr. Repton holds open the front door; Evie Ravensdale passes out. One of the crimson-plushed, knee-breeched menials unfolds the cab doors, and stands with his hands over the wheels while his master springs in; then he closes them to.

"Where to, your Grace?" he inquires respectfully.

And Evie Ravensdale, looking up at his brilliantly lighted luxurious mansion above him, answers somewhat absently, "Whitechapel."

The fit is on him to see and contrast the misery of some of London's quarters with the wealth and the luxury which he has just quitted. Hector D'Estrange's telegram has brought it to his mind. He remembers his last conversation with that dearly beloved friend, and how it had turned on that very point. The splendour of his own mansion, the brilliancy that he saw around him a few minutes since is about to be changed for cold, dark, ill-lighted streets, narrow alleys, and filthy courts. He wants to see it all for himself.

The hansom rattles through the streets. It goes at a good pace, but it seems a long time getting to its destination. At length it pulls up.

"What part of Whitechapel, sir?" inquires the cabman, looking through the aperture in the roof of his vehicle.

"You may put me down here, cabby," answers the young duke, handing him half-a-sovereign; "and if you like to wait for me, I may be about an hour gone. I'll pay you well, if you will."

"You're a genelman, I can sees that pretty plainly," answers the cabman glibly, as he touches his hat, and pockets the half-sovereign. "I'll wait, sir; no fear."

Evelyn Ravensdale wanders through the gloomy, ill-lighted streets. Midnight has chimed out from Big Ben; it is getting on towards one o'clock, and he does not meet many people. A policeman or two saunter along their beats, and turn their lights upon him as he passes. Sometimes a man and woman flit past him, or a solitary man by himself. He passes a dark, gloomy-looking archway into which the light from a flickering gas-lamp just penetrates. He can see a boy and girl with white, pinched faces asleep in an old barrel in one corner, a shivering, skinny dog curled up at their feet. The sight is terrible to him. He steps into the archway, and touches the boy on the shoulder. With a frightened cry the lad starts up and eyes him beseechingly.

"Ah, bobby! Don't turn us out tonight," he says pleadingly. "Maggie's so poorly and sick, she can hardly stand up. See, she's asleep now. Don't wake her, please, bobby, don't."

He starts suddenly, and pulls his forelock as he perceives that it is not a policeman he is talking to. "Beg pardon, sir," he says, "thought it was a bobby."

"Have you no better place than this to sleep in, my poor lad?" inquires the duke pityingly, his hand still on the boy's shoulder.

"Ah, sir! this is a gran' place. We don't allays gets the likes o' this. Poor Maggie, she was so pleased when we found this 'ere barrel. See, sir, how she do sleep."

"Is Maggie your sister?" asks the young duke, with a half-sob.

"No, sir, she's my gal. Maggie and me, we'ves been together a long time now, we has."

"And what do you do for a living, boy?" continues Evelyn Ravensdale gently.

"Anything, sir, we can get to do. It's not allays we can get a job, and then we have to go hungry like."

"My God!" bursts from the young man's lips, but he says no more. The next moment he has pressed a couple of sovereigns into the poor lad's hand, and is gone.

He wanders on through the same street. He takes no note of the name of it. His thoughts are far too busy for that. He is approaching another street, less lonely and better lighted than the one he is in. There are more people about, and he sees several women loitering up and down near the corner. Instinctively he crosses the street so as to avoid them. Two of them are making off after two men that have just passed by, the third is left alone. She spies the young duke at once, and runs across the street to cut him off. He sees he cannot avoid her, and pulls himself together. In another moment she is by his side, with one hand on his arm.

"Won't you come home with me, dear?" she says softly. "Won't you—"

"Peace, woman!" he almost shouts, as he flings off her hand from his arm. She starts back with a low cry, and he sees a face, young still, with traces of great beauty, but careworn and haggard with suffering. His heart is filled with a great pity; he feels that such sights as these are unendurable to him. He feels that he cannot face them.

"Poor thing, poor thing," he says gently; "forgive me if I was rough to you. This is no place for you, my child. You look a mere child; are you not one?"

"I am eighteen," she stammers.

"Eighteen, and so fallen!" he exclaims in a horrified tone. "Ah, child! get away out of this."

"And starve?" she exclaimes bitterly. "Easy for you to talk; you are not starving."

"Starving!" He utters that word with a peculiar intonation. It tells her what pity there is in his heart for her.

"Oh, sir!" she exclaims, "I would not be here if I were not driven to it. I don't want to be here. I hate it; I hate it! It is my hard, hard fate, that I am here."

"Have you no father, no mother to care for you?" he asks sadly.

"No, sir, not to care for me," she answers, with a sob. "Father's in gaol. Mother walks the streets like me, to make her bread. She told me I'd better do so too, unless I wanted to starve. That's how it is, sir."

He covers his face with one hand, and groans aloud. His thoughts have rushed back to the luxury he has but lately quitted; he compares it with the misery he has just witnessed. Once more his hand is in his pocket.

"If I give you this, my child," he says, drawing out a five-pound note, "will you promise me to go home at once, and leave these streets of infamy and wrong; and if I give you my card, and promise to place you in a way of earning an honest livelihood, will you call at my house tomorrow for a letter which I will leave to be given to you? Will you try and get your mother, too, to come with you?"

She bursts into tears. "Ah, sir! may God in heaven bless you. Yes, yes, I will promise; indeed I will. Gladly, too gladly."

He holds out to her the card and the bank-note. As she takes them she bends over his hand and kisses it passionately. He draws it gently away.

"Remember your promise," he says quietly.

"I will," she answers, between her sobs. "Oh God! I would die for you, sir."

He watches her as she turns away and disappears in the gloom. Heavy tears are in his eyes.

"I must go home now," he whispers to himself. "*I cannot see more.*"

VI

"Ten to one bar one, ten to one bar one, ten to one bar one." The ring is roaring itself hoarse over these words; the hubbub is deafening; it reverberates all around; it echoes and re-echoes through the hot June air.

It is Derby Day. The waving downs of Epsom are alive with people; they swarm over every cranny and nook of the wide-stretching space on either side of the straight run-in; they surge to and fro like a sea of dark, moving matter; they contribute to the busy air of life, that has established its reign on all around. It is a great day. Always crowded, Epsom is more than usually so. Old *habitués* of the place declare, that never in their memories—and some of them have pretty old ones—can they recollect such a swarming throng.

But the reason for all this crowd is an excellent one. Have not the people come to see the great horse win?

He is in the paddock now, and is being stripped, for the saddling bell has rung. He is the centre of a pushing, hustling throng, all eager to catch a glimpse of the unbeaten hero of the day; for have not his triumphs been such as a horse and its owner might well be proud of, carrying, as he does, the laurels of the Dewhurst Plate, the Middle Park Plate, and the Two Thousand Guineas upon him?

What a grand-looking horse he is! How his rich, ruddy chestnut coat glistens in the sun like armour of burnished gold! Such a quiet beast, too, neither snatching, nor stamping, nor doing aught that a restive or vicious racehorse would.

"He can't be beat!" exclaims a young man who has been standing silently watching the stripping process. "I'll be a man or a mouse, Florrie; I'll stand every penny I've got on him or lose all, hanged if I won't!"

"Don't be a fool, Reggie," answers the lady addressed. She is close beside him, and has laid her hand on his arm. It is Flora Desmond.

"Fool or no fool," he answers quickly, "I mean to have this dash. I tell you he can't be beat. It's only a question of pluck laying the odds. Hanged if I won't stand every penny of the £100,000 which I have got on him. They are taking twenty to one now."

"Suppose he is beaten," she says quietly?

"Then I shall be a beggar," he answers, with a laugh; "but I'm not afraid. By God! I'll stand my chance."

He turns as he speaks, and tries to get through the crowd. What can she do? She has little or no influence with him, and if she had, this is no place in which to reason and argue with him. She feels downcast and sad; for although she, like everyone else, has little doubt in her mind that Corrie Glen will win, there is just the chance, ever so slight, that he might not. And if he does not, "well, what then?"

"Ruin!" she soliloquises half aloud, as she puts the question to herself, and answers it in that one word. There is a bitter smile on Flora Desmond's face, for she knows what ruin would mean.

"Are you looking Corrie Glen over, Lady Flora?" inquires a voice at her elbow. She has no need to turn round to discover the speaker, for she knows the voice full well. It is that of Hector D'Estrange.

He has heard the conversation between Sir Reginald Desmond and his wife, and as the former elbows his way through the crowd, he has pushed forward and sidled into his place by her side.

"Yes, Mr. D'Estrange, I am," she answers just a shade wearily. "Like everyone else, I am looking at the crack. I suppose he can't be beat? By-the-bye," she adds hastily, "you've a horse in this race, haven't you?"

"I have a mare," he replies significantly; "and whom do you think is going to ride her, qualified for a jockey's license, and everything on purpose?"

"Who?" she inquires absently.

"Why, Bernie Fontenoy. The boy's a splendid rider, and mark my words, Lady Flora, if he doesn't win, it will be a near thing between my Black Queen and Corrie Glen."

She starts. She has never known Hector D'Estrange to err yet, and her husband's rash act recurs more forcibly to her mind. "May I see Black Queen?" she inquires hastily.

"Certainly," he answers; "come with me."

They push through the crowd, still surging round the chestnut horse, and make their way across the paddock to a quiet spot, where very few people are observable. A coal-black mare has just been stripped, and her jockey is standing close beside her. His colours are tinselled-gold.

"That is Black Queen," observes Hector D'Estrange quietly. "You are a good judge of a horse, Lady Flora; what do you think of her?"

She does not reply, but walks up to within a few paces of the mare, and looks her over keenly. She sees before her an animal which, to her eyes, used though she is to good-looking horses, is a perfect picture.

The mare is coal-black; there is not a white hair on her; she is faultlessly shaped all over.

"I think that I never saw a greater beauty in all my life!" exclaims Flora Desmond, and there is a true ring of admiration in her tone. As she speaks the Duke of Ravensdale comes up.

"So you're going to win the Derby, Bernie, are you?" he inquires jokingly, as he raises his hat to Flora Desmond, and holds out his hand to her. "Nice youngster that," he continues, addressing her. "Gave me no peace till I gave him leave to ride, which I never should have done, had it not been at Hector's request; and now I do believe that he thinks he is going to win!"

"I shall have a good try, Evie," the boy replies in a mettled voice. "I can't do more than ride my very best, can I, Mr. D'Estrange?"

"No indeed, my boy, that you cannot," answers this latter kindly. "Do your best; no one can ask for more."

There is a light in Bernie's eye, a flush on his cheek. Flora notes them both. Full well she knows what they mean.

"Mr. D'Estrange," she says hurriedly, moving a few paces aside, "may I speak to you for one moment?"

He follows her with a grave, inquiring look.

"I know you never bet," she continues quickly, "but do you know what they are laying against Black Queen?"

"A hundred to one," he answers carelessly.

"Then will you do me a great favour?" she says in a sad, pleading voice. "Though you never bet, and I hate it, will you lay me out a £1,000 in the ring, so that if Black Queen wins I shall win £100,000? I wouldn't ask this of you, only you seem so confident in your mare, and, and—"

"I understand," he answers quietly; "I'll do it for you, Lady Flora. The race lies between Corrie Glen and my mare, and I quite understand why you want to back the latter. I couldn't help hearing what Sir Reginald said over there. It's on his account, is it not?"

"It is," she answers bitterly. "As you heard him, you will quite understand."

"Leave it to me," he continues in a kind voice. "I'll just give Bernie his last instructions, and then I'll hurry across and do your commission. Will you come over to the stand with Ravensdale?"

"I will," she answers, with a grateful look in her eyes.

And now Bernie has got his last orders, and the beautiful mare, with its handsome jockey, is moving slowly across the paddock to the course.

The tinselled-gold on the boy's jacket gleams and sparkles in the sun, and many an admiring eye rests on the two as they pass out.

He has come out last, and is at the tail end of the long file of horses parading past the stand. Everyone is so keen on singling out the favourite, that Black Queen at first is not much noticed. Yet the sparkling gold on the jacket is bound to attract the eye, and the fact that Lord Bernard Fontenoy, brother of the Duke of Ravensdale, is riding the coal-black mare, awakens interest in the dark steed.

"Why, it's little Lord Bernie riding, I do declare!" giggles Mrs. de Lacy Trevor to Lord Charles Dartrey, who is leaning over her chair pointing out the horses and jockeys on the card in her lap. "What a duck he looks! Oh, I wish Dodo was here!"

"Can't think what D'Estrange means by putting the boy up. He can't win; and it will only break his heart," exclaimes Lord Charles superciliously.

"How old is Lord Bernie?" queries Mrs. Trevor in an interested voice. "Oh, I do wish the darling would win!"

"That's impossible," says Lord Charles loftily, "nothing can beat Corrie Glen."

They are cantering down to the post now, the favourite with great raking strides covering his ground comfortably, and playing kindly with his snaffle, as his jockey leans forward and eases him a bit. Bernie has not started the Black Queen yet; he is leaning down talking to his brother. All eyes are upon him, however, as they see him squeeze the duke's hand, which is laid on the boy's knee. Suddenly, however, he dresses himself upright.

"I must go now, Evie dear," he says, and there is a tremor in his voice. "Oh, pray that I may win!"

Then he sets the mare into a canter, and follows in the wake of the others.

"My word! that mare moves well," exclaimed Sir Horsey de Freyne nervously; "don't half like the look of her. Think I must have something on her for luck. Belongs to that deuced lucky fellow D'Estrange, too. Shouldn't be surprised to see the gold jacket flashing in first."

"Bosh!" answers Sir Reginald Desmond, who is standing next to him. "My dear old fellow, it's only throwing your money away. Corrie Glen can't be beat."

But Sir Horsey de Freyne is not convinced, and goes off to see what he can get laid him against the mare.

"S'pose you've backed the favourite, old chap?" inquires another shining light at Sir Reggie's elbow.

"Yes," answers this latter shortly.

"Had a plunge, eh?" persists the golden youth, who doesn't know a horse from a cow.

"Have got £100,000 on him," is Sir Reggie's curt reply. He is looking through his glasses, and his face is rather white.

"Oh! I say," blurts out the youth, as he edges off to tell all those who will listen to him; "I say, you know, Desmond's laid out £100,000 on the favourite."

There is a murmur in the stands; it runs through them all like an electric shock. "They're off!" is the hoarse cry that resounds suddenly from hundreds of throats. To an excellent start, Lord Marcovitch Bolster has despatched the lot, and as they all stare through their glasses, they can perceive that Hamptonian has taken up the running, closely followed by Masterman Ready, Holyoakes, and Kesteven. Lying fifth is the favourite, and two lengths behind him gleams a flashing spot of gold. A strange horse is overhauling the lot, Hamptonian drops back, and the stranger creeping to the front makes the pace terrific. But fast as he goes he cannot shake off the chestnut, who apparently without effort is going easily enough, and keeping his place as fifth in the crowd. Now the spot of gold seems nearer up; it passes Corrie Glen, and falls into fourth place, Kesteven retiring to the rear. They are racing down the incline. Masterman Ready begins to tire, and the spot of flashing gold closes up to Holyoakes. These two come along neck and neck, Corrie Glen just behind them, the strange horse still in the van. Tattenham Corner is reached. They round it in the order named, and enter the straight; but here the stranger is in difficulties, and Holyoakes and Black Queen, on which sits the spot of gold rigid almost as marble, begin to close upon him. A little more than a quarter of a mile from home they reach him, and he flings up the sponge, retiring to the rear. There are only three horses left in the race now, Holyoakes, Black Queen, and Corrie Glen. This latter is drawing up to the first two named, with great raking strides he is alongside them, and quickly the three are abreast. A distant roar sounds in Bernie's ears, there is a film over his eyes, his heart feels as if it must stop beating, but he sits very still, and does not attempt to urge his horse any faster. Suddenly he sees a flash on his left. The jockey who is riding Holyoakes has his whip out, and Bernie knows he has nothing any longer to fear from him. He glances to the right; the great chestnut is flashing along; there is no whip needed there.

"Oh God! let me win," bursts from the boy's pale lips, as he tightens his rein ever so little, and touches the mare gently with the spur. He is surprised at the effect. He thought she had been going fast before, but she is going faster now. She is quite a length ahead of Corrie Glen, and the jockey of this latter is visibly surprised. He has begun to ride the horse at last, and his whip is actually out.

"Corrie Glen wins! Corrie Glen wins!" comes the wild shout from the stands, as the noble chestnut, with a supreme effort, closes with the Black Queen. They are hardly fifty yards from the winning post; the roar is terrific. Bernie hears it, but he can see nothing now. He makes, however, a final effort, and calls on the mare once more; he has never used his whip.

"Corrie Glen wins! Corrie Glen wins!" The words pierce to his brain. He has done his best, he cannot do more; he knows this well; yet would to God he could win!

"Corrie Glen wins!" Ah! they don't know the Black Queen. She has answered the boy's last call; she has made one more magnificent effort; and, shooting ahead of the favourite, passes the post a winner by a neck!

What a yell goes up from the ring! Blank deadly consternation is in the faces of the backers. In the stands there is very little cheering. Hardly a soul in all that vast crowd has backed the "dark" black mare.

And Sir Reginald Desmond is still standing where we left him. He is deadly pale; his arms are folded on his chest; there is despair in his eyes.

"Had a bad race, old chap? I fear we all have," says a voice at his elbow. He laughs, and turns towards the speaker. This latter starts as he notices the ghastly, haggard look on the young baronet's face.

"Yes—well, yes, haven't had a good one," answers Sir Reggie coolly, taking out his cigarette-case and leisurely selecting a cigarette therefrom. "Have a cigarette, Fernley?"

"No thanks, Desmond, am just going to have lunch. Wonderful race young Bernie Fontenoy rode there. Won't the brat be proud?"

"Oh! ah! yes, won't he?" answers Sir Reggie absently. His thoughts have wandered again. He is looking ahead into the black future. Now that it is too late, he is cursing himself for a fool and an idiot. Oh! why did he not take Flora's advice?

The stand in which he is, is nearly empty. Everyone is making off to get lunch; in a few minutes it is entirely deserted. He sits on alone in it. The cigarette he had lit so ostentatiously not long since has gone out, but it is still clenched between his teeth.

The future *will* rise to his mind. How can such as he face it? He has never been brought up to do anything; he is ill-read, ill-taught, and ignorant. He has never given his mind to anything but amusing himself; and now if he pays the ring what is justly owing to it he will be a beggar, with nothing to live on and nothing to look forward to but misery, and, in his eyes, disgrace.

Poor Sir Reginald! He feels his position acutely, it is burning itself into his brain. He feels that it is past endurance, that *he cannot* face it.

"I'll go home," he says wearily to himself. "I can't face Flora after this; it's all too dreadful."

He rises wearily and goes out. The back of the stand is more or less crowded by the hangers-on and scum of every racecourse. How he hates and loathes the sight of them now; how their rough, coarse, pleasure-seeking faces bring up to his mind, with haunting horror, the great loss which he has sustained! He is staying near the race-course, and has not far to go, so he hurries through the crowd and makes straight for The Laurels, which is the name of the place. He reaches it, and tries the front door. It is locked; of course no one is expected back yet. He knows of a side-entrance though through the smoking-room. Ten to one the careful servants have forgotten it. He walks round and tries it. Yes, true enough, they have. Very quietly Sir Reginald slips in. In another moment he is upstairs and in his bedroom.

He turns the key in the door, and goes over to the writing table. His face is still deadly pale, and he walks like one who has had too much to drink. He sits at the table and scrawls a few hurried lines. They are as follows:—

"Flora dear, forgive me. I've been a brute and an idiot. Would to God I had taken your advice! But it's too late now. You'll pay the ring for me, dear. Let them know it was my last wish. If I lived we should be beggars, and I can't condemn you and the 'little one' to that. But at my death you'll get all that money that is to come to you and the child. Goodbye, dear old girl. You've been good and kind to me. This is about all Reggie can do to show you he is grateful. Goodbye. Forgive."

She has been looking for him a long time, and so has Hector D'Estrange, but there is no sign of Sir Reginald Desmond anywhere. At last she can stand it no longer.

"I must go back to The Laurels," she says; "perhaps he is there."

Estcourt, who is standing by her, offers to accompany her, and thither they proceed in silence. Of course when they reach the house no one has seen him. The servants assure her ladyship that Sir Reginald has not returned; they must have seen him if he had. They forget to add that the greater number of them have been perched on the high wall surrounding The Laurels, during the greater part of the day, watching the races.

"I'll just run up to the bedroom and have a look," says Flora to Estcourt. "I won't be a minute."

He waits below, but almost directly hears his name called,—

"Estcourt, come here."

He races up the stairs. He finds her standing outside the door of a bedroom.

"I can't get in," she says hurriedly. "I've called, but there is no reply. Oh, Estcourt! do you think he is in there?"

He makes no reply, but runs downstairs. In a few minutes he is back with a hatchet. Curious servants are following him.

"Stand back," he says to Flora. She obeys, and the young man brings the hatchet with tremendous force against the lock. Three, four, five strokes, and he has broken it to shivers. Then he opens the door.

Sir Reginald Desmond is seated at his writing table. His left hand is beneath his chest, his head is resting on the table above it, his right is outstretched and hanging over the side. Just below it on the floor lies a revolver, and drip, drip, drip, dripping on to the chair on which he sits, is a stream of running blood. Who shall judge him as he lays there silent, and fast stiffening? for—

"He is dead, and blame and praise fall on his ear alike, now hushed in death."

Those may do so who can. I cannot.

VII

Were you in the Commons last night? Did you go to hear Hector D'Estrange?"

"Rather; I think all the world was there, or trying to be there. I don't think I have ever seen such a crowd before."

"What a wonderful speaker he is, to be sure!"

"Yes. With the exception of Gladstone, I don't suppose there ever was one like him, or ever will be again. Talk of orators of bygone days! Pooh! they never came up to him."

"Well, the women have got the Suffrage in full at last, thanks to him. The next thing is to see what use they'll make of it."

"Better, perhaps, than we men have."

The speakers are two men, the Honourable Tredegar Molyneux, M.P., and Colonel des Vœux of the Blues. Nearly four years have passed since the events related in the last chapter. The world has been slowly marching forward, and many things have happened between that time and this. In the political world, and in Parliament, like everywhere else, Hector D'Estrange has made a stir. His eloquence and debating power are the wonder of all who hear him, and his practical, sympathetic knowledge of the social questions of the day has made him the idol of the masses. He has just succeeded in carrying his Woman's Suffrage Bill by a large majority, thereby conferring on women, married or unmarried, in this respect, identical rights with men. And now today in the monster Hall of Liberty, which he has founded, and which has been erected by the lavish subscriptions of the women of Great Britain, Ireland, and the world at large, he is to preside at the ceremony of its opening. It *is* a monster building. Talk of Olympia, of the Albert Hall— why, they are dwarfs beside it!

In shape it is circular, and towers aloft towards heaven, its great dome pinnacle crowned by a cap of glass, which report declares to consist of a million panes. Around this glass a gilded crown is twined, and holding it there—one in a kneeling attitude, the other upright, with one hand high upraised towards heaven—are two gilded women's forms. They are the Statues of Liberty.

The interior of this vast structure is wonderful to look upon. The floor or centre is raised, and constructed so as to move on a pivot slowly round. It consists of an immense ring, the middle of which presents the appearance of a giant circus. On the right, or side facing the great entrance, is a monster swimming bath, and exactly opposite, or on the other side of the circus, is a huge platform. Suspended in mid air, a very network of trapezes and other gymnastic appliances hang, while stretched tightly beneath them is a monster net. Around the arena, with a low palisade separating it from the same, is a broad circular horse-ride, and raised slightly above this, running all round in a similar manner, a roomy promenade. Then come tier above tier, tier above tier of seats, amidst which here and there boxes are placed promiscuously, while dotted about all over these countless and seemingly never-ending stories, are cosy platforms enthroned in a wealth of green, where abundance of refreshments are obtainable.

The seats come to an end at last, and are replaced by six broad balconies running entirely round the building, and built one above the other; opening on to these balconies are what appear to the spectator in the arena as thousands of pigeon-holes. In reality they are doors, communicating each one with a tiny but compact room, in which stands a bed, two chairs, a washhand-stand, a small dressing table, and a writing table. It is stated that in all, opening off from these balconies, are ten thousand rooms. These rooms have been included in the building to accommodate women students from all parts of the world, who may wish to take part in the physical drill or educational advantages afforded by this great central institute for the training of womankind. Attached to the Hall of Liberty are large lecture-rooms, studying-rooms, and reading-rooms, and in connection with these a monster library. Outside the building are the stables, one of the wonders of London, the grooms being entirely composed of girls and women; and clustering round the mother structure like a miniature town, are the pretty cottages and dwellings of the immense staff of instructors, teachers, and lecturers connected with the institution. It is a wonderful structure, and its erection is a triumph, the magnitude of which can hardly be measured, for Hector D'Estrange. It was he who conceived it, it was he who submitted it to the approval of his countrymen, and it was he who commanded the expenditure of the voluminous subscriptions, which in answer to his appeal poured in from all quarters of the globe. No less marvellous was the rapidity with which it arose, thousands of workmen having been employed in its construction.

It is finished now; it towers to heaven like a mighty giant from some unknown world. The gilded Statues of Liberty flash back the sun's rays, and stand out to view for miles and miles around. All London is flocking to the ceremony of its opening, for is not the genius that conceived and placed it there to be the principal functionary of the day?

All is orderly in the streets; the vast crowd is held and kept in check by the military and the police. A good-humoured, happy crowd, it seems to be, with here and there occasionally a little rough horse-play. But no harm is done. The people are on their best behaviour, for Hector D'Estrange, the idol of that people, has appealed to them to preserve order.

The vast building is rapidly filling. Since the great doors have been thrown open, it has been one successive influx of people. There is no disorder, for there is a separate passage for the holders of each class of ticket, and along these the incomers are marshalled by the liveried servants of the establishment. It is a wonderful sight to see the people swarming to their places, and all the while through the building trembles dreamy music, which thrills the senses, and makes them all aglow with gentle and tender feeling. At last it is full. There is not an inch of standing room in all that vast space set aside for spectators; every seat is appropriated. Not a vacant one to be seen, and it is computed that there are 50,000.

Every class is there; from the prince and peer, to the labouring man and peasant, all have come, attracted by the all-powerful genius who is to address that monster meeting this day. Imbued with the same feeling, impelled by the same curiosity, attracted by the same sentiment, that crowd of mixed denominations and sexes awaits his coming in breathless expectation.

And it has not long to wait. The clock is striking eleven, when a distant roar is heard, and the strains of martial music come floating from afar. In the great Hall of Liberty a sudden hush has fallen; the dreamy music has ceased abruptly, and a supreme silence reigns.

Again that roar! It is like the booming of a thousand cannons. It is steady now and unceasing; it rushes forward along the dense walls of spectators that throng the streets on either side of the way up which Hector D'Estrange has to pass.

A whisper runs through the vast hall, a whisper of suppressed excitement and expectation. "He is coming; he is coming!" is on everyone's lips, as with eyes aglow and hearts thrilling with eagerness, the people bend forward in their seats to watch for him.

The crowds outside the building have begun to cheer. The martial music is very distinct now. The plaudits are every moment becoming more intense, until they break into a deep and prolonged roar. As they do so, the great folding doors of the Hall of Liberty are thrown open, and the people rise in a body to their feet.

He is entering now. Preceded by the band of the White Regiment of the Women's Volunteer Companies, playing a march triumphant, he passes through the giant portals. His head is bared, and he is mounted on a milk-white horse, which he sits with grace and ease. As he does so the sun shines down on his dark auburn hair, lighting it up with the tints of old-gold that play amidst the curls which nestle on his high, white brow, while the sapphire light in his glorious eyes shoots forth with a gleam of triumph as he surveys the magnificent scene.

He is dressed in the White Guard Regiment uniform of the Women's Volunteer Companies, of which he is Commander-in-Chief; but the regiment itself is his own especial one. It was the first which he established four and a half years ago, when he first took the matter in hand. The idea has prospered since then, and the women enrolled in all the companies of the Volunteer force number 200,000.

It is a fitting uniform for the occasion, one which he has done well to don; for the first business of today's ceremonial will be the march past of the "picked" of the companies of these 200,000.

He has ridden round the broad, spacious horse-ride followed by one or two especial friends, conspicuous amongst whom is the Duke of Ravensdale. The cheering is deafening; it never ceases for a moment. It swells and swells again, like the mighty mid-ocean waves, that bear onwards in their wild career to break on the lone sea-shore.

And now he has dismounted, and, with his friends, has taken his place on the evergreen flower-decked platform. Even as he does so his dark sapphire eyes are raised aloft, and sweep with their dreamy gaze the thousands that throng that vast Hall of Liberty, as if seeking amidst the multitude one especial form. It is even so; and as they roam the sea of faces, all turned to his, they are suddenly brought to a standstill. The anxious, searching look within them dies away, giving place to one of calm contentment and repose, for Speranza is there.

The mother's eyes are fixed upon her child. Through the filmy distance of space cannot Gloria perceive this well? For a moment, one brief moment, the hero of the hour is Gloriana de Lara, in the next, he is Hector D'Estrange. The audience is still cheering,—it seems as though it will never cease,—but he has raised his hand, and like magic a great silence falls.

"Ladies and gentlemen," he begins, and the clear, exquisite voice thrills through the huge building, "I shall have a few words to say to you before I declare the Hall of Liberty open, but first we will witness the march past of the representatives of all the companies of the Women's Volunteer force of which I have the honour to be Commander-in-Chief."

A flourish of trumpets and loud cheering greets this announcement. Once more the great entrance doors unfold, the band of the White Regiment strikes up a march, as through the portals, ten abreast, and mounted on grey horses, that regiment advances at a trot.

And at their head is one whom we have seen before. Very handsome she looks in her uniform of pure white cloth, with the gold facings glittering on her breast, and her sword in its silver sheath dangling sparkling at her side. Flora Desmond is not greatly changed since we saw her last, in appearance certainly, but over her life has come a wondrous transformation. She is Hector D'Estrange's right hand, and in aiding him to carry out his noble aims is thoroughly in her element.

The white troopers advance at a trot rapid enough, but as each line passes the platform on which Hector D'Estrange is standing they break into a canter, increased to a gallop, whirling round the broad-spaced horse-ride in magnificent order. Looking along the serried line of horses' heads hardly a hair's breadth in difference can be distinguished, so compact is the position which is maintained throughout the ranks.

The march strains cease, and give way to a flourish of trumpets. Simultaneously the galloping steeds are reined on to their haunches, remaining motionless as statues. Thus they stand until the voice of Flora Desmond is heard giving the order to retreat, when they fall into position, and retire at the trot, she riding-round to join her chief on the platform.

And in this wise, headed by their respective bands and officers, representative companies of Hector D'Estrange's two hundred regiments march or gallop past him. The ceremony occupies some two hours, but they roll by all too quickly for the spectators, who, spellbound by what they see, watch the revolving scenes with the keenest interest.

The last one closes appropriately. Crashing and rumbling through the wide-opened entrance dash the artillery. They come on at a rapid pace, and wheeling round into the vast arena form up into splendid line. The work of detaching the horses and unlimbering the guns is that of a moment. In the next, a tremendous roar rings forth from the mouths of a score of cannon which have been rapidly charged and fired.

Ere the echoes have died away the horses are again attached, the guns as rapidly limbered up, and one by one the gun-carriages dash from the scene, the great doors closing upon them.

Then cheer after cheer rings through the densely packed building as Hector D'Estrange advances to the front of the platform to speak. But he is raising his hand once more, as though appealing to be heard, and again a great silence falls.

"We are here today," the bright, clear ringing voice declares, "to open a building the magnitude of which cannot be measured by any other in the world. The Hall of Liberty stands here today as a living witness to the desire of woman to be heard. It was six years ago that I first saw it in my dreams. It is reality now, and will endure through all time, as a memorial of the first great effort made by woman to shake off the chains of slavery, that ever since our knowledge of man began, have held her a prisoner in the gilded gaols of inactivity and helplessness. I stand here today prepared to deny that woman is the inferior of man, either in mental capacity or physical strength, provided always that she be given equal advantages with him. I go further still, and declare that in the former respect she is his superior. You deny it? Then give her the chance, and I have no fear but that she will prove that I have not lied. You have today seen passed in review 10,000 representatives of the 200,000 volunteers that in a little more than four years have been enrolled and drilled into the splendid efficiency witnessed on this memorable occasion. Will you pretend or seek to tell yourselves that in warfare they would be unavailing? I laugh such an idea to scorn. One of our most heart-stirring writers—I allude to Whyte-Melville—has left it declared in his writings, 'that if a legion of Amazons could be rendered amenable to discipline they would conquer the world.' He was right. The physical courage, of which men vaunt so much, is as nothing when compared with that greater and more magnificent virtue, 'moral courage,' which women have shown that they possess in so eminent a degree over men; and hence physical courage would come as an agreeable and welcome visitor where hitherto it has been forcibly denied admission.

"Men and women who hear me today, I beseech you ponder the truth of what I have told you in your hearts. You boast of a civilisation unparalleled in the world's history. Yet is it so? Side by side with wealth, appalling in its magnitude, stalks poverty, misery, and wrong, more appalling still. I aver that this poverty, misery, and wrong is, in a great measure, due to the false and unnatural position awarded to woman; nor will justice, reparation, and perfection be attained until she takes her place *in all things* as the equal of man.

"And now, my friends, I will detain you no longer. In this great Hall of Liberty woman will find much which has long been denied her. It is but a drop in the ocean of that which is her right, yet is it a noble beginning of that which must inevitably come. I declare this Hall of Liberty to be open."

That is all. He says no more, but with a stately inclination to the vast audience turns back to where his friends stand. His horse is led forward by a youthful orderly in the uniform of the White Regiment, and as he mounts it the band strikes up once more. Bareheaded as he entered, he rides slowly from the scene of his triumph, and passing again through the portals of the Hall of Liberty comes out into the densely, wall-lined street, amidst the roar of the thousands that are there to greet. Such is the welcome of *the people* to Hector D'Estrange.

VIII

Lord Westray sits alone in his sanctum in Grosvenor Square. There is an anxious expression on his face, for he has been expecting someone who has not turned up. He has already consulted his watch about half-a-dozen times, and he consults it again. Then he gets up and rings the bell.

He can hear it tinkling downstairs from where he sits. "A smart servant," he thinks to himself, "would have answered it quickly." Yet he would think this no longer, if he could only hear "his smart servant's" remark anent that bell.

"James," calls out that worthy, who is seated in the room on an easy armchair in front of the fireplace, with his feet against the chimney-piece, "what bell's that?"

"My lord's, sir," is the laconic reply from the lackey outside.

"Oh! ah! tha-a-anks. Let him ring again."

The bell does peal again, this time furiously, and Stuggins, with a face of disgust, pulls his feet down from the chimney-piece.

"My word! what a hard time of it we have's," he exclaimes to himself, as he rises slowly from his seat to go upstairs.

On reaching Lord Westray's sanctum, however, his face is composed and affable.

"This is the second time I've rung," exclaims Lord Westray angrily. "Surely, Stuggins, there is someone in the house to answer the bell."

"I was in my room, my lord, and did not hear it," responds Stuggins in a conciliatory voice.

"Has no one called yet, Stuggins?"

"No one, my lord."

"Well, he'll be here at any moment now. Mind he is shown up without any delay."

"Certainly, my lord."

And the sleek, over-fed domestic goes off smiling.

Ten minutes later, and there is a ring at the doorbell. Lord Westray starts and listens.

"It's he!" he exclaimes briefly.

And in a few minutes the "he" is politely waved in by Stuggins.

"Mr. Trackem, my lord."

"All right, Stuggins, shut the door. Not at home if anyone else calls."

"Very good, my lord."

The door is shut, and Lord Westray rises and shakes the new-comer by the hand.

"Glad to see you, Mr. Trackem," he observes heartily. "Began to fear you were not coming. A little late, eh?"

"A little, my lord, but I was usefully employed."

"Made out where she is, Mr. Trackem?"

"Yes," responds this latter solemnly.

Lord Westray rubs his hands delightedly.

"Where?" he asks eagerly.

"Near Windsor, my lord. I found it out by shadowing Mr. D'Estrange."

"Capital!" exclaims Lord Westray, with a laugh. "And does she still go under the name of Mrs. de Lara?"

"Yes, my lord."

"Now, Mr. Trackem, what are your plans?"

Mr. Trackem puts on a mysterious look, walks quickly to the door of the sanctum, and opens it suddenly. "What do you want?" he inquires sharply of someone without.

"If you please, sir, I was just coming in to see if his lordship had rung," answers Stuggins stolidly, who had never quitted the outside of the door since we last saw him, and who had been listening intently all the time.

"Lord Westray did *not* ring," answers Mr. Trackem, coldly, "and you are *not* required."

"Oh! very good, sir," and Stuggins retires defeated, and much put about.

Mr. Trackem watches the butler's retreating form till it is out of sight, then he closes the door softly, and returns to his original place near Lord Westray.

"These are my plans, my lord. I propose to take down two of my men by rail. Two will be ample, as more might attract attention and be in the way. I shall send a brougham and smart pair of trotters the day before. I have ascertained by observation that Mrs. de Lara invariably goes for a walk in the evening by herself, that her servants do not sit up for her, as she writes in her study late at night, and I have further ascertained that she is frequently in the habit of leaving the house before anyone is up, and coming up to town. This is a most valuable point, as her absence will attract no attention. But to be safe I have possessed myself of some of her writing paper and a sample of her writing, and a note will be duly left, apprising her maid of her departure, and intention to remain in London for a few days."

"By Jove, Mr. Trackem, you are a smart one! I don't see how your plan can fail," exclaims the wicked earl with a laugh.

"I never fail, my lord, in any of these little businesses," answers Mr. Trackem, with a suave smile.

"But ain't you afraid of the police finding you out?" inquires Lord Westray, just a little nervously.

Mr. Trackem laughs outright. "Police!" he exclaimes contemptuously. "What's the good of them? Think they know a lot, know nothing. Why, my lord, the police are useless in matters of this sort; and as for detectives, why, it's easy to green them up the wrong way. I don't fear them. I'm a match for every noodle detective in and around Scotland Yard, I am," and Mr. Trackem gives a self-satisfied laugh.

"Well, Mr. Trackem, when is it to be?" inquires the earl anxiously, after a short lull in the conversation.

"It's to be the day after tomorrow," answers Mr. Trackem. "Tomorrow my men go down. I shall follow, and just give them a squint at the place, and then they'll be all prepared for the next day. Never fear, my lord; by Wednesday she shall be in your power."

"In *my* power!" The words come triumphantly, though mutteringly, through the ground teeth of the man whom Speranza de Lara had called, and justly so, "a fiend in human shape." Yes, she had spurned him, loathed him, defied him, forbidden him her presence. Through these long years he had striven to regain her in vain, and now—ah, now!—he would be amply and surely revenged.

"Well, I am sure, Mr. Trackem, I cannot thank you sufficiently for the excellent way in which you have laid your plans in order to carry out my commission," he says warmly. "And now to business. I am to give you £50 down now, and the remaining £150 when the transaction is finally accomplished. Is not that so?"

"It is, my lord," answers the vile creature blandly.

Lord Westray pulls out a drawer in his writing table, and taking out a cheque book is not long in writing off an order for £50 to the credit of self. This he hands to his visitor, who accepts it deferentially, and commits it to a greasy pocket-book, after which he takes up his hat and stick, preparatory to leaving.

"Won't you take something?" inquires the earl with his hand on the bell. "A glass of sherry, brandy-and-soda, or what?"

"No thank you, my lord, nothing," answers Mr. Trackem. "Must keep a clear head in my business. Thanks all the same."

They shake hands, these two scheming monsters, both intent on a base and ruffianly deed, yet one of them is regarded as a gentleman, is received and welcomed by society, is high in the graces of the Government of the day, and accounted a clever man and useful statesman. Clothed in these mantles of virtue, he is free to do as he pleases. Wickedness will not bar Society's doors against him, or lose him his high preferments. Is he not a man, one of the dominant and self-styled superior race? Therefore, is he not free to do as he pleases?

THE DAY HAS COME,—a hot July one. Down upon the dusty country roads the sun has burnt fiercely all day long. The cattle and beasts of the field have eagerly sought for shade and refuge from the torturing flies that ever haunt their presence, but evening has fallen at last, and with it relief has come.

It is cool and pleasant along the banks of the old Thames. The silver streak glides sluggishly along, with the moon's pale light playing softly upon it. The stars twinkle merrily forth to endure their brief sweet reign; Nature looks ghostlike in her mantle of sleep.

A fairy cottage, half hidden in walnut trees and clinging ivy, peeps forth upon that scene. The smooth lawns around it gleam white as the driven snow beneath the moon's soft gleams. Tall dark trees rise up behind in ebony framework, making an efficient background, while through the still air trembles and quivers the nightingale's exquisite song.

It would seem, at a first glance, as if all were asleep in that cottage; but no, there is yet a light left in one of the rooms on the ground-floor. Suddenly a pair of window-doors in it are flung open, and a tall, graceful woman steps out through them. Her head is uncovered, the moon gleams down upon the thick masses of pale gold hair that cover it, and shines in her glittering eyes of turquoise-blue. It is Speranza de Lara.

"What a glorious night!" she soliloquises to herself. "I suppose my darling is speaking now. She said it would be about ten o'clock. Oh, Harry! my precious long-lost love, would that you could see *our* child now!"

She has pressed the ring with its glittering brilliants to her lips,— the only ring she wears. The stones flash and sparkle in the moon's light like gems of living fire, beautiful, pure, and shining as the love that is next her heart. Much more than a score of years have passed away since Harry Kintore died in her arms, but if she lived through countless scores of years that love would burn just the same. She wanders along the gravel carriage drive, her thoughts busy with the past. Anon they fleet forward to the future, and then a light of triumph dances in her eyes. But it is with the past that she is chiefly occupied this night, for it is the 14th of July, the anniversary of the day on which her darling died.

She has passed along the shady avenue, and entered a tiny straggling path, shut in by tall dark trees. It is a glade upon which the gardener has not been allowed to bestow his fostering care. He has been forbidden this spot by his mistress, who loves to leave it in possession of the primrose and violet, the wild anemone or dark blue hyacinth that Nature has scattered so plentifully around. It is Speranza's safe retreat, away from the outside world, the spot where she best loves to roam.

All is quiet; not a sound disturbs the tenor of her thoughts as she walks quietly along. Suddenly, however, her eye is arrested by a gleam of light in front of her. The next moment two dark forms spring forward in her path, and she sees that they are men.

Speranza is no coward. We already know that well. Screaming is without her ken, she has no knowledge of it. Of fear, she only knows the name. If it is a thrill that permeates the body from head to foot, and sends the blood rushing through the system with irresistible impetus, then Speranza knows what that strange, mysterious sensation called fear is. But then it only makes her feel defiant. She has no thought of fleeing. Her impulse is to stand and face the danger, whatever it may be.

"Who are you?" she asks in a quiet, measured voice; "and what do you want here?"

"You," is the laconic answer, as the speaker seizes her by the arm, and deftly getting behind her, endeavours to draw her two elbows together. The pain is excruciating, but Speranza's blood is up. She is no weakly woman, helpless with life-long inactivity and want of muscle power. She is strong and flexible as wire, and makes her assailant feel this too, as with a wrench she frees herself, and springs backward behind him, facing them both once more. With a foul oath the man who had first attacked her bares a short, ugly-looking knife, and his companion does so as well.

"No use resisting!" exclaims this latter. "If you do you'll get a taste of these. Better come quietly."

She does not even answer them. Her lovely head is thrown back, her blue eyes shoot defiance, even while in them trembles the look of

LADY FLORENCE DIXIE

despair. Her hands hang clenched by her side, but she never quails for a second.

They rush at her, their knives poised threateningly. She seizes the blades with both her hands, and holds them with the grim clutch of a last great effort. With a brutal laugh they jerk them backwards, and the sharp, keen edges cut clean into her tightly closed palms. Out pours the rich, dark blood from the cruel, gaping wounds, as with a low cry, the first that has escaped her, she lets go her hold. Then, with the ferocity of tigers, they spring upon, and force her to the ground. In another moment the gag is on her mouth, tight straps are round her arms and ankles, and she is a prisoner at their feet.

"Come on quick, now!" exclaims one of the men. "My, Bill! she be a strong, plucky one, and no mistake! If it 'adn't been for that there root we shouldn't have mastered her so easily—no, nor we should."

The root referred to is the jagged, stumpy end of a fallen tree. Against this Speranza's head had struck in falling, rendering her senseless. No wonder they tied her so easily.

They lift her between them, and carry her across the copsewood towards a low hedge, outside which lies the road. Over this they hoist her, and then lay her down on the pathway, one of them giving a long, low whistle.

There is an answering whistle down the road, a rumbling and stamping as of carriage wheels and horses' feet. Two lights gleam through the darkness, like the eyes of some terrible monster, and the next moment a carriage dashes up.

"Got her?" inquires a thin, spare man, jumping out.

"Right as a trivet, sir," they answer.

"Well, put her in! Look sharp; no time to lose. I thought I heard footsteps as I came along," and Mr. Trackem, for it is he, holds open the door.

They obey his orders without more ado, and then he jumps in.

"Now then! look alive, men! One on the box, one in with her and me."

It is done. The men are "sharp uns." They know their master, and he knows his men. The next moment the carriage is bowling along towards Windsor, *en route* for London.

Who will track them, who discover them? Not the detectives of Scotland Yard!

IX

There has been a late sitting in the House of Commons. A protracted debate on the crowded condition of the filthy alleys and slums in that most wonderful city of the world, London, has kept members fully occupied. But twelve o'clock, midnight, has struck, and the Commons are dispersing. It has been a great night for Hector D'Estrange. He has spoken for an hour and a half to a spell-bound audience; for does it not know full well that the subject of that night's discussion is one in which he is no novice, it having been undertaken on his own motion?

He has spoken for an hour and a half, and has told them many things. Has he not a right to do so? None like him have dived into those terrible slums, have visited night after night, as he has done, those abodes of crime, of vice, of wickedness, and of misery. He knows them well, and has depicted them as they *are*, to the wondering representatives of a nation, in language of which he alone is master.

He has seen much, and knows much of the horrors which he has depicted so vividly, yet not even he knows some of the depths of infamy that exist in that cesspool of Modern Babylon. He has yet another experience to incur.

"Dear old Hector, that was a grand speech of yours!" exclaims the Duke of Ravensdale, who, having been an attentive listener during the debate, has run down to join his friend as the latter leaves the Commons. "Come across to Montragee House, and let us have a little supper. Wish you would stay there the night, old man!"

"I can't, Evie," replies Hector. "I have to go down to Windsor by an early train, and must go home and order my things to be packed up; but I'll come across for half an hour or so and have a mouthful, as I went without my dinner."

They walk along, linked arm-in-arm, towards Whitehall, and as they do so Big Ben chimes out the hour of half-past twelve.

"How time flies, to be sure!" remarks the young duke thoughtfully. "Funny thing time is—eh. Hector?"

"It is," answers this latter gravely; "a something without being, shape, or substance, and yet a thing that has been, is, and yet shall be."

"What a happy chap you ought to be, Hector! I don't suppose there's an hour in your life which you can look back upon as having wasted or misspent, save in doing good and trying to help others," exclaims his friend in an almost envious tone. "Would to God I could say the same of myself!"

"Hush, Evie! don't try and make me vain; and don't run yourself down before me. I won't allow it. God knows you are earnest enough in your desire to do good, and, dear Evie, you have succeeded. I don't suppose there's another in your position who has done so much. I never had such a good true friend as you in all my undertakings, except one, and of course I except her."

"Her!" exclaims his friend, in a somewhat surprised voice. "Whom, Hector?"

"My mother," he answers quietly. "She has been my right hand through life. I could not have got on without her."

"Your mother, Hector!" says the duke in a low voice. "Have you a mother alive?"

"Yes, Evie, and one of the best that ever lived. I will introduce her to you some day. She knows you well by hearsay, for I have often spoken of you to her. But a favour, dear old Evie; don't ever mention her to anyone; promise me."

"Of course not. Hector. You know the simplest wish of yours is law to me. Well, here we are; we'll finish our chat inside over some soup and oysters, and anything else you like to have."

The duke's hand is on the bell, but he pulls it very softly.

"Won't do to peal it," he remarks. "The sound would awaken Bernie, he's such a light sleeper; and always will get up to welcome me if he awakes, dear little chap."

"Let's see, how old is he now?" queries Hector D'Estrange; "well nigh sixteen, is he not? He's a dear lad, and I like him especially on account of his love for you. He does love you, Evie."

"Yes," answers the duke softly, "and I love him. Bernie is all I have got to love, unless it be you, Hector."

He does not see the bright flush that rises to Hector D'Estrange's beautiful face, or the passionate look in the sapphire eyes. It might have startled him if he had. But the great massive doors are unclosing now, and he enters, followed by his friend.

"Supper in my study, Repton, please," he exclaims. "Is Lord Bernard asleep?"

"Fast, your Grace," answers that individual confidentially, "His lordship wanted to sit up for your Grace, but when I gave him your Grace's message he went straight to bed."

"That's right," says the duke heartily. "Bernie's a good lad. God bless him!"

The two have moved on into the duke's study, and Repton has hurried off to command his Grace's supper to be served immediately. He has pompous manners, has Repton, a high opinion of himself, and certain notions of his own importance and dignity, but he is a good servant nevertheless, and a faithful one. He is not of the Stuggins' class. He would as soon dream of keeping his Grace waiting for his supper as of jumping over the moon.

The consequence is, that in the twinkling of an eye supper is served in the study. And the two friends, as they sit discussing it, wander off on some favourite theme, so that the time passes quicker than they think. Suddenly they are startled by hearing a bell peal. The duke springs to his feet.

"Good heavens! What can that be?" he exclaims nervously. "Is it Bernie's bell; is the boy ill, I wonder? I must go and see. It's past two o'clock."

"It's the front door bell, I think," says Hector D'Estrange. "Hark, Evie! there are voices in the entrance hall. Open the door and listen."

The duke does so. A woman's voice is plainly distinguishable, appealing to Repton.

"For God's sake," he hears her saying, "let me see the duke. I must see him. It is a matter of life and death. If you tell him it is for Mr. D'Estrange he will see me, I know."

"I have no orders from his Grace to admit you," answers Repton pompously, "and certainly cannot disturb his Grace at this hour. You must write or call again tomorrow morning, and all I can do is to report your wish to his Grace."

He bangs the door to as he speaks, but the next moment steps sound behind him, and Hector D'Estrange has seized the handle and pulled it open. His face is very white, and there is terror in his eyes.

"Rita!" he calls out, "is that you, Rita? My God! what brings you here?"

"Mr. D'Estrange!" she bursts out with a low, glad cry. "Oh, are you here? Thank God! thank God!"

She has rushed forward and seized him by the hand, and the duke, who has followed close behind him, recognises in the youthful, fair-featured girl the sad, haggard, careworn, starving creature whom but a few years back he had rescued from prostitution and degradation. Yet in what a terrible condition she seems. Her dress is torn and mud-stained, her shoes likewise, her fair, soft hair dishevelled and hanging about her face and down her back, while her expression is that of one scared by a terrible fear.

"Come quick, come quick!" she cries imploringly, "before it is too late. Oh, Mr. D'Estrange! they have waylaid her, and carried her off. I saw her bound, with her poor cut bleeding hands, and could not help her; but I know where she is, and can guide you to the place, if you will only come."

"Rita," exclaims Hector D'Estrange, in a voice the very calmness of which fills her with awe, "come into the duke's study for a minute, and explain yourself. Follow me."

He leads the way with Evie Ravensdale following, and she close behind the duke. As for Repton, he is rigid with astonishment.

The three enter the study, and the door is closed. "Now, Rita," queries Hector excitedly, "explain."

"I will," she cries again. "It is your mother. She was out in her favourite walk this evening about ten, and I was coming home rather late from Windsor. I saw her attacked by two men in the spinny, bound hand and foot, after having been knocked senseless. A carriage drove up, and they put her into it. My first impulse was to rush to help her and shout for assistance, but in a moment I reflected how useless that would be. I determined to hang on to the carriage behind, and see where they took her to. It was a terrible drive, but God helped me, and I succeeded, though I'm about done. I saw the house they took her into. I know the spot well; I can take you there straight now. But come, please come, or it will be too late."

There is a look of fury and hatred so intense in Hector D'Estrange's eyes, that the duke can hardly recognise him as the sweet, gentle-featured friend whom he loves so dearly.

"Evie," he says in a strained, unnatural voice, "I can explain nothing now. It is impossible. But you can trust me, Evie. My mother, my precious mother, is in terrible danger. Will you help me to save her?"

The duke's reply is laconic, but Hector knows its meaning. They are simple words, "I will."

"Then come," he exclaims feverishly; "lead on, Rita, brave, plucky Rita! I'll never forget what you have done today."

She does not reply, for they are hurrying out of the room. They are in the hall now, and both Hector and Evie Ravensdale have seized their hats. But the next moment the duke has slipped a loaded revolver into his pocket, and handed another to his friend.

"Take this," is all he says, "You may want it."

There is a four-wheeler at the door. They all three get in quickly. As Rita does so she gives the order, "Whitechapel. Quick," she adds, "and you shall be paid well!"

The cab-horse trots swiftly along. The hope of a substantial fare has given the cabby wings. No well-bred brougham horse could go quicker. He flies along does that old cab-horse.

On the outskirts of Whitechapel Rita calls a halt. "We must get out here," she observes. "Mr. D'Estrange, please give the cabman a sovereign, and tell him to wait."

He obeys her. He can trust her, can Hector D'Estrange. Ever since the day when, at Evie Ravensdale's request, he had appointed her as his own and his mother's secretary, Rita Vernon has served him with a fidelity and painstaking exactitude of which he knows no parallel. She leads the way through dark, uninviting streets. She knows the locality well. She learnt it years ago, before Evie Ravensdale came there to save her from a doom far more terrible than death. She had declared then that she would willingly die for him. The same feeling animates her now. For Evie Ravensdale Rita Vernon would deem it a happiness to die.

They have passed through courts and filthy alleys, through streets well and ill-lighted. Very few people are about. Only a policeman or two on their beats pass them as they move along. Now they are turning into a sort of crescent or half square, with houses superior to those of the localities they have traversed. As they do so Rita turns to the two men following her, and pointing to a house at the further end, exclaims, "There!"

There are no lights in the windows; the place is silent and dark.

"How shall we get in?" asks the duke.

There is a bitter smile on Rita's face as she replies.

"I will show you, but remember you must play your part. I shall pretend I am bringing you here, and that there's another woman coming. I'll order a room, and once in there I know how to find her."

She says no more, but passes swiftly along the pavement, they close at her heels. On reaching the house she pulls the bell softly.

The door is opened cautiously, and a woman's face peers out.

"What's wanted?" she inquires suspiciously.

"I've brought these gentlemen here," answers Rita. "We want a room. Your best if it's empty."

"Can't have you tonight," replies the woman. "The whole house is took."

She is about to shut the door when Rita springs into the opening. The next moment she has the woman by the throat. "Quick!" she cries in a low voice. "Gag her, tie her hands and feet!"

No need to speak further. Both Hector D'Estrange and Evie Ravensdale have obeyed. Three handkerchiefs suffice to gag the woman, tie her ankles together, and her wrists behind her. Then they look at Rita.

"Put her in here!" exclaims this latter, opening a door on the right. "It's dark. Never mind; I know the place; she's safe there."

They lift her in, and lay her on the floor. Rita closes the door, and locks it. A dim light is burning in the hall, but no one is stirring; only in the distance they think they catch a sound of voices.

"Come on," she says excitedly. "I am sure I can find them. They'll be in the best room. Follow me."

She goes up the stairs quietly, her companions as noiselessly following. On reaching the landing she turns down a passage to the right, and comes to a halt opposite a door.

"Listen," she says in a low tone. "*You two should know that voice.*"

But she has no time to say more. Pale with fury, with murder in his eyes, Hector D'Estrange has burst open the door. A flood of light almost blinds him as he enters, but through it all he sees the mother that he loves.

Speranza de Lara is stretched on a sofa. Her ankles are still tightly secured, her wrists likewise. Around her, like a cloak of gold, falls her lovely hair. There is a mad, wild look in her eyes terrible to behold, but her lips are mute and speechless, for she is gagged. And beside her stands that monster, that petted *roué* of Society, that "fiend in human shape,"—the Earl of Westray.

There is a loud cry as a shot rings through the silent house.

END OF BOOK I

BOOK II

I

It is the year 1900. Men are hoping that it will be a peaceful one, after the factious bickerings of 1898–99. While the National party and the Progressists have been snarling over contentious bones, they have omitted to notice in the bye-elections unmistakable signs of public weariness and disgust with squabbles so profitless.

The National party, into which the Unionists have been merged, and the Progressists—a party arisen on the ashes of the Liberals—have failed to take warning by these signs. Woman's Suffrage, established as law by the action of Hector D'Estrange, has materially altered the aspect of the old state of things, and brought about a thorough and healthy change of thought in many places. The women have given their aid enthusiastically to Hector D'Estrange, and worked heartily in support of the youthful reformer. Almost every bye-election has returned a D'Estrangeite candidate.

Now at length the General Election is over, and the Parliament returned is a curious one. Including the Irish, Scotch, and Welsh Home Rulers, the D'Estrangeite members are in a majority, the Nationals coming next, and the Progressists last.

And yet the majority referred to is a somewhat precarious and unworkable one, for if the two latter parties choose to combine, they can wreck the new Government completely. No one knows this better than Hector D'Estrange, who, having been invited by his sovereign to form a Cabinet, has succeeded in doing so, and occupies the proud position of Prime Minister at the age of twenty-eight.

Only sixteen years since Gloria de Lara made her vow to the wild sea waves,—and now?

Has the prayer that accompanied that vow been answered?

Not yet.

"Is it not tempting defeat, my child, to introduce the bill at so early a date?"

"Mother dear, it is my only opportunity. The position I hold is, I know, quite untenable for any length of time. The Government may be defeated at any moment, and then my chance is gone. Though I have not the slightest hope of carrying the bill, I shall yet gain a tremendous point by its introduction. I shall be defeated on it without a doubt, but it will be before the country, and I can appeal to the country upon it."

"Ever right, my child."

The speakers are Speranza and Gloria de Lara. The former is now fifty years of age, but years sit lightly on her shoulders. The new century beholds her as lovely and youthful-looking as ever; time has not played havoc with that fair face.

And the pale golden hair is golden still. No sign of whitening age is discernible in the thick tresses. It seems as though fair youth will never quit her side, for Speranza is unchanged.

Unchanged in all save one thing. Since that terrible day, upon which the last chapter closed so abruptly, there has dwelt in Speranza's lovely eyes a hunted, haunting look of fear. She has never quite recovered from the shock of that most awful trial, and none dare mention to her the name of Lord Westray.

He has never been heard of since that day. His disappearance at the time caused the greatest excitement. Men declared that he must have been foully murdered, and his body secreted by the murderer or murderers. Of course the blame was thrown on the Irish, with whom Lord Westray was no favourite. Not long before his disappearance he had been appointed Chief Secretary for Ireland, an appointment that had given the greatest dissatisfaction to the Irish. There was nothing beyond surmise, however, to account for his fate.

They are sitting in Speranza de Lara's private room in Montragee House, which has been her home ever since the terrible day above referred to. Apartments in the huge building have been set aside for her use, for it is the delight of Evie Ravensdale to lavish upon the mother of his dearest friend on earth all the affection and love of a son. And his love is returned indeed, for Speranza's heart has gone out to him with all the love of a mother, a love only surpassed by that which she feels for her child.

The great day has come at last, when Hector D'Estrange is to introduce to Parliament his bill for the absolute and entire enfranchisement of the women of his country. The bill, it is whispered, is not a mere stepping-stone to future power for the sex, but a free and unfettered charter of liberty, a distinct emancipation from past slavery, a final and decisive declaration that women are not man's inferiors, but have as clear and inalienable a right as he to share the government of their country, and to adopt the professions hitherto arrogated by men solely to themselves.

LADY FLORENCE DIXIE

Hector D'Estrange's colleagues have been made aware of the bill's contents, and have loyally and nobly elected to stand or fall upon it. They have all been selected for their singularly wide and sympathetic views, and are not likely to forsake their chief in the moment of trial. So also can he depend upon all the D'Estrangeite members, without a fear that there will be a single seceder from their ranks; but he knows that the defeat which he expects will come from the united forces of the Progressists and Nationals, who for a time have buried their feuds and disputes, in the desire to defeat the revolutionary schemes of Hector D'Estrange.

There is a knock at the door, and, in response to Hector's invitation to enter, it opens, and a young man comes in. It is Lord Bernard Fontenoy, very much grown since we saw him last. He is eighteen now, but looks older, and is the Duke of Ravensdale's Secretary, the duke being Minister for Foreign Affairs.

"A telegram, Mr. D'Estrange," he observes. "Will there be any answer?"

Hector takes the missive and opens it. It is from Flora Desmond, and runs as follows:—

"The ten regiments have marched in from Oxford, and are quartered in the Hall of Liberty. Twenty-seven miles completed in eight and a half hours; not a single private fell out of the ranks. Will be down to see you in an hour or so."

"No, Bernie; no answer, thanks. Is Evie in yet?" queries the recipient.

"I'll go and see," answers the youth, vanishing as he speaks.

"Dear mother, I must leave you now, but will see you again before I go to the House. Estcourt and Douglasdale will be here directly, and the latter is to escort you tonight," observes Hector D'Estrange, rising and kissing Speranza.

The mother throws her arms around her child. The anxious look in her eyes is intensified.

"My darling, may all go well with you tonight. It is foolish, I know, but there is a foreboding of evil next my heart which I cannot shake off, try as I may. Ah, Gloria! if aught should happen to you, my precious child, what would your mother do?"

"Why, mother, what ails you, dearest? Evil happen to Gloria? What fancy is this? Of course I expect defeat; but that will not be evil; merely the beginning of a great end."

"I do not allude to that, dear one, but to something quite different. Gloria, I had a terrible dream last night. I saw him close to me, the being that I loathe. He had you down, and stood above you with a naked sword raised threateningly. I rushed to save you, but ere I could avert his arm he had pointed it straight down at you, and pierced you to the heart."

"Tush, mother, a mere dream, that's all. You must not dwell upon it. Dear mother, put it from your mind."

"Would to God that I could, Gloria! But it haunts me like a spectre, and will not pass away. However, my child, I must not damp your spirits with my fancies. Go now to your duties, from which I must not keep you, and mother will do her best to drive the dream away."

"That's right, motherling. Do, for Gloria's sake."

He kisses her tenderly and goes out, for he hears Evie Ravensdale's step approaching. The two friends and colleagues meet just outside the door.

"Let's go to your room, Evie," he says gently, "and let us have a chat before I go to work. Chats with you are a luxury now. We don't find much time for them, do we? By-the-bye, I have just had a telegram from Flora Desmond; the regiments have reached the Hall of Liberty. She reports the last march of twenty-seven miles in eight and a half hours, with not one single fall out from the ranks. Yet they would have us believe that women are weak, feeble creatures, unable to endure fatigue. There is the lie direct."

They pass on into the duke's study, a room full of pleasant memories for Hector D'Estrange. Many a happy hour has he spent here with the truest and best friend of his life, the one man whom he loves above all things, and, with the exception of Speranza, the only being to whom he is passionately attached. A big oil painting hangs above the fireplace. Two figures are represented on the canvas. One is a tall, dark-haired, dark-eyed man, with long silken moustache and aristocratic mien, the other of shorter and slighter build, with a face of exquisite beauty. The features are those of a very young man, the eyes are sapphire-blue, the glossy, close curling hair of a deep old-gold colour. It is easy to recognise the former as Evelyn, Duke of Ravensdale, the latter as Hector D'Estrange. The picture has been executed by the duke's order, and represents the two friends first meeting—ever memorable for both.

They sit on alone together, these kindred spirits, happy in the communion of each other's thoughts. They are seeking to scan the future and what it will bring, diving into the days that have yet to come. With Evie Ravensdale, it is a firm belief in the ultimate success of Hector

D'Estrange's scheme, a supreme and absolute confidence in his young chief's ascendant star.

"I wonder who will be the first woman Prime Minister," he observes dreamily. He is looking into the glowing coals, and does not notice the flush that rises to Hector D'Estrange's cheeks.

"Ah, yes, who indeed?" echoes the latter quietly.

"Sometimes I think, Hector, that I can see her. Certainly I have seen her in my dreams," continues the young duke softly.

"Can you describe her, Evie?" asks his friend.

"Ask me to paint your face. Hector, and then you have her in living life. Yes, my woman Prime Minister is an exact counterpart of Hector D'Estrange. Ah, Hector! if you were only a woman how madly I should love you; for love you as I do now, it can never be the same love as it would be if you were a woman."

It is fortunate that the shaded and softly subdued lamps in Evie Ravensdale's study are low, or certainly the look in Hector D'Estrange's face would have betrayed the secret of Gloria de Lara. As it is, he only laughs softly.

"So I am your woman's ideal, am I, Evie?" he asks in a would-be bantering tone.

"Yes, Hector, you are. Your face is too lovely for a man's. You ought to have been a woman. and yet if you had been, the glory of Hector D'Estrange would be an untold tale. There is, alas! no woman living, I fear, who would have been able to beat down the laws that held her enchained as you have done. How the women worship you, Hector, and rightly."

The front door bell is pealing. In a few minutes the study door is opened, and Lady Flora Desmond is announced.

She comes in easy and graceful, her White Guard's uniform fitting to perfection her supple and agile form. People have grown accustomed to Hector D'Estrange's women volunteers. The uniforms no longer strike them as strange and unfeminine, for custom is the surest cure with offended Mrs. Grundy.

"What a dense crowd there is, to be sure!" she exclaims, after first greetings have been exchanged. "I had hard work to get my guards through it. But they are in order now, and a clear way is kept right up to Westminster, so you will have no difficulty in getting your carriage along, Mr. D'Estrange."

"Is it so late?" he inquires in a surprised tone. "Evie and I have been talking away, and did not notice how the time was slipping. Pray wait here. I shall not be many minutes dressing. I must wear my White Guard's uniform tonight, you know."

"Very well, Mr. D'Estrange. I will wait for you here," she replies. There is a ring in Flora Desmond's voice which tells how happy she is. She has never dreamed of seeing such a day as this.

HE IS STANDING ON THE steps of Montragee House, clad in his White Guard's uniform. A long line of the White Regiment keep the road clear to Westminster. The crowd is dense all round. Nothing but a sea of faces can be seen, and the cheers of the people have grown into a hoarse, continuous roar. Thousands and thousands of women are amongst that crowd, women with hearts full of love and devotion for their hero; women who would account it a happiness to die for him at any hour; women who are strong in their gratitude for what he has done, and is trying to do for them. He has entered the carriage that stands in waiting in front of the ducal mansion, and with Evie Ravensdale has taken his seat therein. As it drives rapidly towards Westminster the mighty volume of cheering is again and again renewed, a few hisses being here and there noticeable.

How describe the scene within the House of Commons? To attempt to do so would be but to court failure. The precincts are thronged until there is no standing room. There is eager expectation on every face.

The roar of the crowd outside has penetrated the vast building, and tells those within that he is approaching. A thrill runs through that assembly of princes, peers, commoners, and ladies who are there to await his coming, and then the silence of intense expectation falls on all around.

He is entering now, and walks slowly forward to take his seat. He is received with a burst of enthusiasm by his own colleagues and party, and is watched with interest by every woman who looks down upon him from the spacious galleries that at his instance have been erected for ladies, in place of the wild beast cage originally considered by men as good enough for the inferior sex. And now he has taken his seat while awaiting the usual formalities, and the eyes of the House are upon him. It would be a trying position for an old Parliamentary hand, one used to many years of debate. Is it not just a shade so for Gloria de Lara, as she sits there under the name of Hector D'Estrange preparing to do battle for her sex?

But she has risen now. The silence of death has fallen once more on the House, for the clear, beautiful voice is speaking at last, and this is what it says.

LADY FLORENCE DIXIE

II

M r. Speaker, I make no apology to you, sir, or to Honourable gentlemen for the bill which I am about to introduce to the House. It is a bill embodying a simple act of justice to woman, a tardy though complete offer by man to repair the wrong which he has done her in the past. Now the bill is simple enough, and contains no ambiguous clauses. It states in terse, clear language what it is that we propose to bestow on woman, the rights to which she is entitled, and the manner in which we suggest that they should take effect.

"We have rightly, though tardily, bestowed the suffrage upon her. That was an act which should have been performed years ago, but one which has been delayed by much of that unwieldy and unworkable machinery that clogs and hampers the operations of the Westminster Parliament. I refer to the numerous local affairs of England, Scotland, Ireland, and Wales, which, as you know, I have frequently expressed as my opinion, might be more profitably, efficiently, and quickly disposed of in the separate countries named, leaving the time that is consumed here in attending to them free for the consideration of great Imperial and National social questions, which are, alas! and dangerously so, being pressed into the background.

"The bestowal of the suffrage on woman is a practical acknowledgment by man that woman has a right to be considered as a being who can reason, and who can study humanity in its various phases, and act on her own responsibility. It is not for me here to seek for the causes which have hitherto led man to believe to the contrary. His belief, in a great measure, has been due to woman's weak acceptance of his arbitrary laws; for I do not suppose it will be pretended by anyone that the laws laid down for the sacrifice of woman's freedom were the creation of a woman's brain. But this weak acceptance of these arbitrary laws cannot fairly be ascribed entirely to the fault of woman. 'Slavery in no form is natural;' it is an artificial creation of man's; and woman's slavery cannot be taken as an exception to this maxim. She has, in point of fact, been subjected to bondage, a bondage which has, in a manner, become second nature to her, and which custom has taught her to regard as a part of the inevitable.

"But if honourable gentlemen will believe me, Nature is stronger than custom, and more powerful than law. Nature is a force that cannot be repressed finally and absolutely. It is like an overwhelming torrent against which you may erect monster dykes, which you may dam up for a time, but all the while the waters are rising, and will find their level in the end. Through countless years woman has been repressed. Every human force and ingenuity of man have been employed to establish her subjection. From religion downwards it has been the cry 'Women, submit to men!' a cry which I may safely say was never originated by herself.

"Now Nature has established a law which is inviolable. It has laid down the distinction between the sexes, but here Nature stops. Nature gives strength and beauty to man, and Nature gives strength and beauty to woman. In this latter instance man flies in the face of Nature, and declares that she must be artificially restrained. Woman must not be allowed to grow up strong like man, because if she did, the fact would establish her equality with him, and this cannot be tolerated. So the boy and man are allowed freedom of body, and are trained up to become muscular and strong, while the woman, by artificial, not natural laws, is bidden to remain inactive and passive, and in consequence weak and undeveloped. Mentally it is the same. Nature has unmistakably given to woman a greater amount of brain power. This is at once perceivable in childhood. For instance, on the stage, girls are always employed in preference to boys, for they are considered brighter and sharper in intellect and brain power. Yet man deliberately sets himself to stunt that early evidence of mental capacity, by laying down the law that woman's education shall be on a lower level than that of man's; that natural truths, which all women should early learn, should be hidden from her; and that while men may be taught everything, women must only acquire a narrow and imperfect knowledge both of life and of Nature's laws.

"I maintain to honourable gentlemen that this procedure is arbitrary and cruel, and false to Nature. I characterise it by the strong word of Infamous. It has been the means of sending to their graves unknown, unknelled, and unnamed, thousands of women whose high intellects have been wasted, and whose powers for good have been paralysed and undeveloped. To the subjection and degradation of woman I ascribe the sufferings and crimes of humanity, nor will Society be ever truly raised, or ennobled, or perfected until woman's freedom has been granted, and she takes her rightful place as the equal of man. Viewing this great social problem in this light, we have deemed it our duty to present to Parliament a bill, establishing as law, firstly, the mixed education of the sexes, that is to say, bringing into force the principle of mixed schools and colleges, in which girls and boys, young men and young women, can be educated together; secondly, the extension of the rights of primogeniture to the female sex, so that while primogeniture remains associated with the law of entail, the eldest born, not the eldest son, shall succeed the owner of property and titles; also that all the professions and positions in life, official or otherwise, shall be thrown open as equally to women as to men; and thirdly, that women shall become eligible as Members of Parliament, and peeresses in their own right eligible to sit in the Upper House as well as to undertake State duties. Such is the drastic, the sweeping measure by which we desire to wipe off forever and repair, though tardily, a great wrong. Honourable gentlemen will perceive that we take no half-way course. We are not inclined to accept the doctrine of 'by degrees,' believing that this would only prolong the evil and injustice which daily arise from the delay in emancipating the female sex; and I will now as briefly as possible set forth to honourable gentlemen the arguments in favour of the three clauses contained in this bill.

"With regard to the first one, namely, the advisability of educating girls and boys, young women and young men, together, it is necessary to point out that the system of separating the sexes throughout their educational career has arisen chiefly from the totally different forms of education meted out to each. We hold that these different forms are pernicious and morally unhealthy, calculated to evilly influence the sensual instincts of the male sex, and to instil into the other sex a totally wrong and mischievous idea of the right and wrong side of Nature. We are convinced that this system has been productive of an immense amount of immorality and consequent suffering and degradation in the past, and that the system of elevating Nature into a mystery is the greatest conceivable incitement to sensuality and immorality. We hold that there should be no mystery or secrecy anent the laws of God. We hold that in creating mystery we condemn God's law— namely, Nature, to be what it is not—indecent; and we hold that the system of separating the sexes, of telling all to the one and enshrouding everything in silence and mystery to the other, has had the evil effect of producing immorality, so wide and far-spreading as to be frightful in its hideousness and magnitude; while it has been productive of millions of miserable marriages, of disease, and of evil immeasurable and appalling.

"Nature tells us truths which we cannot condemn as falsehoods, however much we may avert our eyes from their light. Nature tells us that it is natural for the male and female sex to be together. If we bring up the young to face this truth, if we bring up the young to accept as natural and rational the laws of pure and unaffected Nature, they will accept it as it is. But if we clothe it in boys' and men's eyes in fanciful garments, and leave girls and women in ignorance of its truths, we must expect the terrible and horrible results which have followed such unnatural teaching through centuries of time.

"We therefore emphatically in this clause record our protest against the system of teaching the young to regard Nature in a false light, in other words, to judge of God's laws as impure. We believe such a system of education to be, as we have said, an incentive to the male sex to do wrong, while totally unfitting the female sex to do right. The beginning of all immorality on woman's side has sprung from ignorance, and from the system of mystery and the tendency to declare indecent that which cannot be so, being God's law. In regard to the physical condition of the sexes, we hold that where equal opportunities are afforded to both of strengthening, developing, and improving the body, little material difference will be found in the two. There are many strong men in this world, and there are many strong women, as there are weakly men and weakly women. I have never heard it yet argued, that because a man is not strong in body he is therefore unfitted to take part in the affairs of State. Yet woman's weakness is one of the reasons adduced for excluding her therefrom. We believe that in a big public school, say, for instance, at Eton, if girls and boys were admitted together, that girls would very soon prove that neither physically nor mentally were they inferior to boys, nor should such a pernicious doctrine be ever inculcated into the boy's brain. He should not be brought up as he is now, to look down on his sisters as inferior to him, nor should those sisters be told that he is their superior in strength and mental capacity. It is a doctrine the perniciousness of which is far-reaching, and a distinct infringement of the natural.

"This leads us to the consideration of the second clause, the adoption by women of those professions hitherto arrogated to themselves solely by men. We are of opinion that, granted a similar education as men, women are in every way as fitted to occupy those professions. I may be allowed here perhaps, to refer with pride to that magnificent body of women over 200,000 strong who are now enrolled in the regiments of the Women's Volunteer forces, of which I am proud to call myself a member, and whose uniform I am fittingly wearing on this occasion.

We have before us a splendid evidence of woman's power to combine and come under discipline. These regiments are kept up to their full force, and are all due to individual effort and womanly sacrifice. There is no State aid in the question, and yet the efficiency of each regiment is perfect. Disbanded and scattered, they can be summoned to their ranks at a few days' notice, without fear that they will fail. I point to this as a brilliant example of what women can accomplish in so short a time, by self-sacrifice and simple determination. The same argument of their efficiency to enter the army applies to the navy, and to any other profession hitherto occupied solely by man.

"But, believing as I do, that with the admission of women into the conduct of affairs of State, wars, and all their attendant horrors, would quickly become a thing of the past, I dwell shortly on the second clause, passing on to the third, which, in conjunction with the first, I regard as the most important part to be examined.

"It is now eleven years since County Councils were established. At the very first elections women were chosen as representatives, but on an appeal to the law they were ousted from their seats. We have wisely remedied that state of things, and no one thinks it odd or extraordinary now, to see women sitting in these County Councils as members. On the contrary, it is tacitly acknowledged that their presence is, and has been, productive of much good. Well, will honourable gentlemen tell me in what great particulars these County Councils differ from Parliament?

"Both are debating assemblies, and both are conducted on almost similar lines. What is there preposterous and appalling in the suggestion that women should become Members of Parliament, and when, by genius or talents, they can attain to such, assume Cabinet rank, and claim the right to carry on the affairs of their country? It is merely custom that now debars them, a custom established by the selfishness and arrogance of man, and accepted by woman in the same manner as slaves in the past, from long custom, accepted the lash from their taskmasters. The taskmasters had established the right to flog their slaves; they had dammed up the slowly rising waters of rebellion, but these rose to their level at last, and overflowed and slavery is no more. The analogy holds good in the case of woman, whose greater slavery is not yet entirely overcome. That it will finally be, is as certain as that the hours of Time never go back. You may fight against it, you may pile the dykes higher, you may go on damming the rising waters as you will, but the time must inevitably come, when those dykes and dams will crumble away beneath the overwhelming flood, which your own efforts will have entirely accumulated and brought to its tremendous and irresistible strength. We may be met with many arguments in condemnation of this bill. One will be that it will obstruct the rite of marriage. We deny this. We grant you that it may diminish the number of marriages, but we contend that this will be a blessing rather than a curse. Thousands of miserable unions are yearly effected in consequence of woman's unnatural and one-sided position in Society. In all these cases she does not marry because, with a knowledge of the subject, with every profession thrown open to her and chance to get on equal to men, she is satisfied that she prefers married life. No. In the cases referred to, she marries for money, or for position, or to escape the restraints of home, or because she has no chance of making her way in the world, and the result is that these marriages are miserable failures, and the offspring of such either diseased in body or in mind, or condemned to grow up to a life of misery, and in thousands of cases, immorality and crime.

"There is a problem creeping gradually forward upon us, a problem that will have to be solved in time, and that is the steady increase of population. If it advances at its present rate, the hour will come when this earth will not be able to contain it. What then? We may possibly by that time have arranged, with the aid of science, for conveyances which shall carry our superfluous population to other realms of light, but it is equally possible that if this be so, those realms may not consent to receive the emigrants. What then? I believe that with the emancipation of women we shall solve this problem now. Fewer children will be born, and those that are born will be of a higher and better physique than the present order of men. The ghastly abortions, which in many parts pass muster nowadays, owing to the unnatural physical conditions of Society, as men, women, and children, will make room for a nobler and higher order of beings, who will come to look upon the production of mankind in a diseased or degraded state, as a wickedness and unpardonable crime, against which all men and women should fight and strive. The emancipation of women will, I am convinced, lead up to the creation of the great and the beautiful, to higher morals and nobler aims.

"Yet, as we are now, what is the sad reality? In this huge, over-crowded city alone, the greatest the world has ever known, amidst rich and poor alike, teems immorality awful and appalling in its magnitude. Deeds are committed of which even some of the most vicious have no idea. Thousands are born in our midst who should never see the light of day.

Born in disease, these miserable victims of vice and immorality grow up to beget to others like horrors, and in the teeming millions of this vast city alone exist misery and sin too terrible to contemplate.

"We submit, therefore, to honourable gentlemen that the first step towards the regeneration and upraising of mankind is the emancipation of woman, and with her emancipation the careful training of the sexes together. Convinced that the time has come, when it would be dangerous to delay this emancipation, we have made it the plank on which the Government of the day intend to stand or fall. We would further, perhaps, overstep the bounds of custom, and ask that the fate of the measure be decided tonight by a vote taken on it immediately. If the vote be adverse, the Government will at once resign, and appeal to the country on the clauses of the bill. They are clauses which I think, tonight, it would be but waste of time to discuss. They can be discussed before the country if the bill be rejected. Yet, ere I sit down, I would beg of honourable gentlemen to consider the few words which I have had the honour, and, I thank God, the opportunity to make to them. I would appeal to them to put aside party feeling, and vote for the common good as their consciences dictate. I solemnly warn them, however, that they cannot put back the hand of time, and that the hour must be reached at last when the cause of woman will triumph; for, as I have already remarked, Nature is like the rising waters of a great flood, which the hand and ingenuity of man may restrain for a time, but which must find a level at last and overflow. The course of Nature is unconquerable; no art of man can defeat it, wrought as it is by the hand of God."

He has sat down. He has been heard throughout in death-like silence, but now the Ministerialists and D'Estrangeites are cheering him again and again. Yet chill as ice are the Nationals and Progressists. They cannot rise to the height of generosity to which he has appealed. In this moment of uncertainty for many, Hector D'Estrange knows that the bill is doomed.

THE HOUSE HAS DIVIDED. IT has recorded its vote. The numbers for and against the emancipation of women have been announced. The author of the bill was no false prophet when he predicted defeat. By a majority of 120 it has been rejected.

Then the rafters ring with the wild cheering of the victorious Opposition, of that strange medley of parties, that hating each other cordially, yet hate still more the high-souled, far-reaching, justice-loving principles of Hector D'Estrange. Again and again the cheering is renewed, drowning in its volume the counter-cheers of the D'Estrangeites, wild, almost ungovernable in its elation, full of bitter meaning, echoing with sneering emphasis the triumph of selfishness over right.

He sits very quietly through it all, hardly seeming to notice this outburst of the victors. He does not grudge them their momentary triumph; his thoughts do not dwell upon the defeat which he has just sustained. They are far away, out beyond the portals of the present, clasping the warm hands of the future, reading the bright letters that twine their golden circlet round its brow, as they flash their meaning forth in the one word "Victory!"

Be of good cheer, brave heart, for victory is at hand!

The House has adjourned; it is five minutes past twelve. As the Prime Minister passes out he is joined by Evie Ravensdale, who at once links his arm within that of his friend and colleague. Although the duke's carriage is in waiting, these two purposely refrain from entering it, so as to avoid the crowd and the inevitable demonstration which would follow recognition thereby. In this manner they escape detection by the populace.

Not entirely, however. Sharp eyes have recognised Hector D'Estrange, He has not gone many steps when a hand is laid on his shoulder.

"Mr. D'Estrange," he hears a voice saying, "I arrest you in the name of the law."

"On what charge?" he inquires in a quick, startled voice.

"On the charge, sir, of murdering Lord Westray," is the reply.

In a moment his quick brain has taken in the situation, and he knows that resistance is useless.

"Very well," he answers quietly, "I will go with you. Evie," he adds, in a calm, composed voice "please go at once to my poor mother."

III

S ay, prisoner at the bar, are you or are you not guilty of the murder of Lord Westray?"

"Not guilty."

The answer comes in a clear and distinct voice, a voice in which there is neither faltering nor evasion. It is a voice singularly rich and melodious, a voice which one would think could not readily lie.

A hum runs through the crowded court, an indescribable buzz and movement of excitement, but there is joy and relief on many a face, where hitherto doubt and perplexity had reigned.

The court is crowded to suffocation. All the well-known faces of the day are present. The rush to obtain admittance has been unprecedented, and the excitement and popular feeling in regard to the case is unparalleled in the annals of the law courts.

He stands there very quietly, but erect as a dart. His arms are folded on his chest, and his whole carriage is one of easy dignity. None, looking at the beautiful face, with its clear, radiant complexion, magnificent eyes, and high, pale, thoughtful brow, around which the old-gold curls lovingly cluster, could bring themselves to believe that that man is a murderer.

Yet, as we have seen, of crime so terrible Hector D'Estrange stands accused. Since that fearful night when, with murder in his eyes, he had burst into that room of ill-fame, and found his beloved mother in the power and at the mercy of the man who had blighted her early life, and who had pursued her with such relentless vengeance, neither Hector D'Estrange nor society at large had seen Lord Westray. As we may remember, the former in that moment of horror and fury had been tried to the highest pitch. A shot had rung out through the silent house, followed by a loud cry, and that was all.

He stands accused not merely of murder, but of having secreted the body of his victim with intent to avoid detection. At the coroner's inquest evidence had been forthcoming to show how, acting upon various anonymous communications received, the heir-at-law of the deceased had placed the matter in the hands of the police, who thereupon had discovered the body and clothes of Lord Westray buried deep in the ground at Mrs. de Lara's residence near Windsor. Evidence had likewise been forthcoming to prove, that Hector D'Estrange was the last person seen in the company of Lord Westray, and the clothes of the murdered nobleman had been fully identified by his valet and others as those in which he was last seen alive. The body was, of course, past recognition. Two years in the earth would necessarily render it so; yet on the skeleton little finger of one hand a plain gold ring had been found, as also around the skeleton's neck a gold chain and locket, the latter containing a faded portrait of the late Countess of Westray, the earl's mother. It had been proved that Lord Westray always wore this ring, chain, and locket, and his valet had sworn that he was wearing them the very day on which he disappeared. Public opinion was perplexed. Even those who would glory in Hector D'Estrange's innocence found it difficult to believe him so. Everything appeared so clear against him, so unanswerably conclusive, that men and women shook their heads and sighed when hopes of his acquittal were expressed. But the day of trial had come at last, and Hector D'Estrange was there to confront his accusers.

In face of the terrible charge preferred against their chief, the members of the Ministry have unconditionally resigned, and a provisional Government, pending an appeal to the country, has been hastily constructed from the National party. The Government of the day is therefore known to be rabidly antagonistic to the late revolutionary Prime Minister, who now stands accused of murder. The counsel retained for the prosecution by the Crown is the Attorney-General, aided and assisted by two Q.C.'s, but Hector D'Estrange has retained no one to aid him. He defends himself.

And now with a flourish and many theatrical attitudes, Sir Anthony Stickleback begins the case for the prosecution. Sir Anthony is fond of rhetoric, and he airs it to the court, fully to his own satisfaction. He has many long-winded phrases to get through before he closes with the main point, which may be briefly told in his closing summary of the statements contained in his opening address.

"I shall therefore, my lord, call witnesses who will speak to the evident intimacy which has existed between Mr. D'Estrange and Mrs. de Lara through so many years. These witnesses will be able to show moreover, that on several occasions Mrs. de Lara received visits from her late husband, Lord Westray, during Mr. D'Estrange's absence; that she was frequently in the habit of mysteriously disappearing from her residence near Windsor on visits to London, and that on one of these occasions— the occasion, in fact, when Mr. D'Estrange followed her—she actually left a note for her maid, acquainting her with her departure. I shall show how Mr. D'Estrange, having surprised her in the company of Lord Westray, deliberately fired his revolver at that nobleman. The last thing seen of this latter unfortunate gentleman was in the company of Mr. D'Estrange, who had announced his intention of taking him to his home in Grosvenor Square. It is needless to say that from that day forward Lord Westray bas never been seen in living life, though, in consequence of several anonymous communications received, private inquiry was set on foot by those who have been determined to bring the murderer to justice, and which has resulted in the discovery of the body and the clothes which Lord Westray was wearing when last seen, buried deep in the earth, in the private grounds near Windsor belonging to Mrs. de Lara. I will now, my lord, proceed to call the witnesses for the prosecution."

And one by one the witnesses are brought forward to swear away the life of Hector D'Estrange.

Charles Weston deposes that he was for many years Mrs. de Lara's butler, and that he frequently admitted Lord Westray to her house, but always in the absence of Mr. D'Estrange. Only on one occasion did Mr. D'Estrange come in while Lord Westray was in the house, and he recalls high words passing between the two, followed by the hasty departure of Lord Westray, whose brougham was awaiting him at Mrs. de Lara's door. This was when she resided in London. After this Lord Westray always came on foot, and he, Weston, had strict orders to keep a sharp look out for Mr. D'Estrange, so as to give the two full warning. He remembers perfectly well bringing Mrs. de Lara a note from Lord Westray the very day on which she disappeared from her Windsor residence, and the same on which Lord Westray was murdered, and he also remembers a note being left that night by Mrs. de Lara for her *maid*.

Cross-examined by Hector D'Estrange. "Are you not a discharged servant of Mrs. de Lara's, Weston?"

"No, sir," answers this person with cool effrontery. "I gave notice myself."

"You will swear, Weston, that Mrs. de Lara did not dismiss you for drunkenness and gross impertinence?"

"Certainly, sir. Mrs. de Lara told me I had had too much to drink, and I told her I would leave. I gave a month's notice."

"Thank you, Weston, I have no more to ask you." Hector D'Estrange's voice has a peculiar ring of unutterable contempt in it. The wretch winces as he receives the order to "stand down."

Victoire Hester is next called. She deposes to being Mrs. de Lara's late maid. She corroborates Charles Weston's evidence. Asked if she remembers the writing paper used by Mrs. de Lara and Hector D'Estrange, "Perfectly," is her reply.

"Can she select a specimen from amidst the packet of letters handed her?"

"Certainly," she replies again.

In a few minutes she has picked out three letters all written in the same hand and on a similar stamp of paper.

"This," she declares, "is the paper used by Mrs. de Lara and Mr. D'Estrange all the time that I have been in Mrs. de Lara's service."

Asked again if she recognises the handwriting on the letter, she unhesitatingly declares it to resemble Lord Westray's. Asked if she received a note from Mrs. de Lara, acquainting her with her sudden departure for London the night of the murder, she answers, "*Yes!*"

Cross-examined by Hector D'Estrange.

"Victoire Hester, are you not engaged to Charles Weston, and were you not dismissed by Mrs. de Lara?"

"No, sir," she unblushingly replies. "I gave notice same as Charles did, because Mrs. de Lara behaved so improperly to me."

"Victoire Hester, you say that Mrs. de Lara left a note for you on the night of the supposed murder of Lord Westray, informing you she had gone to London?"

"Yes," is the reply.

"But was she not in the habit of frequently going up to town in the same way without leaving notes?"

"Yes, sir."

"Then how is it she should trouble to do what she had never done before, Victoire Hester?"

The maid is visibly flurried.

"I don't know, sir," she stammers.

"Thank you, Victoire." The cold, calm, contemptuous voice comes again, and the maid in turn steps down.

Alfred Hawkins corroborates Charles Weston's evidence, as to driving Lord Westray to Mrs. de Lara's South Kensington residence on one occasion. He states that he was groom to the late lord, and is still so to his successor.

"I call for Mr. Trackem," enunciates Sir Anthony Stickleback in an important voice, "since the accused does not wish to ask Alfred Hawkins any questions."

Mr. Trackem enters the witness box. He is extremely well dressed, and has an air of importance about him. Like Sir Anthony, he has evidently a good opinion of himself.

"Mr. Trackem, you own a certain house in Verdegrease Crescent, do you not?" inquires Sir Anthony blandly.

"I do, sir," answers Mr. Trackem.

"Have you or have you not admitted Mrs. de Lara to the house?"

"Frequently, sir," answers that individual.

"Presumably for what purpose?"

"On each occasion, sir, to meet Lord Westray."

"Do you, Mr. Trackem, know anything of Rita Vernon?" asks Sir Anthony.

"Certainly, sir. She used frequently to visit my house."

"Will you name the last two occasions you have seen her, Mr. Trackem?"

"Well, sir, the first was on the night of the 20th of June, 1894, and the last on the night of Lord Westray's murder," answers Mr. Trackem.

"Was she with anyone on those two occasions?"

"Yes, sir, each time with the same person."

"And that person, Mr. Trackem, was?"

"The Duke of Ravensdale," answers the scoundrel quickly.

A movement of intense surprise pervades the court.

"Will you describe to his lordship and the jury all you know about the terrible occurrence of which Lord Westray was the victim, Mr. Trackem?" commands Sir Anthony Stickleback, folding his arms.

"I will do my best, sir. On the afternoon of the day on which Lord Westray disappeared, I received a note from Mrs. de Lara, sent especially by Rita Vernon. In this note she instructed me to retain my house free for the night, and to admit no one but Lord Westray. I acted as requested, and she and his lordship arrived about half-past one. I retired to bed, there being no one in the house but two men-servants and a woman. The men, like myself, had retired to rest. Suddenly I was startled by hearing a shot, followed by a loud cry. I jumped out of bed, slipped into my trousers, and called my two men. We proceeded to the room in which were Lord Westray and Mrs. de Lara. On entering, we found it in possession of Mr. D'Estrange, the Duke of Ravensdale, and Rita Vernon. The two latter were beside Mrs. de Lara, who was lying on a sofa. Lord Westray was stretched out on the floor, blood issuing from a wound in the throat, and above him stood Mr. D'Estrange, with a discharged revolver in his hand."

"I at once rushed up to him, and accused him of attempting to murder Lord Westray. He replied that he was sorry for what he had done, but that he did it in a moment of passion. He declared that he did not think he had seriously hurt the earl, and that he would take him to his home if I would procure a cab. At the same time he begged the Duke of Ravensdale and Rita Vernon to take charge of Mrs. de Lara. I was getting seriously alarmed at the turn affairs had taken, and upon Lord Westray expressing a wish to get home, I acceded to Mr. D'Estrange's request. Two cabs were procured. In one of them Mr. D'Estrange and Lord Westray took their departure, in the other Mrs. de Lara, the duke, and Rita Vernon. I saw them off from the door, and then re-entered the house. As I did so, I heard a groaning in a room on the right. I procured a light and opened the door, the key of which was turned in the lock. To my surprise I found my woman servant laid out on the ground, bound hand and foot with handkerchiefs, while a third gagged her mouth. I produce these handkerchiefs now. One has a ducal coronet on it, the other H. D'Estrange worked on it, and the third the name of Rita Vernon. Next day I received a letter, apparently in Lord Westray's writing, begging me to keep strict silence on all that had occurred. He declared that if it leaked out his reputation would be lost, and he informed me that he intended disappearing for a couple of years, at the end of which he would return. He enclosed me some money, and promised to continue the donation quarterly, on condition of my silence. I received six donations in all, and three letters. At last the donations ceased, and I began to grow suspicious."

"What first made you suspicions?"

"Well, sir, I noticed one day that the paper on which these letters were written was exactly similar to the quality used by Mrs. de Lara in her note to me on the afternoon of the day when the murder was committed, and I also thought Lord Westray's continued absence after the time specified was suspicious. Finally, I went and made a clean breast of it to the present earl, who I found in receipt of various anonymous communications declaring the murder, and indicating where the body and clothes were concealed. He employed me to find out all I could. I set to work, sir, communicated with the police, and investigations were set on foot, with the result as we all know it."

"Ah! you combine the work of a private detective with your other business, do you, Mr. Trackem?" inquires the Attorney-General graciously.

"I do, sir."

Cross-examined by Hector D'Estrange.

"Have you the letter which you allege Mrs. de Lara wrote you?"

"The counsel for the prosecution has it, sir," answers Mr. Trackem.

"Is it not a little strange you should have preserved that letter all these years, in view of the fact that you thought Lord Westray alive, and is it not a little strange that your communication to the new Lord Westray should have been almost simultaneous with the receipt by him of anonymous information?" pursues the accused.

It is Mr. Trackem's turn to look confused, but he quickly pulls himself together as he answers, "No, I do not think so."

Other witnesses are called to corroborate Mr. Trackem's statement in some particulars, and to testify to the discovery of Lord Westray's body and clothes, the latter being produced in court, this production causing much excitement.

Walter Long is next called. He identifies the chain, locket, and ring found on the skeleton as belonging to his late master, and he also identifies the clothes. He swears positively that Lord Westray was wearing all these things the day he disappeared.

"These, my lord," declares Sir Anthony, "are the witnesses for the prosecution."

And with this statement the Court adjourns for luncheon.

On reassembling, Hector D'Estrange opens the case for the defence.

"I shall not," he observes quietly, "detain the Court at any length with my opening statement. I have been charged with undue intimacy with Mrs. de Lara. The charge is stupid and disgusting, and when I inform your lordship and the gentlemen of the jury that Mrs. de Lara is my mother, this will at once be evident, and show the groundlessness of the charge. I deny the statement that Lord Westray was a frequent and admitted visitor at my mother's house, though he made many endeavours to be one. Only once he obtained ingress, and was ordered out both by Mrs. de Lara and myself. He has been the curse of my mother's life. The sufferings of Lady Altai must be green in the memory of many, while the fate that befell my father at his hands is matter of history. I shall call Mrs. de Lara, who will deny having written either to Mr. Trackem or to her maid. She will explain how these so-called mysterious visits to London were solely to see her child. She will describe to you how it was her custom to walk out at night in her grounds at Windsor, and how on the evening of the day on which I am accused of murdering Lord Westray, she was set upon by two men, gagged, bound hand and foot, transferred to a carriage, and taken in it to London, where, at the house of Mr. Trackem, she was handed over to the mercy of Lord Westray, from whom God in His mercy enabled me to rescue her in time. This evidence will be corroborated by Rita Vernon, who will explain all she was eyewitness to. She will tell you how she clung to the back of the brougham which contained Mrs. de Lara all the way to London, and having taken note of the house—which, alas! she knew too well—hurried to Montragee House to apprise the Duke of Ravensdale, whom she knew to be my dear friend, of the terrible occurrence. There she happily found both him and myself, and we at once proceeded to my mother's rescue. Effecting an entrance into the house, we gagged and bound the woman who let us in, and then, guided by Rita Vernon, stole noiselessly upstairs to what Rita styled the best room. On reaching the door she halted, and bade me listen to a voice, which I recognised as that of Lord Westray's. Mad with fury, I dashed open the door—what to find? Why my mother, gagged and bound, a prisoner in the hands of the scoundrel who had wrecked and ruined her life. My lord, would not the sight have driven you mad? I drew my revolver, and shot him where he stood. He uttered a cry and fell. Quickly the duke and I cut the thongs that bound my mother. Her hands were cramped and saturated with blood, across both palms extending a ghastly gash. We carried her tenderly downstairs, procured a cab, and in Rita Vernon's and the Duke of Ravensdale's kind care she was transferred to Montragee House. I then went back to the room where Lord Westray was lying, where I found him alone with Mr. Trackem. I offered to call the police and state what had occurred. Lord Westray was seated on the sofa, and begged me not to do so. He declared the wound was nothing, and requested me to leave him, and on no account to disclose what had occurred. For my mother's sake, and yet on another account, I agreed. Next day I called upon Mr. Trackem, who informed me of the letter he had received from Lord Westray, the contents of which he has communicated in his evidence today. I regret, however, to have to say that the greater part of the remainder of his evidence has been falsely given, why, I am at a loss to understand, as beyond the encounter in the house in Verdegrease Crescent, I had no quarrel with him whatsoever. I propose now to call my witnesses."

Mrs. de Lara is called. Her appearance in court excites the greatest interest. For though few have seen the beautiful Lady Altai of former days, the story of her marriage, her flight with Harry Kintore, and the tragic sequel in which Lord Westray figured so prominently, is well known in Society. So this is Speranza de Lara, mother of Hector D'Estrange?

"No wonder he is handsome, with such a mother as that!" gasps Mrs. de Lacy Trevor. "Dodo dear, it's the same lovely woman we met him riding with on the Burton Course long ago, at Melton, don't you remember? The mystery's cleared at last."

She stops abruptly and stares at her friend, for Lady Manderton is scarcely heeding her, and there are large tears in her fine, handsome eyes.

"Why, what is the matter, Dodo?"

"Nothing, Vivi, nothing! There, don't attract attention," she answers hastily.

She is thinking though, how wasted has been her life. She has heard Hector D'Estrange's statement, and believes it implicitly. She is thinking that others may not, though. If Hector D'Estrange is condemned, well, Dodo Manderton feels that she would die to save him.

IV

"Mrs. De Lara," queries Hector D'Estrange, in a voice in which respect and tenderness are mingled, "you have heard the statement for the prosecution in which you and I are accused of undue intimacy? You have heard my reply, in which I declare you to be my mother? Which statement is correct?"

"Yours," she replies in a firm, clear voice. "I am your mother."

"And my father?" he again asks.

"Was Captain Harry Kintore."

"Both Weston and Victoire state that they gave you a month's notice. Is this a fact?"

"It is not," she replies firmly; "it was I who gave it to them. To Weston for being drunk and impertinent, to Victoire for the latter fault."

"It is stated by Weston that you were in the habit of receiving frequent visits from Lord Westray? Is this so?"

"It is not," she answers quickly; "the statement is a wicked falsehood. Only once he obtained admittance, when he came to insult me with the proposal that I should re-marry him and forget the past. You came in when he was there, and requested him to leave the house."

"Did he do so?"

"At once," she replies.

"Since then have you been annoyed by his presence, or in any other way?"

"By his presence, no, until the night on which he is alleged to have been murdered, but by letters, yes."

"You have kept or destroyed those letters?"

"Everyone is destroyed!" she replies almost fiercely; "most of them unopened."

"Can you remember the date when Rita Vernon first came to you, and who sent her?"

"Yes, well," answers Speranza. "It was the 21st of June, 1894. She brought a letter from you, written at the instance of the Duke of Ravensdale. I at once made her my secretary and general amanuensis."

"Has she served you faithfully?"

"None more so," she replies.

"Mrs. de Lara, you have heard Mr. Trackem's statement, that you sent her with a note to him on the day of the supposed murder. Is this true, or false?"

"False!" she replies sternly.

"And you have heard Victoire's declaration that you left a letter for her, apprising her of your departure for London the night of the supposed murder. Is this true?"

"It is not," she answers. "I wrote no letter."

"Will you give his lordship and the gentlemen of the jury your version of what occurred on the night in question."

She gives it in a firm, clear voice, without hesitation or faltering. She tells the facts as we have described them in a former chapter. A shudder runs through the court at their mere recital. Is it possible that such horrors reflect the truth? Sir Anthony smiles superciliously.

"Hallucination," he mutters audibly. "Many women are subject to it."

She looks at him contemptuously, but scorns to further notice the great man's brutality.

"You swear, Mrs. de Lara, that what you have stated is absolutely correct?"

"Absolutely," she answers calmly; "I swear it."

Cross-examined by the Attorney-General.

"You will swear that you were not in the habit of receiving Lord Westray, Mrs. de Lara? Now, pray be careful, very careful."

Again the same contemptuous glance, as she proudly replies, "I swear it."

"And you mean to say that you never sent Rita Vernon with a letter to Mr. Trackem, or left a note for Victoire Hester on the day of Lord Westray's murder? Again I ask you to be careful."

"I did not!" is her fierce reply.

Sir Anthony puts his hands on his hips. There is a self-satisfied smile on his face as he glances round the court, but he questions no further.

"I have no more to ask the witness," he remarks jauntily.

Rita Vernon is next called and questioned. She describes her first meeting with the Duke of Ravensdale, and what followed. She gives in simple, unaffected language the story of the attack on Speranza and the part she played in it. Again Sir Anthony is heard to mutter the word "hallucination." He has no questions to put to the witness—yet stay—as she is about to leave the box he jumps up.

"One moment please, Miss Vernon," he remarks in a suave voice. "I presume, of course, that you are grateful to the Duke of Ravensdale for all his kindness?"

There is a flash in her grey eyes, but she answers quietly,

"Need you ask it, sir? I would die for his Grace."

The next witness is the duke himself. He corroborates the statements made by Hector D'Estrange, Speranza de Lara, and Rita Vernon. His evidence is listened to with marked attention, and the keenest interest by the Court. Sir Anthony does not cross-examine him.

As he steps down, Hector D'Estrange's voice is heard speaking.

"I have one more witness to call," he is saying. "This will be my last, my lord. I call for Dr. Merioneth."

A white-haired man enters the box and is sworn.

"Dr. Merioneth, do you recall attending Mrs. de Lara many years ago?" inquires the accused.

"I do," replies the witness.

"Will you state for what purpose, and how many years have elapsed since then?" is the next question.

"I attended Mrs. de Lara in her confinement, and it is twenty-eight years ago," answers the old doctor.

"Where, Dr. Merioneth?"

"At Ancona, sir, on the Adriatic."

"The child was born well and healthy, I believe?"

"A beautiful child indeed," replies the doctor. "I wish all children resembled it."

"Thank you, Dr. Merioneth."

"Stay, I have a word, please, to put to you," exclaims the Attorney-General, jumping up. "You have not told us the sex of the child, doctor."

For a moment the old man hesitates. Then he looks sadly at the prisoner.

"A girl it was," he replies in a low voice.

"Ha! a girl you say?" echoes the counsel for the prosecution in a loud voice, as he looks round the court with a knowing air. "Thank you, doctor. I am greatly obliged to you for that information."

This concludes the evidence for the defence.

Then Sir Anthony rises slowly and portentously. His hands are behind him, he leans perilously forward, and his gown is stuck out behind like a lady's dress-improver. He appears thoroughly satisfied with the appearance of importance which he believes this attitude gives him, but it is not so certain that others share that opinion.

"My lord, and gentlemen of the jury," he begins in a somewhat pompous voice, "the case before us is a very peculiar one, yet I hope to detain you at very little length in reviewing it. The prisoner, Mr. D'Estrange, is accused of a base and horrible murder, and it is my painful duty to endeavour to bring home to the jury the absolute certainty of his guilt. It will be necessary in so doing to show motive for the crime, and I think I shall be able to point to this motive as conclusive, jealousy prompting and being at the bottom of it. It is now, my lord, and gentlemen of the jury, nigh on thirty years ago that Mrs. de Lara, then known as Lady Altai, broke faith with her husband, whom in wedding she had sworn to love, honour, and obey, and shamelessly fled with her lover. Captain Harry Kintore. It is known that Lord Altai, who was devoted to his wife, pursued the two, coming up with them at Ancona. Here, having confronted them, a fierce dispute ensued. It is said that Captain Kintore drew a revolver, and in self-defence Lord Altai fired at him, unfortunately with fatal effect. I wish to dwell as lightly as possible upon a matter so terrible, and therefore pass on to the next event in this painful story, namely, the birth of a child. Dr. Merioneth has been called, ostensibly to bear witness to that birth. Unfortunately he has marred the case for the defence by informing us that the child to which Mrs. de Lara gave birth was a female. Now, my lord, one of the chief points of Mr. D'Estrange's defence is, that the intimacy which we declare has existed between him and this lady for so long a time is impossible, inasmuch as Mrs. de Lara is his mother. She has herself so stated this, and furthermore pointed to Captain Kintore as being Mr. D'Estrange's father. This statement must fall to the ground in face of what Dr. Merioneth has told us. So much for that portion of the defence, as I do not suppose Mr. D'Estrange is going to pose before us as a woman. It would appear that Mrs. de Lara is not averse to this mode of life. She married Lord Altai by her own free will. Next we find her leaving him and electing a new lover in the person of Captain Kintore, and of late years we have direct evidence that Mr. D'Estrange has been the favoured man. Yet not only this, but the evidence sworn to by Charles Weston, Victoire Hester, and Mr. Trackem points to the existence of a secret intimacy carried on by this lady with her divorced husband, Lord Westray. Both she and Mr. D'Estrange now tell us that only once did the late earl obtain admission to Mrs. de Lara's house, and then it was in opposition to the latter's wishes. I leave you to judge if this statement be possible of either acceptance or belief, in face of what the witnesses referred to have told us.

"We have heard some evidence likewise of the way in which Rita Vernon became introduced into Mrs. de Lara's household. It appears that she was formerly no novice to Mr. Trackem's house. She does not deny this. In fact, how could she? Does it not strike you, gentlemen, that Rita Vernon was just a peculiar class of young woman to put in the responsible position described by Mrs. de Lara, and does it not seem very clear that the use to which her services were put was of a totally different nature? We were told distinctly by Mr. Trackem that Mrs. de Lara sent him a note by Rita Vernon on the day of the murder, instructing him to retain his house for her and Lord Westray. Mrs. de Lara denies having written this note. I produce it, and it runs as follows:—

SIR,
      Please to reserve the house tonight as usual for Lord Westray and myself. We shall arrive between twelve and one.
                                                            S. DE LARA

"What is to be thought, my lord, of the veracity of such witnesses as Mrs. de Lara and Rita Vernon, for the girl denies having delivered this note? Yet here we have it, and we have furthermore the fact, that on the night when Mr. D'Estrange shot Lord Westray, Mrs. de Lara was found alone with that nobleman in Mr. Trackem's house. And, gentlemen, as against this very clear and circumstantial evidence, we are asked by Mrs. de Lara and Rita Vernon to accept a romance which all sane men can only regard in the light of hallucination, if not, as I regret to believe, downright deliberate falsehood. We are asked to believe that Mrs. de Lara was waylaid in her own grounds at night, overcome by ruffians, and carried off bound hand and foot to London. We are asked to believe that a slight, frail girl like Rita Vernon performed a task which a man of herculean strength would have found almost beyond his power to accomplish. We are asked, in fact, to believe that Rita Vernon, whom you have had an opportunity of seeing, could cling to a brougham between Windsor and London, and then sum up sufficient force to make her way to Montragee House at half-past two in the morning, where of course, like in a fairy tale, she finds the Duke of Ravensdale and Mr. D'Estrange all ready to accompany her to the release of the lady fair. The story defeats its own end by its wild improbability, unsupported by fact, and establishes at once the reasonable and circumstantial evidence of the side for the prosecution. I maintain that there is proof positive that Mr. D'Estrange, assisted by Rita Vernon,—who in this instance betrayed her mistress,—came upon the unfortunate earl with intent to murder. He admits that he shot him, but he declines to give any further information as to what he did with Lord Westray after leaving the house in Verdegrease Crescent. We find, moreover, that the three letters purporting to come from Lord Westray, and addressed to Mr. Trackem, are all written on paper which Victoire Hester has identified as the quality and class always used by Mr. D'Estrange and Mrs. de Lara, and exactly similar to the paper on which the notes to Mr. Trackem and Victoire Hester were penned on the day of the murder. The writing of the last note is denied. Again I meet that denial by producing the note. It runs thus:—

HESTER,

I have gone up to town for a few days, will let you know when to expect me back. Miss Vernon has accompanied me.

Faithfully yours,

S. DE LARA

"Such facts leave very little doubt in my mind but that Mrs. de Lara had arranged to meet Lord Westray, and that Rita Vernon betrayed her intention to Mr. D'Estrange. Such facts convince me that this latter resolved on vengeance. He deliberately went to Verdegrease Crescent, and shot Lord Westray, and finally, under cover of repentance, decoyed him from the house, and got rid of him somehow and somewhere. What follows? A letter arrives for Mr. Trackem, who is frightened out of his wits at the turn affairs have taken—a letter purporting to come from Lord Westray. By a strange coincidence, this letter and others following are all written on the same class of paper as that used by Mr. D'Estrange in Mrs. de Lara's house. Lastly, the very suit which Lord Westray was known to have been wearing the night he was shot at, has been found buried deep in the ground on the property of Mrs. de Lara at Windsor, bearing evidence of having been a long time under the earth, and in close proximity to it the body of a man reduced to a skeleton was also discovered. Around the neck of this skeleton a gold chain and locket was found, and on the little finger a plain gold ring. These have been identified by the late earl's valet, who has sworn to seeing them on the earl's person the day he disappeared.

It would be superfluous for me to detain you with further details, the points of evidence which I have submitted being, it appears to me, too clear for it to be possible to draw any other conclusion but the one that Mr. D'Estrange deliberately, and of malice aforethought, did shoot at Lord Westray with intent to kill, and did afterwards, in some manner not yet unravelled, make away with the life of that unfortunate nobleman. I ask you, therefore, to put aside from your minds Mr. D'Estrange's high position and social status, and to find a verdict in accordance with the evidence before you."

The great man sits down hastily, and glances round the court. An almost unnatural stillness reigns therein. Every eye is bent on the prisoner, and then on the beautiful, pale, gold-headed woman, whose gaze is riveted on her child's face with an intensity terrible to witness. But there is nothing but calmness on the features of Hector D'Estrange, in whose eyes the confident, triumphant expression shines, which conscious innocence alone could create.

"I will endeavour, like the Attorney-General," he observes, "to detain the Court as shortly as possible. But at the very outset I would wish to point out to you that the evidence of Weston and Victoire is not trustworthy, as being that of discharged servants. Mrs. de Lara has told you most emphatically that Lord Westray paid her no visits, save the one referred to by the coachman, Alfred Hawkins. She has told you how that visit was forced upon her, and how Lord Westray was ordered out of the house by myself. There is absolutely no evidence corroborative of that given by Charles Weston, which I can only characterise as pure and malicious invention, the same remark applying to the false testimony of Victoire Hester. This woman has declared that Mrs. de Lara wrote her a note the night of the supposed murder apprising her of her visit to London. Yet these visits with Mrs. de Lara were of frequent occurrence, and she had never before found it necessary to acquaint Victoire of her movements. My lord, I declare the letter to be a forgery, as I also declare the letter to which Mr. Trackem refers as coming from Mrs. de Lara to be likewise. My lord, and gentlemen of the jury, the Attorney-General has passed a cruel and unnecessary sneer on Mrs. de Lara's account of the ruffianly and brutal attack made upon her by the undoubtedly hired scoundrels of her most bitter foe. He has attributed all to romance, hallucination, deliberate falsehood. His insinuations are brutal and cowardly. My mother, like myself, *would scorn to tell a lie*. We leave that to the poltroons and cowards who seek by forgery and perjury to swear away the life of one who is innocent. I maintain that Mrs. de Lara's account and description of what took place is in every essential particular true, while the corroborative evidence of Rita Vernon bears it out in every detail. The Duke of Ravensdale has clearly stated to you how the poor girl sought him at Montragee House, and the state she was in after her terrible drive. The Attorney-General smiles scornfully at the idea of a woman being capable of such pluck and heroism as Rita Vernon evinced on that occasion. I cast back the slur into his teeth. I tell him that if he wishes to find true courage and heroism combined, he must go to a woman to discover it. But it is not to such as he, that women will go for justice.

"And now, my lord, and gentlemen of the jury, I ask you to put yourselves in my place. Had you been called to that house of ill fame, and there found a being whom you honoured, loved, and respected, in the hands and power of her bitterest enemy, bound hand and foot, gagged, bleeding, and helpless, would you not have acted as I did, and in the fury and horror of the moment lost all power of restraint? I admit that I shot Lord Westray; I have never denied it. But I do deny that I caused his death; and what is more, *I confidently believe that he is alive at this moment*, and that this foul accusation is a plot to ruin me, to be, in fact, revenged on yonder noble lady, who has through life resented his brutality, defied and scouted him, and refused to submit to his hideous desires. I make no pretence of being able to account for his disappearance, for the alleged discovery of his body and clothes, for the letters written in his handwriting on the paper used by myself and Mrs. de Lara. I am unable to understand it all save in the light of a base, foul, and detestable plot which has for its object revenge. Of that I know him to be perfectly capable.

"And now, my lord, and gentlemen of the jury, I have but one more statement to make ere I close these remarks. I once more positively affirm that Mrs. de Lara is my mother, and that the intimacy of which I am accused is a base and unfounded fabrication."

He has folded his arms, and his voice has ceased. A burst of applause greets him as he stops speaking. Vainly the judge calls for order.

"This is an exhibition that I will not tolerate," exclaims that worthy functionary. "Another such a disgraceful proceeding, and I will cause the whole court to be instantly cleared."

This produces silence. Sir James Grumpy is a bit of a martinet. The public knows that he means what he says.

And now he proceeds in his summing up. Very carefully he goes over all the points advanced by both sides, but it is apparent to all, from the first, that the summing up is most unfavourable to the accused. It takes him about an hour to get through his task, and all the time Hector D'Estrange stands motionless, with folded arms and immovable features. Only now and again the dark blue eyes wander to where Speranza is sitting, with the Duke of Ravensdale by her side.

The summing up is over at length, and the jury have retired to consider their verdict. Apparently, however, they had made up their minds beforehand, for they do not keep the Court long waiting. In a few minutes everyone has reassembled.

"Gentlemen of the jury, have you considered your verdict?" rings out a harsh, sing-song voice.

"We have," answers the foreman.

"You find the accused guilty or not guilty of the murder of Lord Westray?"

Amidst a silence, terrible in its intensity, comes the answer—

"Guilty."

A thrill of horror runs through the court. There is hardly a dry eye within it. The duke has got Speranza's hand in his, but she never moves.

"Hector D'Estrange, have you any reason to give why sentence of death should not be passed upon you?" again inquires the harsh, sing-song voice.

"I have," he answers, with a low musical laugh. "My reason is, that if I am put to death, murder will indeed be committed, for I am guiltless. I wish to add also one word of explanation, for I see the time has come. Both Sir Anthony and the learned judge have laid great stress on the apparent falsehood of which they allege I have been guilty, in declaring that I am the child of Captain Harry Kintore and Mrs. de Lara. They point to the fact that Dr. Merioneth has declared that the child born at Ancona was a girl. Has it never struck you, my lord, and gentlemen of the jury, that a girl could do what I have done in youth, a woman accomplish what I have accomplished in maturer years? No. I plainly see that this has not struck you, for you are men. You will not acknowledge that a woman can equal man, and with fair opportunities rise to power and fame. Yet such has been my aim in life to prove, for this I have struggled; and had it not been for the base machinations of enemies, would assuredly have lived to triumphantly achieve. Know, however, that Hector D'Estrange is no liar. If for sixteen years he has practised on Society what may be called a fraud, it was for the sake of righting a terrible wrong. My lord, and gentlemen of the jury, I again declare myself to be the child of Captain Kintore and Mrs. de Lara, but I confess my sex. In Hector D'Estrange the world beholds a woman— her name, Gloria de Lara."

Amidst confusion and excitement unparalleled sentence of death is passed. Yet, as the judge's words come to a close, a voice rings through the court, a voice in which defiance and love are mingled. It is a woman's voice. Many recognise it as Flora Desmond's.

"As there is a God above," it cries, "Gloria de Lara shall not die!"

But even as all eyes are turned in search of the speaker, Flora Desmond has vanished.

V

"Guilty!" "Condemned to death!" "Hector D'Estrange a woman!" The words have passed through the court, along the corridors, and out into the street beyond, where the crowds press eagerly forward to hear the news. It is received at first with astonishment and incredulity. Some people call it a hoax, others laugh at the statement as a wild improbability, and wonder what the real truth is. But even as they discuss the rumour, a movement is visible opposite the court, as an officer of the White Guards' Regiment makes her appearance outside. An orderly mounted on a grey horse is holding an empty-saddled white one in readiness, and as the officer makes her appearance, brings the steed alongside the steps leading up to the entrance.

The officer is no stranger to the crowd. Flora Desmond's features are well known to it. Is she not the leader of Hector D'Estrange's especial regiment, a regiment entirely drawn from the women of "the people"? Whatever may be the feeling of the middle-class and a portion of that one which claims to rank above it, in regard to Hector D'Estrange, one thing is certain, that amidst the poor and the needy, amidst the suffering and the struggling, that name is a talisman to conjure by.

She comes down the steps hurriedly, and mounts her horse in haste. The crowd sways and presses towards her in spite of the efforts of large numbers of police to repress them.

"The verdict?" they shout inquiringly. "Tell us the verdict!"

She stands up in her stirrups and looks at that sea of faces. Enemies there may be amongst them, hundreds, perhaps, antagonistic to Hector D'Estrange, but amidst the rough faces of the thousands that press around her, she knows that the majority are true as steel.

"Guilty!" she calls out. "He is condemned to die! I mistake the people, however, if they will believe the verdict or acquiesce in the sentence. Say you, whom he loves, whose hard lot he has struggled to raise, will you permit it?"

"Never!" comes the fierce shout from hundreds, nay, thousands of throats. "Hector D'Estrange shall not die!"

"I knew it," she replies proudly. "Justice shall be upheld. I knew the people would be true to him, men as well as women. He shall not die!"

They cheer and cheer again as she makes her way through the crowd followed by her orderly. It gives room to her willingly, and opens a passage for her horse. She rides along rapidly in the direction of a quiet side street, well away from the thronging crowd of people. Even as she does so the rumbling wheels of the prison-van strike on her ear. She can see it approaching, surrounded by a strong force of police, and as she does so, she urges on her horse.

Flora Desmond passes rapidly along the quiet, deserted street, until she nearly reaches the end, and then turns her horse down a narrow alley leading therefrom. This brings her into a wide, spacious yard, around which a big square building is built, in the centre of which is a large archway with strong iron gates, guarded by two mounted sentries. They salute her as she rides up, and the iron gates are unlocked at once. She rides through them, and enters what appears to be an immense riding-school, in which are drawn up a hundred troopers of the White Regiment. Her eye scans them keenly and rapidly. They are in perfect order, and look fit for any work. Every face is turned towards her.

"Hector D'Estrange has been declared guilty," she says in a clear, distinct voice, "and is condemned to die! I am here to lead you to his rescue. If anyone is to die, it shall be we who will do so, not him. Follow me, guards. There is not a moment to be lost."

She places herself at their head. They pass out into the courtyard, and the gates are locked behind them. The sentries fall into their places, and the troopers, six abreast, follow in the wake of their gallant-hearted leader. At a smart trot they pass down the quiet street. In the distance they can hear the roar of the crowd, which is cheering loudly; and they know that Hector D'Estrange is being removed to the prison from which his accusers hope never again to see him issue.

They are nearing the crowd now, for it is surging their way. The prison-van is coming along at a smart pace, guarded by its bevy of policemen. It is not a hundred yards from where Flora Desmond, at the head of her hundred and two guards, sits motionless on her horse, for she has called a halt, and is awaiting their coming.

Suddenly she stands up in her stirrups and turns to her troopers. At the same moment she draws her sword.

"Forward!" she cries, waving it above her head. "Forward, guards of *his* regiment; rescue him or die!"

She has put her horse in motion as she speaks, and with the rush of a whirlwind the White Guards bear down upon the prison-van. The policemen catch sight of them coming, and close around it manfully. The driver whips up the horses, and urges them along at a canter. "Of what avail?" The White Guards are upon them; nothing can withstand the charge. It is the work of a moment.

"Sever the traces; cut the horses loose!" shouts Flora Desmond, as she gallops up alongside one of the animals, and, seizing its rein, brings it up on to its haunches, one of the troopers doing likewise by the other.

They obey her promptly and rapidly, while the remainder engage the police escort, who resist gallantly. "Of what avail?" The crowd has closed round, willing and eager to assist in the work of rescue. The odds are too great to allow the representatives of law and order to prevail.

Twice over Flora Desmond has summoned the policeman inside to unlock the door of the van, but he stands to his guns and refuses. "If you do not," she cries, "I shall be forced to fire through the lock until I break it, and the bullets may injure you. Come, man, no use resisting now."

But the policeman is staunch in the performance of what he considers his duty, and remains firm in his determination not to betray his trust.

"Then throw yourself flat on the ground, my man," again calls out Flora Desmond, "for I am going to fire."

She pauses for a moment to give him time to obey, then raises a revolver, and fires once, twice, thrice through the lock, which gives way at last. The crowd cheers loudly, the door of the van is flung open, and in a moment Flora Desmond is beside Gloria de Lara.

"Thank God!" she exclaims. "Here, come this way. I have a horse all ready for you."

The policeman is lying motionless on the floor of the van. The two step across him, and pass quickly out of the wheeled prison. As they do so the people press forward to welcome their hero, for to them, in spite of the rumours, Gloria de Lara is still Hector D'Estrange. She has mounted her horse, and raised her hand to enjoin silence. The police escort has been overcome; its members are passively accepting what to them is the inevitable. They have sought to do their duty. They can do no more.

"Friends," she calls out in the voice they know and love so well, "I have been unjustly accused and unjustly condemned. If it were not so, I would not accept the rescue brought me by my faithful women guards, aided by your kindly and generous devotion. My enemies are those who would fight against true progress, and the abolition of scandals and wrongs which must destroy this great nation with their wickedness, unless abolished in time. I have sought to probe to their root these scandals and these wrongs, have sought to submit to you the quickest and surest way to remedy them. I tell you that the greatest evils we have to face are the social ones. To them I ascribe all the sufferings and sins of the poor, the sins and false position of the rich. There are bad laws which must be done away with, good ones which must be set up to accomplish such social reform. Before you can do this you must set Nature on an even footing, and do away with the artificial barriers which you have raised against woman's progress and advancement; for until she has the same powers and opportunities as man, a thorough and exhaustive reform of the evils which afflict Society, will never be efficiently undertaken."

"And now, my friends, we are on the eve of a great revolution. If the people will stand by me, I will stand by them. Let us loyally determine to carry this great question to a successful issue, nor rest till it has been accomplished. I am going to trust myself amongst those whom I have ever loved, whose condition I have sought to raise. Yet ere doing so, I have one confession to make to you. Hector D'Estrange, whose advancement has been rapid and unparalleled almost in the annals of statesmanship, must be no longer known to you under that name. The time has come when I must confess myself. Before you you see one of the despised and feeble sex, the unfitted to rule, the inferior of man. *I am a woman!* Henceforth I am no longer Hector D'Estrange, but Gloria de Lara."

She has ceased speaking, and begun to move her horse through the crowd. Men and women press round her to kiss her hand. Poor men are more generous than rich ones. With rare exceptions, the fire of suffering purifies from self, and makes the heart appreciate true worth more readily. It is the people's voice that generally forces on all great reforms; it is the people's will that carries everything before it, when the reform required is a just one.

It never enters these men's minds to depreciate her deeds, to belittle her acts, because she is a woman. Their reason tells them that she understands their wants, that her great heart is in sympathy with their needs, that she has sought to help them when in power, and that now her enemies have got the upper hand, all their loyalty and devotion is needed to support the cause, which she has told them lies at the root of all future social reform, which means progress, comfort, and happiness for the toiling millions. But there is a sound of many horses' feet coming towards them, and all eyes are turned in the direction whence the sounds come. The ever-increasing crowd sways to and fro, expectant and anxious, instinctively apprehending what is to come.

"Form up, guards!" Flora Desmond's voice is heard shouting. "Close round her, and defend her with your lives. It is not we who seek to spill blood, but if our rulers will have it so, then let it be. We will show them that woman is not the helpless coward they imagine. If necessary, we will fight to save her. Retreat in good order on Montragee House."

They close round her, obedient to the order. The movement is executed silently but swiftly, and with an exactitude which speaks volumes for the discipline of the White Guards. "Shade of Whyte-Melville," could ye arise now, you would behold your prophecy an accomplished fact, for the Amazons, whom you predicted, if rendered amenable to discipline, could conquer the world, are before you there. The sounds have assumed shape, and a troop of Horse Guards Blue, hastily turned out to support the arm of the law, are in view now. The horses have been ridden at a good pace, for the foam studs their black shining coats. At the word of command the troopers rein up.

The position is a difficult one. Between them and the White Guards a dense, impenetrable crowd is surging. To charge that crowd means death to many, yet it can only be compassed in this manner. The order which the officer in command has received is, however, specific. It is to disperse the crowd, to give every assistance to the police, and to recapture the prisoner at any cost.

It is a soldier's duty to obey superior orders, nor question the why or wherefore. It is no part of a soldier's duty to use his own discretion.

"His not to reason why, His but to do and die."

So at least thinks Colonel Jack Delamere, as his quick eye takes in the scene. Duty is a strange thing. It nerves the heart not only to physical but to moral deeds of courage. Surely it is no insignificant act of the latter which draws from that gallant officer the command to obey an order which he loathes, for, apart from all other considerations, Jack Delamere loves Flora Desmond, and knowing her as he does, he is aware that the order will probably mean death to the being for whom he would willingly sacrifice his own life.

"Make way, my friends," he calls out imploringly to the people. "Make way, I beseech of you. My orders are to disperse the crowd, and I must obey them. If you do not make way, I shall be forced to order my men to charge."

A loud shout of defiance is the only reply which he receives. There are heroes and heroines in that crowd. They are resolved that only over their trampled and crushed bodies, shall Jack Delamere and his Blues come up with the White Guards, who are retreating in good order with Gloria de Lara in their midst. Every minute is precious for this latter, and the crowd will do its best to afford these precious minutes.

There is a tremor in Jack Delamere's voice as he once more puts his request. The crowd mistake it for a sign of anger, and defy him with jeers and sneers.

"Then be it so," he says sadly, as with a heavy heart he gives the order which must bring death to many.

His men obey. The black horses charge into the swaying mass, and men and women go down before them. Some make a desperate fight for it before they succumb, clinging to the animals' bridles, and attempting to force them back from their onward career. But the troopers have their swords out, and the unarmed cannot prevail over the armed. Nevertheless there is no surrender, no cry for quarter or mercy. The crowd are in earnest in their desire to let the White Guards get away with their beloved charge, and their resistance is dogged and determined.

The police have joined in, and are using their batons freely. Shouts and cries resound, and the crowd grows denser every moment, swelled by the numbers that have hastened to the scene. Dead and dying are lying on the cold stone pavements of the street. Even the latter are forgotten in the fierce fight that is raging, a fight undertaken by the people that the idol of their hearts may live.

It is an unequal contest, and can only end one way. Nigh every trooper has cut his way through at the expense of many a life. They are re-forming now, and with Jack Delamere at their head set off in pursuit of the White Guards, the crowd following as best it can in the rear.

But its devotion and sturdy resistance have given the start to Gloria de Lara's escort, and ride as they may, the Blues on their black horses cannot come up with the lightly mounted greys of the White Guards. These flash along Whitehall at full speed, with their precious charge in their midst. Another moment, and the hoofs of the horses are clattering through the entrance to Montragee House. It is the work of an instant for the great folding doors to unclose. Once through them, and Gloria de Lara is safe. Flora Desmond has laid her hand on the bridle of this latter's horse.

"Quick!" she exclaims. "Pass in there, Gloria. Ah! do not delay. Remember that your life means liberty to thousands. It is not a question of self. I know well how you would wish to stay and help us, but your duty is to preserve your life first. No one doubts your courage."

"God bless you, Flora! Yes, I will do my duty, for the sake of the great cause that shall triumph."

She springs from her horse as she speaks, and as one of the troopers leads it towards the stables, she turns to the others. "Brave guards," she exclaims, "none know better than you that Gloria de Lara is grateful for your devotion and staunch loyalty."

"We would die for you!" they shout enthusiastically, and many of their voices tremble. Even as they cease, the Duke of Ravensdale is on the threshold of his noble mansion. His hand is on Gloria's arm.

"Great God be praised!" bursts from his white lips. "Gloria, they shall never touch you here!"

He draws her gently into the great front hall, and the door is closed and barred behind them. There is a triumphant smile on Flora Desmond's features; her quick ear has caught the sound of galloping horses. "Do you hear them?" she laughs defiantly. "They come too late. Brave people! They have done their part well, and she is saved. Now follow me, guards. She has no need of us just yet. We must seek a safety for the future good that we may do, and for the sake of the cause we love. There is work ahead of us—hard work, and plenty too, for the revolution has begun!"

VI

"M y dear, how did you ever manage to get here? How could you venture out? Isn't it terrible, my dear?" exclaims Mrs. de Lacy Trevor, as her friend Lady Manderton enters her boudoir in the snug Piccadilly mansion, already introduced to the reader, on the morning following upon the events related in the last chapter. Outside, the streets are filled with an angry and excited crowd. The rougher element have taken advantage of the *mêlée*, to introduce themselves into its midst, and are parading the streets, causing confusion and terror to the more respectable and orderly portion of the crowd, whose presence is to be accounted for by totally different circumstances to those which have attracted the irredeemable portion of Society. The news of the verdict and sentence on Hector D'Estrange, the confession as to sex of the late Prime Minister, the daring and masterly rescue of the prisoner by Flora Desmond and her White Guards, the devoted resistance of the crowd to the charge of the Blues under Colonel Delamere, and the ultimate escape of Gloria de Lara from her pursuers, has spread like wild-fire through the metropolis. London has been in a state of the greatest excitement throughout the night. The most startling and improbable rumours have been afloat as to the intentions of the Government, while the people are loudly clamouring for a squashing of the verdict, an annulment of the sentence, and a free pardon for their idol, to many more than ever popular now that her sex is disclosed. For, let it be whispered, that this disclosure has operated in winning over to Gloria de Lara's side many a wavering mind, which is able now to recognise in the brilliant successful life of Hector D'Estrange, the unanswerable and irrefutable proof of woman's power to equal man in all things, provided fair play and equal opportunities be given to her. Of the murder of Lord Westray, her adherents believe her to be absolutely guiltless, and are loud in condemnation of the verdict.

Such is the position of affairs on the morning in question,—a position sufficiently grave, to warrant the calling out of the troops to assist the police in maintaining order, amidst this wholly unparalleled scene of public protest and sympathy.

There is a quiet smile on Lady Manderton's face as she answers her friend.

"I came here on foot, Vivi, and I have come to say goodbye. Ah, Vivi! you need not stare, dear. I'm not the old Dodo you have been accustomed to. Great God! why were not my eyes opened before, all the time that Hector D'Estrange has been working for us? But it is not too late. I can retrieve the past even yet, by working on behalf of Gloria de Lara's cause. Ay, Vivi, it is a cause well worth dying for."

"Why, Dodo, you must be clean gone cracked! What are you going to do?"

Lady Manderton takes a newspaper out of her pocket, and hands it to Mrs. de Lacy Trevor. "Have you read this?" she inquires at the same time.

Mrs. de Lacy Trevor opens it and reads.

THE GREAT D'ESTRANGE TRIAL

SPEECHES OF THE ATTORNEY-GENERAL AND
HECTOR D'ESTRANGE.
THE JUDGE'S SUMMING UP.
VERDICT AND SENTENCE.
EXTRAORDINARY CONFESSION OF THE PRISONER.
SENTENCE OF DEATH.
DARING RESCUE OF THE PRISONER
BY LADY FLORA DESMOND AND WHITE GUARDS.
DETERMINED RESISTANCE TO THE MILITARY.
GREAT LOSS OF LIFE.
DEATH OF THE POLICEMAN FORTESCUE, WHO WAS IN
CHARGE OF THE PRISONER.
WARRANTS OUT FOR THE ARREST OF GLORIA DE LARA
AND LADY FLORA DESMOND.

Beneath these startling announcements Mrs. de Lacy Trevor further reads much of which she did not know. Then she lays down the paper.

"My dear, it's like a dream," she exclaims. "What will happen?"

"What has happened already," answers Lady Manderton. "Revolution. Vivi," she continues eagerly, "I suppose it's no use asking you to take the step I'm going to? I'm going to throw in my lot with Gloria de Lara, and help her by every means in my poor power."

"Dodo! what do you mean?" cries her friend in a horrified voice.

"I mean what I have said, Vivi," answers Lady Manderton in a quiet, sad voice. "Vivi, I can't tell you how terribly I feel my past wasted life.

But it was not all my fault. I was brought up to nothing better, and probably should never have realised it, if Hector D 'Estrange had not been born. Ah, Vivi! Gloria's life has opened my eyes. I see now that if woman had fair play, women in the position of you and I, Vivi, would never throw away and waste our lives as we have done. But, thank God, there is a chance of remedying it. At any rate, I'll do my best. For Gloria de Lara's noble cause I would die willingly a thousand times."

She has taken her friend's hand as she speaks. "Goodbye, Vivi," she says gently.

But Vivi has risen and thrown her arms round Lady Manderton's neck.

"Don't, don't, Dodo! You mustn't go! There are going to be terrible doings; I can see that plainly. Oh, Dodo! please don't go."

There is just a slight curl of contempt upon the lips of Lady Manderton's handsome mouth as she kisses the weak, timid woman, whom all these years she has been contented to call friend. Then she gently undoes the tightly clasped hands of Vivi Trevor from around her neck, and presses her firmly but kindly back into her seat. "I have no fear, Vivi. There, now, don't cry; you will hear of me soon, dear—God grant better employed than I have been. There now, think of what I've said. Goodbye." The next moment she is gone, and Vivi Trevor is left alone.

For a time she sits like one in a dream, then she rises and walks to the window. The crowd is still surging to and fro. All traffic is rendered impossible save on foot. Mounted policemen and military patrol the street, interfering as little as possible with the people, who, save for the rougher element already mentioned, are orderly enough, albeit excited and angry.

"What will happen?" mutters Vivi to herself. "What a strange sight! Never realised before what a number of people London contains, and what a strange-looking lot, too! Didn't think there were such people in existence."

There is a knock at her boudoir door as she stands thus soliloquising to herself.

"Come in," she answers.

It is Marie, the French maid, and she is the bearer of a note.

"A letter for madame," she says.

"Marie, what a fearful crowd!" exclaims her mistress. "What will happen? Have you ever seen anything like it before?"

"Mais jamais, jamais de ma vie, madame," answers the Frenchwoman shuddering. "C'est terrible."

"Marie, you can bring me my coffee and bread-and-butter now," continues Vivi, as she turns the note over in her hand and looks at it curiously. It is from Mr. Trevor.

"Madame will have to take *café noir* this morning," remarks the maid gloomily.

"*Café noir?* You know I hate it, Marie."

"Tant pis, madame," replies the woman, with a shrug of the shoulders. "But no milkman has called, and there is no milk in the house."

"But we shall starve, Marie!" exclaims her mistress.

"Je le crois bien, madame," is all the other replies as she leaves the room. Marie is not a stranger to revolution. She was in Paris as a young girl during the revolt which cost Napoleon III his throne. She knows well the suffering which an upheaval of the people always brings with it. She will be astonished at nothing that may come. Has she not been detailing her experiences downstairs to the frightened servants, who are undergoing *their* first hardships in Mr. and Mrs. de Lacy Trevor's luxurious service by having to go without milk in their tea that morning? Do they, by any chance, cast a thought to the suffering thousands who have no tea into which to put either milk or sugar,—those suffering thousands whose condition and very existence has given the brain of Gloria de Lara many a racking thought, as—when in power—she has pondered the problem, so far unravelled, of their amelioration and upraising? Not a bit of it. These servants do not realise a suffering which they have never seen. It is just the world's way. Not one half of it knows how the other half lives.

Left alone, Vivi Trevor opens her husband's note. She thinks it strange he should write to her. He has never written to her before while staying under the same roof. She has not set eyes on him since the day before, when he parted with her after the trial, conviction, and sentence of Hector D'Estrange. He had not come in to dinner that night, nothing out of the way to Vivi, the comings and goings of her husband being of small importance or interest to her. These two have drifted more than ever apart since the days when Mr. Trevor first had his eyes opened by the Eton boy's article in the *Free Review*. He has never sought to interfere with his wife's goings on, feeling that to do so would only make his desolate home more unhomely and comfortless than ever. It is therefore with some surprise that Vivi reads the following:—

My Dearest Vivi,

You will wonder at these few lines, but I feel I owe you
some little explanation, though whether you will care about
it I know not. Our lives as regards one another have not
been over happy; at least I can speak for myself in saying so.
I do not blame you, Vivi, for the want of affection you have
always shown me, or for your goings on with other men.
The fault lies in your bringing up, and the false position in
which your sex is placed by man's unnatural laws. I learnt to
recognise this long ago, and to acknowledge the teaching of
Hector D'Estrange as true and just. That noble genius, now
unveiled to a wondering world as Gloria de Lara, is paying
the penalty of her attempt to naturalise woman's position
in this world, as a lead up to many and much-needed social
reforms. I feel strongly that in this moment of trial she
should receive the support of all men and women, high and
low, rich and poor, who feel with her, and I have determined
to place my services at her disposal. This, Vivi, will naturally
take me away from you for a time, perhaps forever. Who
knows? Only God. You will not miss me, for I have never
been anything to you. I do not blame you, dearest, for I
ought never to have married you. Still I loved you, and love
you still; that is my only plea, and I ask your forgiveness. You
will perhaps accord it when you realise that I am giving my
life to the upraising of your sex, and to attaining its freedom,
thereby accomplishing the first great step in the direction of
social reform, on which the gaze of Gloria de Lara is fixed.
How this struggle will end I know not. It will be the greatest
revolution this world has ever known,—far-reaching in its
results, and, let us hope and pray, bringing about a final, fair,
and lasting settlement of that all-momentous question, which
has given to the world its noblest woman in Gloria de Lara.
Goodbye, Vivi.

Your ever-devoted husband,
Launcelot Trevor

She lays the letter down on her lap, and sits staring at it. Her thoughts
fly back across the years of her wedded life, years spent in vain amusements
and false excitements. She cannot recall a single kindly or unselfish

act on her part towards the man who has loved her so devotedly and tenderly, nor can she lay hold of one single act of usefulness upon which she can look back with either pleasure or satisfaction. Very acutely she feels this now; and yet has it been entirely her own fault?

"What else could I do?" she murmurs to herself. "I was never brought up to think of anything else. Mother bade me marry well and quickly. That's exactly what I did do. What other opening was given me None. If I had been a man, and properly educated, I might have done something; but as it was, what else could I do?"

Her thoughts are flying on ahead now, to that vague future of which she can know nothing till it comes. Yet what hope does that glance ahead bring to Vivi Trevor? Absolutely none. In the past her life had been wasted, and now the future, when regarded, brings her nothing But the vague dread of growing old and *passée*, with nothing to turn to when that time comes, nothing to console her for the gay, giddy life which she has led in the past.

She is beginning to understand Lady Manderton's words and action better now. Launcelot Trevor's note has opened her eyes very wide. Vivi vividly sees what she has never seen before, for she is beginning to think for the first time.

She throws herself face downwards on the sofa upon which she had been reclining so daintily, when Lady Manderton called in upon her but a short time since. There is a big black void all round Vivi Trevor's heart, a dull, hopeless feeling of despair. Large tears are welling up into her beautiful eyes, and bitter sobs shake her slight, girlish frame.

Poor Vivi! She is truly miserable, and yet she has no idea how to end that misery. In a like position. Lady Manderton had risen equal to the occasion; but then the latter is of different stuff to her hitherto gay, unthinking friend, a woman of stronger brain and sterner mould, one who is able to make up her mind, and act promptly when occasion requires it.

There she lies, this victim of neglected childhood and unfair, unnatural laws. She lies there, a living protest against the selfishness and conceit that have built up that wall within which she lies imprisoned. Of what good is life to such as she, whose education since childhood has been vain, mindless, ephemeral? If Vivi Trevor had never been born, the world would have lost nothing. And yet, as a drop is to an ocean, so is the life of this one despairing soul to the thousands who, like her, have gone down to their graves in uselessness and obscurity, not because in natural body and mind they were unfitted to work in the great army of man, not because in desire and willingness they were found wanting, but because of that barrier, that artificial mountain which one sex has forbidden the other sex to climb, which one sex has erected in the face of Nature, to shut out the operations of Nature's laws.

These words but reflect the thoughts of thousands, who, wearily struggling along the path of life, ask themselves wonderingly, "Why existence, if this is all it brings?" Many a tired and saddened soul has lain itself down to die, with the undefined feeling that the wasted life left behind might not have been if only—only—ay, if only what? Gloria de Lara, Flora Desmond, and others, could answer that vague, yearning cry. They would reply, "If only Nature had been obeyed." Therein lies the secret of the troubles of this world, the suffering, agony, and misery that millions have to put up with, while a clique lives and reigns, making laws and leading the multitude by the nose under the guise of liberty and freedom! For every happy heart, thousands there are of wretched ones; for every well-fed mortal, thousands there are who starve and suffer. The world is old, its years unknown to the ken of man. Through all these years man has ruled therein, and this is what he has brought it to! Can he do nothing better? Yes, but only hand in hand with woman. Nature declares it; and he who would fight against Nature, must create the evils that torture the world.

VII

Downing street is awake betimes, and within the precincts of the residence of the First Lord of the Treasury an unusual stir and signs of an unwonted anxiety are perceivable. Seated around a long oblong table in a singularly doleful-looking room, are a baker's dozen of gentlemen, apparently in eager discussion. Perplexity and anxiety is on every face, not unmixed, in some cases, with vacuity. A stranger dropped from the clouds, and unaccustomed to the ways, and manners, and customs of our planet, might innocently inquire who these disturbed-looking personages are, and what their business? He would be told in reply that the personages are nothing more nor less than the Sovereign of Great Britain's Ministers, their business, the holding of a Cabinet Council. But at such an hour, nine o'clock in the morning! Why, in the ordinary course of affairs, poor old Lord Muddlehead, the Secretary of State for the Colonies, would be adjusting his night-cap, and turning over for his second sleep in bed, and that excellent nonentity, Lord Donothing, Lord President of the Council and Privy Seal, would be sweetly dreaming of rest and peace, well merited and well earned, after the arduous and fatiguing duties attaching to his noble office!

However, a matter of importance has shaken sleep from their eyes, as they have been summoned post-haste to attend their chief on urgent public business.

The chief in question, the first Lord of the Treasury, the Prime Minister of Great Britain and Ireland, is the Duke of Devonsmere, a tall, aristocratic-looking man, with thick moustaches, whiskers, and beard, in which the grey hairs of advancing age are rapidly gathering. He has thick lips, a not very pleasant eye, and a forehead chiefly remarkable for the crease or wrinkle, which, starting from the centre, runs down perpendicularly to meet the nose. He has a voice far from genial; and, in fact, his manner all round is cold, and haughty, and unwinning.

The duke is a good speaker. That is his chief *forte*. He has not particularly distinguished himself through life as a great politician, though he has held high posts in various Ministries. He has been Secretary for War in a former Ministry, but seceded from his chief when this latter brought in his Irish Home Rule Bill. No one has ever been able to accuse the Duke of Devonsmere of attempting to aggrandise himself. In politics he has been strictly honest according to his lights, though many believe that in the old days of Conservatives and Liberals, he would have graced more appropriately the ranks of the former, which as a Unionist he eventually joined. However, those days are past. There are no Liberals, or Conservatives, or Unionists now. The former having adopted the Progressist title, the two latter become merged in the National party, of which party the Duke of Devonsmere is the head.

The position which he holds at this moment is an awkward one. His is only a provisional Ministry, held together by the temporary support of the Progressist party, the natural and avowed enemy of the Nationals. But the hatred of the Progressists for the D'Estrangeites is so intense, that for a time their minor enmity with the Nationals is merged and forgotten in this new and greater one. It is, therefore, with such assistance as this, that the duke, with a Cabinet chiefly distinguished for its dulness and want of perspicacity, is endeavouring to cope with the extraordinary state of affairs, that has arisen on the defeat of Hector D'Estrange's policy, and the revolution which has resulted from the events following upon that defeat.

Gloria de Lara is at large. Although warrants have been issued for her arrest as well as that of Lady Flora Desmond, no traces of either have yet been discovered. Of course the officials of Scotland Yard surrounded Montragee House, and demanded admission soon after the former's rescue; but when at length the great front door was thrown open for the admittance of the officers of the Law, they were received only by Lord Bernard Fontenoy, who smilingly regretted that he could afford them no information or assist their search in anyway. All he knew was that his brother had left him in charge of Montragee House during his unavoidable absence. Clearly there was very little to be extracted from the youthful lord.

The Home Department Minister is speaking now, but apparently affording but cold comfort to his colleagues. Mr. Mayhew belongs to the English bar. He is an excellent speaker, but that is all. It would have been better if he had stuck to his profession exclusively, and left politics alone, for he has not shone in them. He is a weak man, and an obstinate one, and can never be got to acknowledge having committed a mistake. He has held office before in a Conservative Ministry in the same department, which did not profit much by his supervision, or attain any particular distinction for efficiency. He is the best man, however, that the Nationals have at their command for the post, which is not saying much for the existing state of things.

"Detectives are at work in nearly every great centre, and the police are fully instructed how to act," he assures his colleagues.

"Don't you think, Mayhew, that Hector D'Estrange, or, as I suppose we must now call her, Gloria de Lara, has many secret friends in the force? There is no doubt she has the mass of the working classes of the country on her side—certainly nearly every woman amongst them. Depend upon it your detectives will not trace her, and it seems to me you are all of you vastly underrating her power."

The speaker is a man of about fifty years of age, with a fine forehead, rather scant hair, prominent, intelligent eyes, a sallow complexion, and somewhat of the middle height. He looks younger than he really is, and it is probably his long thick moustache that gives him a little of the military appearance. But Lord Pandulph Chertsey is no soldier. He is every inch a politician, living for nothing else but politics.

While we can pass over the remainder of the Devonsmere Cabinet without notice, because of the extreme mediocrity of talent displayed therein, a glance at the character of Lord Pandulph Chertsey is necessary. The extraordinary point which first strikes one is—why is not Lord Pandulph Prime Minister? Clearly amongst all those thirteen gentlemen he is the only one possessing a large grasp of thought, or a power to look at events and regard them as they are. Few men have been more abused than Lord Pandulph; and yet he has done nothing to merit that abuse beyond showing a certain independence of mind and an inclination to follow the dictates of conscience before party. He has been accused of ambition. It is certain that if he had been less honest in his political career, and less straightforward, he might have risen more quickly to supreme power. But though doubtless ambitious—and what sin is there in that?—he has known how to subordinate his ambition to the dictates of his conscience in all matters, which, according to his lights, he believes affect the welfare of Society. He sees clearly now what the high and dignified Duke of Devonsmere, old Lord Muddlehead, Lord Donothing, and their colleagues do not see in the least. He sees that Gloria de Lara, though she may have many an enemy in the country, is yet a power which must not be despised. Lord Pandulph has no sympathy with her cause or her teachings; but that is no reason why he should ignore the fact that there are thousands who have, and who are prepared to support her. Mr. Mayhew shakes his head. We have said he is an obstinate man, and obstinacy is more or less a sign of weakness.

"No, no," he says hastily. "I think it is you, Chertsey, who overrate her power. Of course she has a few friends, but not many. I always said D'Estrangeism was ephemeral. You will see how quickly the storm she has raised will become subdued. I have not the slightest doubt on that score. But for the sake of law and order we must strain every nerve to arrest both her and Lady Flora. It is a terrible business, but murder cannot go unpunished, that is very clear."

Lord Pandulph laughs, as he glances at the duke, who is sprawling back in his chair with his legs stretched out. Mr. Mayhew's remarks appear to him ridiculous. "Depend upon it," he exclaims again, "that you are utterly underrating her power. We know enough of Hector D'Estrange to be pretty well certain that Gloria de Lara will not remain inactive. You talk of your detectives and police, but let me remind you that there are scattered throughout the country those companies of Women Volunteers, whom she can call out at any moment. Surely you do not underrate their power for mischief?"

But Mr. Mayhew does, and so do the rest of the Cabinet, including the Duke of Devonsmere. This latter is a bitter opponent of Gloria de Lara's advocacy for woman's freedom. He is quite convinced that the sex is hopelessly inferior to his own, and regards their emancipation with the same horror as did the South in the American Civil War when the North upheld the abolition of slavery.

"I think we are straying wide of the mark, Chertsey," he observes rather gruffly. "The policy we have got to decide on, is how the riotous crowds that are paralysing public freedom are to be suppressed. There is no doubt that for the moment this adventuress has a strong party in her favour, but I think, with Mayhew, that all sympathy with her will quickly subside, especially if the Government show a bold and determined front to the mutineers. The most strenuous efforts must be made to arrest those two women, and so put an end to the mutiny which they have provoked. I consider, therefore, that the military ought to be employed to assist the police, and I have little doubt that in a very short time order will be restored. Do you all think with me?"

The eleven satellites do, but not the independent planet. Lord Pandulph does not agree, and he says so plainly. He thinks it will be madness to employ the military, and thus provoke civil brawls, and perhaps civil war. He cannot make himself responsible for such a state of things.

"I am very sorry," he says gravely, "but I am quite unable to fall in with such a policy, which, if pursued, I believe will entail lamentable results. Do your best if you think it possible to arrest the leaders of this movement by means of detectives and police, but for goodness' sake keep the soldiers out of the fray. However, if you persist, I can make way for a fresh Secretary for India. I can resign."

"That is an old game with you," remarks the duke drily. "It will not be the first time you have left your colleagues in the lurch."

"Say rather not the first time that I have refused to stifle conscience for the sake of office, or to make over my honest opinion to the care of others," answers Lord Pandulph somewhat hotly, nettled no doubt by the duke's unfair remark. "However," he continues quietly, "I have no wish to mar the unanimity of these proceedings, and will withdraw. My reasons for resignation can be fully explained in the proper place."

There is a significant ring in his voice which cannot be mistaken. The Duke knows perfectly well that with Lord Pandulph out of his Cabinet, this excellent clique will be little less than a group of mechanical dolls. To lose Lord Pandulph means discredit to his Ministry, and a considerable loss of confidence outside it. He feels he must temporise.

"Really, Chertsey, I don't understand what you want," he observes impatiently. "A short while ago you were making fun of the detective force, and assuring us we had underrated Gloria de Lara's power. Now that I propose to take decisive measures to arrest that power, you object to them. Will you propose a policy yourself?"

"Well, I will, as you invite me to do so," answers Lord Pandulph, with a smile, "but I do not suppose you will adopt it. However, here is my opinion. I am not in sympathy with Gloria de Lara's desires, but I fully recognise that her doctrines are accepted by thousands. I am not likely to forget that it was she who raised the Hall of Liberty, who drilled into efficiency a large Woman Volunteer Force, and who has worked her way into the affections of vast numbers of the working classes. Having read the evidence at her trial, I am extremely dissatisfied with the verdict, while in regard to the death of the policeman in the prison-van, I do not look upon Lady Flora's act as murder. We are assured by members of the police force, that she fired through the lock of the van, only after giving the policeman full warning of her intention to do so. She naturally supposed he had lain down as she bade him; and though his death is most grievous, really she cannot be accused of murder. Looking at matters in this light, I think the wisest thing the present Government can do is to appeal to the country to decide the question, revoke the warrant against Lady Flora, and offer

Gloria de Lara a fresh trial. Such a policy may be out of the way, but we must not forget that we are now facing a state of affairs unparalleled in the world's history. For my part, I cannot take the responsibility of deciding for the country. It is the country which should be appealed to, and allowed to decide for itself."

He has spoken as befits a statesman, who is able and willing to look upon the people as the proper tribunal to decide the policy to be pursued. But the Duke of Devonsmere, unlike Lord Pandulph, has never and will never be able to quit his aristocratic perch in order to descend to the people's level. He is willing to give them a policy and ask them to accept it, but he cannot realise that the masses are able to produce one for themselves. It is not wonderful that he thinks as he does, for he is not, and never has been, in touch with the people.

Like Mr. Mayhew, he shakes his head.

"Your proposal is simple madness, Chertsey. I, for one, cannot fall in with it."

He looks sternly at the eleven satellites who are regarding him. They thoroughly understand that look.

"Nor we," they murmur deferentially, apeing the abject acquiescence of poor old Lord Muddlehead.

Again Lord Pandulph laughs. Words would not measure the contemptuous ring that there is in that laugh.

"And you will pardon me if I say that I think your proposal madness also. I cannot agree to it, and it is best I should resign," he says quietly.

"Very well," answers the duke coldly. "As you are determined, so be it, Chertsey."

Lord Pandulph rises. He accepts his *congé* willingly. It has been gall and wormwood to work with such colleagues as these. He is out of place, and he feels it. He knows that he ought to be where the duke is sitting. Undoubtedly he ought.

"Then it is understood? I shall tender my resignation without any delay, so that you will be able to nominate my successor. This being so, it is better I should retire at once. Good-morning, Devonsmere." And without deigning recognition of the eleven satellites. Lord Pandulph leaves the room.

"Really, Chertsey is about the most insufferable fellow to deal with I have ever known," murmurs Lord Hankney, the Minister for Agriculture, adjusting his eyeglass. "We shall do much better without him, Devonsmere."

So they sit on in council these strange twelve, a Ministry misrepresentative of the people. The policy against which Lord Pandulph warned them, they agree to adopt. The military is to be ordered out, a direct incentive to civil war, while the warrants for the arrest of Gloria de Lara and Lady Flora Desmond are to remain in force. It is the old story, merely history repeating itself, of a group of men omitting to consult the people—whose paid servants they are—before acting. Office, unfortunately, nowadays is too much considered as the happy hunting ground of a clique or class, to the exclusion of the people's acknowledged representatives. So the wrong men step in, and take upon themselves responsibilities for which they are totally disqualified and unfitted; and thus are mistakes committed for which those who pay the taxes have to suffer. The case in point is a good one. Such a decision would never have been come to had the Duke of Devonsmere's Cabinet contained some of the people's representatives.

VIII

"What news, Evie?"

The speaker has risen from a low wooden stool just outside the verandahed porch of a pretty, straggling, rambling cottage, hidden amidst many and various creepers, whose parasitical arms interlace with each other in bewildering confusion. All around stretch dark pine woods far as the eye can reach, as it scans their broad expanse through the cuttings in the forest, fashioned by the hand of man.

Gloria de Lara it is, who thus questions the newcomer. A tall, powerful-looking man, with thick, bushy beard and whiskers, and a clean-shaven upper lip. He is dressed in the habiliments of a navvy, and carries on his back a bag of tools. These he throws down as he replies,

"News, Gloria? Much what I expected. You are to be hunted down by every means at the command of Scotland Yard. Warrants are out not only for your arrest but for Lady Flora's as well, and the military are to be employed to assist the police in suppressing the 'riotous crowds,' as such are termed the people who are agitating in your favour. Pandulph Chertsey has resigned. Bernie was in the House last night to hear him give his reasons. He says Chertsey made a splendid speech, in which he advocated an appeal to the country to settle this question, and a fresh trial for you. His remarks were received in gloomy silence by both Progressists and Nationals, though loudly applauded by the D'Estrangeites. But the two former have no intention to appeal at present. They hate you and yours too much, Gloria. They want to crush you first before they do anything else. To accomplish this, dog and cat though they be, they will be amicable in order to attain their end."

"I know that," she answers, with a sad smile; "but I will do my best to baulk them until my work is done. Then, they may do as they please."

"Hush, Gloria!" exclaims Evie Ravensdale, with a shudder. "Do not speak of harm befalling you. O God, forfend it! I could not survive it."

She smiles again, still sadly, as she lays her hand on his arm, and looks at him with the dark sapphire eyes that have haunted him day and night for many a year with a strange, yearning love, which he often found hard to fathom. He understands it all now, however. There is no mystery about that love any longer. Its cause, Gloria de Lara.

"It is I who should say hush, Evie dear," she says gently, "and it is you who must not speak thus. Remember the great cause we have both at heart, the glorious cause that must and shall win! On its behalf are we not ready to face trial and trouble, and many an anxious hour? Ah, Evie! remember our vows."

Yes, he remembers them well enough. Is he not striving to fulfil them even now? But the future, threatening, as it does, the person of all that he holds most dear, is dark and fearsome in Evie Ravensdale's anxious mind.

"Did you manage to see Flora Desmond?" she inquires, breaking thus the silence which has followed her last words.

"Yes, Gloria," he answers; "and that reminds me that I have much to tell you. Lady Flora has not been idle. She is indeed a most wonderful woman. There she is working away in the heart of London, with the warrant for her arrest duly out, with detectives and police in every direction, and yet not an idea have they where she is, thanks to the people's loyalty."

"God bless them!" is all Gloria says. She is eagerly awaiting the information he has to give her.

"She is not working single-handed either. Who do you think has joined the White Guards, Gloria? You will never guess."

"Who?" she says anxiously.

"Why, Lady Manderton! and Launcelot Trevor has offered his services to Lady Flora."

"Lady Manderton!" Gloria can hardly believe her ears. She looks incredulously at the speaker.

"It is true, Gloria, however impossible it may seem; and a real enthusiastic worker she is. However, to business Lady Flora told me to tell you, that she has sent picked messengers from the White Guards to everyone of our Volunteer centres, so as to be able to keep up active communication with them all. The code adopted works admirably, and has been arranged with extreme skill and forethought. In a few days all will be ready for your campaign. She suggests that you should hold a first meeting in the Hall of Liberty. The White Guards will be in readiness for that one. If the police and military interfere every means for escape will be at hand. Before they have time to look round you will be heard of at York, where you will be attended by the Women's Rifle Corps, and so on. Rapidity of action will be the characteristic feature of your campaign—a regular Will-o'-the-wisp crusade, in fact. Of course it will be attended by a good deal of risk; but it is quite certain that the people must be appealed to, and those who are supporting you now not left in the lurch. God grant there may be no more blood shed!"

"Yes, God grant it indeed!" she answers fervently. "Nevertheless, Evie, 'twere better thus to shed one's blood than to submit any longer and without protest to the present state of things. Whatever may be the outcome of this revolution, I have no fear but that it will lead up to victory in the future. I may never see the day. What matter? *It will come.*"

She laughs softly, a low triumphant laugh, as her mind's eye strives to pierce the murky darkness of the future. Instinctively she realises what lies behind that impenetrable veil, and sees with the glance of prophecy the promised land beyond. It is thus with all reformers. If to them was only vouchsafed the cold, sneering support which the world generally bestows upon early effort, they would sink and die beneath the venomed shafts of the unbelievers; but these latter do not see the noble visions which are given to the pioneers of the future, visions which beckon them forward, and unfold to their eager gaze the triumph of their labours in the establishment of that for which they have given their lives.

"Well, I will go and get rid of this disguise," observes the duke, with a smile. "This beard and these whiskers are uncommonly hot, Gloria. By-the-bye, when does Mrs. de Lara sail?"

"In two days, Evie, she goes by the White Star Line," answers his companion. "I left her in the study just before meeting you. Go in and see her before you change."

He passes on through the porch, outside of which he had found her sitting on his arrival, and enters the cottage, and Gloria takes up her old position to ponder and think over the situation of affairs, which her trusty messenger has brought to her from the outside world.

We have not seen her since that eventful evening, when she was rescued by Flora Desmond and her White Guards from the arm of the law, and safely escorted to Montragee House. Here a hasty consultation had been held, and it was at once decided that without delay she must quit the duke's mansion. Within an hour of her entrance she had left the ducal residence, and in a suit of plain dark clothes had sought a safe asylum with humble friends, in a quarter of the city where no one dreamed of searching for her. The duke himself had quitted his home to avoid awkward questions, leaving it in the care of his brother, and Mrs. de Lara had repaired to her Windsor residence. Communication had been maintained through loyal and trustworthy friends, and from her refuge in the mighty city, Gloria had rejoined her mother and the duke at "The Hut," a tiny out-of-the-way residence belonging to the latter, situated in the heart of the pine forests that clothe the country for miles around, between Bracknell and Wokingham. From this secluded nook she could hold communication with her friends through the medium of Evie Ravensdale, who in various disguises passed to and fro between Bracknell and London daily.

Meanwhile the Devonsmere Ministry has been active. Supported by the Nationals and Progressists, a Bill has been hastily passed through the House of Commons, and sent up to the House of Lords for approval. It grants the Government exceptional facilities for suppressing the public meetings, which may be held by Gloria de Lara's supporters. A large number of special constables have been enrolled, and entrusted with extensive powers. The military have been ordered to hold themselves in readiness to support the police, and a special proclamation has been issued, offering a large reward for the delivery up to justice of the persons of Gloria de Lara and Flora Desmond, or any man or woman found actively espousing the former's cause. Armed with these tremendous powers, the Devonsmere Ministry are confident that the revolution will be summarily suppressed, and the chief actors brought speedily to justice. In vain Lord Pandulph Chertsey has warned them against the course they have resolved upon. He is unheeded, for the Ministry have a majority in their favour in both Houses, and are determined to enforce their policy rigidly and unrelentingly.

All this Gloria de Lara knows full well. The situation is thoroughly understood by her, and the risk fully appreciated, but she knows also that she will be faithful to her vow. She is of the same mind now as she was when, as a child, looking over the lovely Adriatic, that feeling had entered her heart which had bidden her go forward and struggle for the cause, even though the struggle should end in death. She made a vow then; through all these years she has kept it. Now that danger and death stare her in the face, will she draw back appalled? No, ten thousand times no.

Her plans are fully formed, and none so fit as Gloria to carry them into effect. In every part of the kingdom she has faithful emissaries at work. Aided by them, large open-air meetings are to be convened, which she will address in turn, vanishing as quickly and mysteriously as she appears. In this way she will be able to hold communication with the people in every part of the country, and scatter broadcast the seeds of her great doctrine. She knows full well that aid and sympathy will come to her from all parts of the world. She is sending messengers in every direction, Mrs. de Lara having volunteered to visit America on behalf of her child's cause. She knows that the flame once kindled, will never more be extinguished, until victory waves aloft the wand of peace. If in the struggle she be doomed to fall—what matter, so that the great cause triumph?

She has the law against her, but law is only strong so long as the people acknowledge it to be just, and agree to obey it. No law is binding or sacred which has not been ratified by the people's approval. There is no natural Divine right which gives to a few men the power and authority to impose on millions a command to obey. Might alone can force it. It has been declared that might is right. What if the people defy might, and struggle against its tyranny for the triumph of right?

She sits on alone, revolving this truth in her mind. Thought absorbs her with its dreamy influence, carrying her on beyond the present into the great unfathomed future before her. She sees the storm which she has raised angry and defiant, the elements thereof tossed and buffeted, but she knows that after that storm the waves of fury will be stilled in a great calm.

"Dreaming, Gloria? Of what, pray?"

She starts. The voice thrills her, for she loves it well. Gloria's contact with the world in her self-imposed duties has not blunted or dulled the instincts of Nature. In past days, it was a favourite remark with our grandmothers and grandfathers, that woman's connection with the coarser things of life would degrade her by constant familiarity with them. Poor things! They judged of Nature from the narrow-minded platforms on which they had been educated, knew nothing of and cared nothing for the sighs of liberty, or the rights of Nature.

Yes! though her life has been one of constant intercourse with man, though she has been and is familiar with the coarser things of life, Gloria loves, and loves truly and well. Hers is not the love of a timid, ignorant girl, longing to escape the captivity in which she has been reared, or the selfish, guilty love of the *intriguante*, whose love would fade and disappear were it not deemed unholy. Hers is the love of one who, knowing the world well, understanding the character of man, drilled to a knowledge of the laws of Nature, yet elects to love one being above all others. Gloria's love is one that once given, can never die.

As with her, so it is with Evie Ravensdale. The world has courted his love, but its wiles have not awoke it. Often, when in loving commune with his friend Hector D'Estrange, the thought would flash through the young duke's mind, that if Hector had been a woman, the great love of which he felt himself capable, would have gone out to her absolutely and without reserve. What was the subtle power that had attracted him to Hector D'Estrange, which had made him pause on the verge of pleasure's precipice, and, casting to the winds his hitherto selfish existence, had made him body and soul the devoted adherent of the young reformer?

Evie Ravensdale knows the reason now. From the moment that he learnt that in Hector D'Estrange was embodied the person of Gloria de Lara, he understood that the influence of a noble, high-minded, and genuine woman, had allured him from the false glare and glitter of the world, and had given him an aim in life.

"Ah, dear Evie! have I not much to think of? In such times as these, thought does not take much rest."

She rises as she speaks, and links her arm in his. Men have often watched Hector D'Estrange and the Duke of Ravensdale in this friendly attitude before. Such an ape is Fashion, that it has become the *proper thing* for men to walk arm-in-arm. Doubtless, however, in view of the change which has come about in the altered fortunes of Hector D'Estrange, it will be suddenly discovered that such an attitude is both unbecoming and improper. So much for the monkey Custom and its cousin ape Fashion!

"Let us go for a stroll, Gloria," he pleads, "the evening is so glorious; and it may be long before we have the chance again of a quiet chat together. We used to enjoy those *tête-à-têtes* at Montragee when you were Hector D'Estrange, did we not?"

"Yes," she says quietly. "I did love them, Evie. In fact, I think I set too great a store upon them, more than was good for me to do; but they were a true rest and pleasure after toil and anxiety, and I accepted them as such."

They have descended a gentle slope as she speaks and entered a glade in the forest. The warm, red glow of the setting sun pierces in parts the thickly grouped pines, and plays upon the ferns and bracken that grow in green luxuriance beneath. The evening commune of the birds is dying into a low twitter, and the rabbits have commenced to peep forth from their burrows to see if all is still, preparatory to indulging in the evening meal, as is their wont and custom at this hour.

What is it that throws its shadow across the glade in the wake of Evie Ravensdale and Gloria de Lara? As the two saunter slowly along the forest's green pathway, the figure of a man suddenly presents itself at the entrance to the glade, and stands motionless gazing after the retreating pair. Only for a moment though, as with a low laugh he turns quickly in the direction of "The Hut." His movements are peculiar. He does not walk openly up to the cottage, but, concealing himself behind the rhododendron bushes which surround it in thick luxuriance, he stealthily and silently gains the porch, outside of which Gloria de Lara was sitting on the arrival of Evie Ravensdale.

Passing noiselessly along the verandah which runs round "The Hut," the man suddenly comes to a halt outside a half-opened window, and peers in. A logwood fire burns cheerily on the hearth, but there are no lamps as yet in the room, and this is the only light that irradiates it. It is sufficient, however, to enable him to make out the form of a woman seated by the fire. Her elbows are resting on her knees, and her head is bent in her hands, and through the half-opened fingers she is gazing into the glowing blaze. A single ring flashes on the third finger of her left hand; one ring only, but no more. The man's eyes dilate with passion and fury as they watch her. The expression is that of a wild beast gloating upon its prey. This man, too, has a smile of triumph upon his coarse, sensual lips, mingled with malignity and hate.

A quick shudder runs through Speranza de Lara—for this lonely woman is no other than she—as with a sudden impulse she raises her head and looks towards the window with a scared and startled expression. The man draws quickly back from his post of observation, and passing rapidly along the verandah disappears amidst the thick bushes already mentioned. Too late, however, to conceal his features from the gaze of the woman, who, alas! knows them too well. With a cry of horror she springs forward, and pushing open the window makes her way out on to the verandah. Two minutes later, and the tongue of a little tower bell rings out half-a-dozen sharp, warning notes. Evie Ravensdale and Gloria de Lara know full well their meaning. Their sound heralds the word "danger," and brings them sharply to attention. When, a few minutes later, they reach "The Hut," they find Speranza anxiously awaiting them.

"Evie and Gloria," she says in a quiet, self-possessed voice, in which all trace of excitement is absent, "this is no longer a safe place for either of you. It must be quitted at once. I have just seen him."

"Him! Who, mother dearest?" inquires Gloria anxiously.

"The worst enemy I have ever known, and therefore yours too, my darling," answers Speranza, with a shudder. "Ever right, my child, were you when you said he was not dead, for I have just looked on the face of Lord Westray."

As she speaks the distant sound of a galloping horse strikes upon their ears.

"Evie," says Gloria coolly, a quiet smile lighting up her face, "will you see to the horses being saddled at once?"

IX

The roar of London's traffic has died away, for a few brief hours, peace has spread her mystic wings o'er the city of wealth and poverty, pleasure and suffering, joy and pain, virtue and crime. In the sumptuous dwellings of the wealthy, the gentry stretch their pampered bodies on the soft couch of ease and warmth, imitated to a nicety by their dependents. In the dwellings of the middle class, comfort if not absolute sumptuousness is displayed and enjoyed. In the dwellings of the working class, overcrowding and limited space is the chief characteristic, while in the dwellings of the helpless, homeless, and foodless, the vault of heaven is their canopy, the cold flag-stones their couch of rest.

Yet above these scenes, so diversified and strange, peace for a few brief hours has spread her wings. The tramp of the tired horse is silent, the patter of millions of feet is still. Even the wandering, homeless, hungry cur is curled up in some byway fast asleep, dreaming, no doubt, of the rich steaks of meat upon which his poor famished eyes had been fixed this afternoon, when the cruel butcher drove him so mercilessly away.

But there is a faint glimmer of light stealing through the fast-closed shutters of Mr. Trackem's private room, in Verdegrease Crescent, and if, like the fairy of old, we obtain ingress therein in some mysterious manner, we shall find that worthy seated in a comfortable armchair, with his head thrown back against a soft cushion, his legs crossed, his elbows firmly planted on the chair's arms, and his hands lightly joined together. A warm fire glows in front of him, and the smile on his face betokens a thorough satisfaction with things in general, and especially with himself.

On the opposite side of the hearthrug is another armchair, likewise occupied, but by a man apparently in by no means so placid and contented a frame of mind as Mr. Trackem. He wears a rough coat and waistcoat of Cheviot wool, and his cord riding breeches and black top-boots are covered with mud and mire. There is blood on his spurs too, which betokens a hard usage of the poor beast that has lately carried him. On the floor lies a brown slouch hat and riding-whip, while by their side is a soft satin cushion, similar to the one against which Mr. Trackem's head is reclining, and which his visitor has disdainfully tossed on one side.

The manner of this man is excited, and he is leaning forward, and speaking fast and rapidly. He is a handsome man, but has not a nice face, and grey hairs are beginning to mingle in his thick beard, whiskers, and moustache, as well as amidst the once raven locks of his hair. He has thick sensual lips, two rows of fine white teeth, and a restless, roving expression in his dark eyes.

"I tell you, Trackem, I have seen them all three, and I greatly fear that Mrs. de Lara recognised me. Maybe she did not, for the moment she looked round I made off as hard as I could, and have ridden straight from the spot to this place. But if she did, there will be great danger of our plot being discovered, and the idea to me is simply maddening after all I have done, and risked, and put up with to carry it successfully to an issue."

Mr. Trackem refuses, however, to get excited.

"Pray listen, my lord," he says suavely. "I think it is extremely unlikely that Mrs. de Lara recognised you. But even if she did, of what avail? She cannot prove it, and her statement would only be regarded in the light of falsehood, invented to screen Gloria de Lara, or else in the light of hallucination. We managed that point very well at the trial. No, no; have no fear on that score. The only point to be looked at is this. If Mrs. de Lara recognised you, or even took alarm at seeing a stranger in her child's place of refuge, she, and those with her, have in all probability sought a fresh hiding-place. If this be so, their arrest will have to be postponed, until we can lay hands on the spot of their new asylum. It is a pity, for my efforts appeared to be on the verge of crowning success. However, cheer up, my lord. Trackem has never yet failed in any of his jobs, and will not in this one."

"I was a fool to act as I did!" exclaims Lord Westray, for it is no other than he; "but I could not resist the impulse, Trackem. How do you propose to act if tomorrow we find the birds have flown?"

"I propose this, my lord," answers Mr. Trackem in a decided voice. "I intend to send round information to Scotland Yard of their whereabouts. Should this information prove too late, I propose to proceed in this wise. I have in my employ a young woman of extremely prepossessing appearance, and without doubt the cutest of all my staff. She has never failed me yet, and I am not apprehensive that she will on this occasion. My instructions to her will be to ascertain Gloria de Lara's whereabouts, to join her in this rebellion—to be, in fact, one of her most devoted adherents, until such time as I shall require her to be otherwise. When she has been thoroughly entrusted with the rebel secrets, nothing will be easier than to transmit them to us; in fact, I think you know what I mean, my lord."

"I understand," mutters the other moodily. "You mean to set her to the informer's trade. A female Judas, in fact."

"You have it, my lord, extremely well expressed. Ha, ha!" laughs Mr. Trackem quietly, as he rubs his hands together, and nods approvingly. "And what does your lordship think of my little plan?" he continues inquiringly.

"Damned clever and diabolical, Trackem, if you want to know the truth," answers Lord Westray a shade bitterly. He has fallen pretty low, but this seems indeed the lowest depth of the abyss into which he is invited to plunge, for the being who is an accessory before the fact is every whit as villainous as the being performing the deed. Of course he knows this.

"Clever, I grant you, my lord. It is my business to be so. Diabolical I demur to. All is fair in love and war. But pardon me, excuse a moment's absence," and Mr. Trackem, as if struck by a sudden idea, rises and leaves the room.

Lord Westray rises, too, and begins pacing up and down it. There is a dark, angry look in his eyes, and a cruel smile on his thick lips.

"All fair in love and war," he exclaims savagely; "that is a true saying. I loved her—yes, I did love Speranza once, but she scorned and flouted me, and I could not forget that. Even after I married her I loved her, I believe, though she complained that I treated her cruelly. And what if I did? She was only a woman, and my wife. What business had she to complain? What business had she to take the law into her own hands, and go off with that fellow? Ah! I think she counted without her host there, but I was revenged,—yes, yes, I took ample revenge. And then, when she might have made it up, when I offered to remarry her, she flung me from her path, and that girl of hers, whom I thought then was a man, ordered me out of the house. Ah! but I think there again I have come off the victor. I think it is I who have scored. The world believes me dead; Hector D'Estrange, now Gloria de Lara, is my murderer. If we lay hands on her, the Government is bound to make her pay the full penalty of the law. It will break Speranza's heart, and I, I shall triumph and be revenged. None shall flout or scorn *me* without rueing it. By God! no one ever shall."

The laugh is a horrid one with which these last words are accompanied. It is hard to believe the man a human being. Character of this description is false to Nature, surely? Yes, but the education which produced it was false and unnatural too. Human character depends greatly on early teaching. The parent has a heavy responsibility in the moulding of youth's first impressions. Lady Westray, if from the grave you could arise and look upon your handiwork, perhaps even you, shallow, vain, heartless as you were in life, might shudder and repent!

At this stage the door opens, readmitting Mr. Trackem. He walks over to his seat by the fire and reoccupies it.

"I have sent for her, my lord," he informs Lord Westray in a businesslike voice. "It has struck me that it will be best to employ my female Judas without any delay. Second thoughts convince me that it would be mere waste of time to communicate with Scotland Yard. I have not the smallest doubt that, as Mrs. de Lara caught sight of you, 'The Hut' is vacated ere this. At any rate, we will put Léonie on the track, and start her from there. I have no fear that she will disappoint us. She has a marvellous genius for the discovery of the hidden."

"A human bloodhound and Judas combined in one," laughs Lord Westray. "I am curious, Trackem, to behold this monstrosity."

"A curiosity which is about to be gratified," remarks the other coolly, as a low tap is heard on the door of the room in which these two men are hatching their diabolical plans. "Come in, Léonie."

The door opens softly, and a woman glides in. She is small and of slight build, with a bright, fair complexion, even, firm mouth, dark grey eyes fringed round with a wealth of lashes, which at once attract the onlooker by their extraordinary thickness. Her hair, which is cut short, is soft, glossy, and wavy, and is parted on one side, clustering upon her forehead and around her face. On this face play the lights and shades of a constantly changing expression, and if ever genius told its tale in eyes, it is indelibly stamped in these.

Mr. Trackem smiles covertly as he glances at Lord Westray, and notices the expression of surprise in this latter's face. Léonie has walked straight over to Mr. Trackem's chair, and is standing beside him.

"You want me?" she inquires in a matter-of-fact voice. Apparently the break of dawn summons is not in the least strange to her.

"I do, Léonie," answers her master quickly. "I have a little job on hand that I think I can entrust to you, and I rely upon you to carry it out successfully. There is, as you no doubt know, a large reward offered for the apprehension of the adventuress Gloria de Lara, or for such information as may lead to that apprehension. Now I see no reason why my clever little Léonie should not be the person to win that reward, or at any rate a part of it. My commission to you is this. First of all get speech with this Gloria. This necessitates finding her out. Next, worm yourself into her confidence by a display of zeal which I can perfectly trust you to simulate. Keep me informed of her plans and movements as soon as you are able to speak with certainty of them, and be ready to act as I bid you on receipt of any communication or instruction which I may desire to send you. Now, Léonie, remember I trust this job to you, because there is none so fitted as you to undertake it. I have every faith in your sagacity and prudence. I have heard a good deal of Gloria de Lara's wonderful cleverness; I am mistaken if my little Léonie is not her match."

There is a glitter in the girl's dark grey eyes, a quiet smile on her lips.

"You may trust me," she remarks laconically.

"I know I can," answers Mr. Trackem gravely; "I know that very well. Now, Léonie, your work begins at once. Gloria de Lara, her mother Speranza de Lara, and the Duke of Ravensdale were seen at a little place called 'The Hut,' near Bracknell, belonging to the duke. I have reason to think, however, that they have fled that place this very night. You had better go straight there, and take up the scent from the spot. I leave all to you. You can draw upon me, you know. Keep me advised of your whereabouts, stick to the letter of my instructions, and send me good news as quickly as possible. I have no more to say, unless it be that you are to effect that which Scotland Yard cannot."

"I will," answers this strange laconic creature, as with a slight inclination she turns and leaves the room.

"Well, I'm blowed, Trackem, if that is not the queerest elf I ever set eyes upon in my life!" exclaims Lord Westray as the door closes. "Where on earth did you raise her from?"

"A pretty elf, too, eh, my lord? Hardly a monstrosity," observes Mr. Trackem drily. "Where did I raise her from, you ask? Well, that's just the point. I don't care to tell you who she is, but I'll tell you this much. She's the daughter of a customer of past days. Her father was a great man. At least the world said he was. She's got plenty of blue blood in her veins; she's well bred enough. Her mother died here. The great man forsook her, and the child was left in my hands. I found her pretty, remarkably intelligent, and quick-witted. I determined to train her to be useful, and I think I have succeeded. She has certainly proved a most profitable speculation, and repaid the excellent education I have given her. I have no reason to repent my philanthropic act," and Mr. Trackem laughs drily.

"Well, you are a clever fellow, and no mistake, Trackem. I gave you credit for a good deal, but not for rearing detectives from childhood. I thought I knew pretty nearly everything, but this is a new experience," remarks the earl, fairly surprised.

"Yes, my lord, you have seen a good deal and know a good deal. I admit your experience is wide and varied. But not even you know half that goes on in this wonderful city. There's many a queer thing takes place about which outsiders know nothing. It's only natural. What else can you expect in a place like this? And now I think I have no more to communicate for the moment. It will be daylight soon, and I feel I want a snatch of sleep. I will bid you goodnight therefore; and I don't suppose you will be sorry to follow my example. You have had a pretty long, tiring, and eventful day. Goodnight, my lord."

Saying which, Mr. Trackem rises from his armchair, takes hold of a small hand-lamp standing on a table close by, and with an obsequious bow to the patron, for the sake of whose gold he is serving, leaves the room.

For yet another hour that patron paces up and down it, absorbed in moody thought. It is hard to draw the picture of this man, when one thinks how otherwise it might have been had the passions of his youth been curbed, his early life disciplined, and his powers for good fostered and encouraged. If the dream of Gloria de Lara be realised, the time will come when character such as this will know an existence no longer; but this can only be when the standard of morality is placed on a higher pedestal, and the laws of Nature are acknowledged and upheld.

X

Quitting the presence of Mr. Trackem and Lord Westray, Léonie has hurried to her bedroom, from which the former personage had so unceremoniously summoned her. The bedroom in question is small and plainly furnished. A scant, square piece of carpet covers the middle of the floor. There are two chairs in the room, a tiny iron bedstead, a washhand-stand, and a large wardrobe. This latter article takes up an ungenerous share of the space which the little room affords, but it is evidently an article of some importance, for Léonie goes straight to it and throws it open, displaying to view some half-a-dozen shelves, upon which a number of suits of clothes of varied and multifarious shapes, are neatly arranged.

After scrutinising them for a few minutes Léonie selects a strong dark-coloured pair of riding breeches, gaiters to match, and a loose jacket and waistcoat of the same material, which she lays on the bed. To these are quickly added a grey flannel shirt and a complete silk under riding suit. She then proceeds with her toilet, and when dressed looks every inch a comely lad of some seventeen summers, smart, neat, and natty.

Her next act is to pack a small saddle portmanteau with a change of underclothing, toilet and washing articles, which completes the outfit of Mr. Trackem's youthful detective; for Léonie, though a slave, is not unmindful of her personal appearance. She knows she is pretty, and likes to look so, a vanity for which the looking-glass is largely responsible. A small oil lamp burns fitfully in one corner of the room. She fills a tiny kettle with water, and placing it on a miniature stand, sets it to heat above the flame. Then she makes her bed, and tidies up her room with business-like alacrity, and as the kettle begins to hiss, she takes from the chimney-piece a cup and saucer, a small tin of preserved coffee and milk, and a spoon. In a few minutes this Bohemian girl has mixed herself a steaming cupful of the beverage, and abstracting a couple of biscuits from a small paper parcel also on the chimney-piece, proceeds to enjoy her somewhat camp-like meal.

But she wastes no time over it. Léonie is essentially a business-like person. She has settled in her mind the exact hour at which she must set out, and she knows she has not many minutes to spare.

In effect, grey dawn is beginning to streak the murky sky with light. She can hear a distant tower clock chiming the hour of five, and she sets down her cup on a chair close by and takes up the little portmanteau. "Time I started," she mutters to herself, as she cons in her mind Mr. Trackem's instructions. Léonie is a most perfectly disciplined young lady; she has thoroughly learnt the lesson of obedience. It has never entered her head to disregard or evade her master's commands. Mr. Trackem has certainly succeeded in teaching her to take a pride in her work, and in training her to a faithful discharge of duty. He has reason to congratulate himself, and to boast that this girl slave has never failed him yet.

She passes along the passage leading to the staircase, and descends this latter noiselessly. All is silent throughout the house as she lets herself out of the front door and closes it softly behind her. Then she sets off at a smart walk along the Crescent, and gaining a side street turns down it.

The street in question is more or less a mews, but as yet there are very few signs of life within it. Léonie, however, seems quite at home in this place, for she walks down it unhesitatingly, until at length she comes to a halt opposite a stable door.

Drawing a key from her pocket she unlocks this door and lets herself in. There are some half-a-dozen horses tied up in an equal number of stalls, and they greet her with neighs and a good deal of grunting and stamping about. A rough shaggy-looking dog, with the coat and body of a staghound, and the head and drooping ears of a bloodhound, rises from a bed of hay in the corner of the stable, and comes up to her with wagging tail and a doggy smile on his rough and shaggy face. She pats him kindly. "Come on, Nero," she says at the same time; "I shall want you." Then she goes to the corn bin and measures into the sieve a feed of oats, which she takes over to a bay horse at the far end of the stable. This produces a loud protest from the remaining five animals, which to anyone acquainted with horse language is unmistakable.

Perhaps there is a kind corner in Léonie's heart. Maybe it is only to secure quiet. Who knows? But she fills up the sieve brimful once more, and divides the oats amongst the five protesting animals. At any rate, it gives them contentment for a while, judging by the crunching and munching that goes on.

A little harness-room adjoins the stable, and Léonie dives into this, and unearths a neat light man's saddle with grey girths and a pair of bright small steels. The saddle is quickly girthed on to the bay horse, and then a plain double snaffle is produced from the same quarter to be

LADY FLORENCE DIXIE

slipped in the animal's mouth directly he has finished his meal. Léonie is anxious to be off before the stable men come in, which will be about six o'clock.

Consulting her watch, she sees it is nigh on half-past five. As the clock chimes that hour the girl leads the horse out into the mews, followed by Nero. Closing the stable door and locking it, she turns to her steed, and gathering the reins in her left hand puts her foot in the stirrup, and swings herself lightly on to his back.

"Come on, Nero," she calls again to the dog as she puts her horse into a trot and leaves the mews behind her.

Her course is taken for Waterloo Station. None whose gaze fall upon her as she rides through the awakening streets, followed by her shaggy companion, would take her for what she is, a female detective in the employ of Mr. Trackem. But then a well-got-up detective ought to be unrecognisable, and Léonie, the handsome, gentlemanly youth to all appearance, is well got up.

On reaching Waterloo, Léonie sees to the boxing of her horse and dog. She elects, too, to travel with them in the horse-box as far as Bracknell, which place is reached at nine o'clock. Here the horse-box is run into a siding.

Léonie loses no time, for she knows that every moment is precious. She sees to the unboxing of the horse, and before remounting him slips a shilling into the porter's hand.

"How far is 'The Hut' from here?" she inquires as she does so.

"What, the Duke of Ravensdale's Hut, sir? Oh, nigh on two miles. But there's no one there, sir. It's shut up; there's only the forrester and his wife."

"Just the persons I want to see. You mean of course—, there now, the name has quite slipped me," exclaimed Léonie, with well-feigned appearance of annoyance at the name having just that moment escaped her memory.

"Why, Miles Gripper, old Miles Gripper and his wife, sir," puts in the porter, eager to supply the young gentleman's defective memory. "They are well known to the country round, sir."

"Of course, of course; how stupid of me to forget!" answers Léonie briskly. "Well, now, my man, just tell me how I must frame for 'The Hut.'"

"Just cross that there bridge, sir," explains the porter, pointing upwards, "and bear away down to the right. Keep straight on that road, sir, till you can't go no further; there you'll see a road going left and right. Take the right turn, sir, and after that the next right turn what ever is, and then stick to that road, and never mind any turns that you see, until you come to two cross-roads, the left one with a signboard directing to Aldershot. Don't you go taking either of those two turns, sir, but ride on another fifty yards, and you'll see a small wooden gate on the left. That leads to 'The Hut'. It's away in the forest."

"Thank you, my man," says Léonie politely. "I think I understand. I go up over that, bridge, bear to the right, keep straight on till I must turn right or left, then take the right turn, and the very next that is, ride straight on until I reach the cross-roads, then about fifty yards further, where a gate on the left leads up to 'The Hut.' Is that it?"

"Exact, sir. You couldn't have it more exact, sir. If you follow those directions you can't mistake," answers the porter glibly. The shilling and the young gentleman's whole appearance has impressed him.

"Well, good-morning, my man, and many thanks," says Léonie, as she begins to move her horse away. She is surprised when the next moment the porter comes up alongside her.

"Beg pardon, sir, no offence, sir, but be you a friend of the duke?"

Léonie is perplexed, but she answers evasively, "What do you want to know that for, my man?"

"Because," answers the honest fellow with an eager look in his eyes, "because, sir, I've been reading all about how the Government is a-hunting of him and that great man Mr. Hector D'Estrange. Least they say Mr. D'Estrange is a woman. I don't know, and I don't care. I don't see what it matters whether Mr. D'Estrange is a man or a woman, sir. He's the people's friend, sir; he wants to help us poor folk. There is no humbug about him, sir, and we love him for that, we do. If you know them, can you tell me if they are safe, sir? Forgive a poor fellow asking this, sir—but oh! I'd die for them, I would, sir!"

The blood rushes to Léonie's face. What is it that brings it there? Perhaps a vague, undefined feeling of shame that she should be bent on an errand so degrading with the true words of the honest working man ringing in her ears.

"Yes, they are safe," she says hurriedly. "Here, take this, my man."

She throws him another shilling, and as he stoops to pick it up, she puts her horse into a quick trot, and widens the distance between herself and her interlocutor. What does Léonie know of goodness, gratitude, or any high and noble virtue? In that young, cold, calculating heart of hers, what room is there for devotion or love? She wonders, as she rides along, why that man's words brought that flush to her face, and what that strange feeling was that made her heart beat and her pulse throb. She puts it down to a fear that her object and mission might be recognised.

"I'm getting nervous, I believe," she laughs to herself. "That will never do. Mr. Trackem has always told me to be cool and self-possessed. What a fool I was to let that man see he had flustered me! Léonie, you are an idiot!"

She tightens her horse's rein, and just touches him lightly with her heels as she speaks, and the animal breaks into a canter. Nero gallops happily by her side. The dog is enjoying his outing in the country. Two miles at this pace is quickly got over, but Léonie draws rein as she reaches the cross-roads. To the left stands a signboard, and "Aldershot" is written on it.

"Fifty yards further on," mutters the girl as she trots forward. The porter's directions are very exact; the wooden gate is before her.

She rides through it, and enters a narrow carriage drive, closed in on both sides by tall pine-trees. Thick rhododendron bushes fill up a few open spaces here and there. The little road is steep and precipitous, leading sharply upwards. Léonie throws the reins on her horse's neck and gives him his head. She has no fear that her four-footed friend will stumble. Horse and rider know each other well.

Suddenly, however, she picks up the reins and urges him forward. A sudden thought has struck Léonie. She must not be caught napping. The time has come to employ her detective wiles, and she acts on the impulse that has seized her. Such a pace up such an incline is naturally trying to her steed. Thus, when rounding a sharp turn in the forest road she comes into full view of 'The Hut,' her animal's sides are heaving pretty freely, and he is decidedly blowing.

She brings him up to the little front entrance at the same pace, and reins him up abruptly. In another moment she has pealed the bell.

She can hear a slight scuttling inside, and voices whispering, which causes a delay not at all in keeping with her plans, so she peals the bell again.

Then steps come rapidly forward, and an elderly man in a dark green cord suit and brass buttons opens the door.

"I have a message for the Duke of Ravensdale," exclaims Léonie in a low, confidential voice. "You are Miles Gripper, are you not? Ask his Grace if I can see him. It is of the utmost importance, admitting of no delay."

Miles Gripper scratches his silver head and looks perplexed. He is a faithful servant and an honest one. His instructions have been most specific. He has been told to feign absolute ignorance of the duke's movements or whereabouts, though he knows them well. But Léonie's words have staggered him.

"Gracious!" he exclaimes. "But his Grace is not here, sir."

"Not here!" gasps Léonie, with well-feigned dismay. "Good God! what is to be done?"

"Is his Grace in danger?" blurts out the forrester tremulously. "Oh, sir! what is it?"

"Danger!" echoes Léonie. "I should just think so. Look here, my man, I have come post-haste from London to see him. He must be warned, or both he and Gloria de Lara will be in custody before the day is down. Can I trust you to take his Grace a message? I was told you were a faithful and trustworthy servant of his."

Miles Gripper is completely taken in. His honest heart bounds with loyalty at Léonie's words.

"Ah, sir! and that's just true. His Grace has no one more devoted than old Miles Gripper. I'd give my life for his Grace, I would. But, God forgive me, how can I take your message, sir, in time? He's far from here by now."

"What! far from here?" again gasps Léonie; "but not out of riding distance, surely? Tell me where he is, and, tired as my horse is, I'll do all that is in human power to reach him. God grant I may not be too late!"

What does Léonie know of God? Still less does she care about Him. God, to Léonie, is an expression, a forcible expression, and no more. The expression serves her well on this occasion, however. Miles Gripper's honest heart is no match for detective acting. Believing that he is serving the duke, he passes the secret, which he was bidden to keep, into the care of this apparently devoted and self-sacrificing adherent of his master.

"And drat ye for a big-headed fool, when his Grace express forbade ye say aught of his whereabouts save to the Lady Flora," Léonie hears a sharp, angry woman's voice exclaiming. But she waits to hear no more. She is on her horse, and trotting quickly down the hill with the secret she had been puzzling her brains how to win, safe in her keeping. Small wonder at Dame Gripper's ire.

"Come on, Nero, laddie," laughs the girl detective. "I thought I should want you, doggie, but I can do without you now. However, come along."

She rides back to the cross-roads and the signboard. On one of this latter's arms is printed "Marlow."

"That's it," she mutters to herself, as she turns her horse's head into the long straight road, which, girt on either side by tall dark trees, stretches far as the eye can reach. "I'm safe on the track now, I am."

Léonie is happy. One of the most difficult obstacles in her path has been lightly cleared, and quite unexpectedly too. Yes, she is happy, if it be possible for one so hard and callous to be so. Perhaps the dawn of a better day is coming for this child of an unholy love. As she rides along in the bright spring morning however, with her rough dog galloping by her side, she has no higher aim in life than to carry out successfully the "little job" which Mr. Trackem has confided to her care.

END OF BOOK II

BOOK III

I

It is the last day of summer, and the evening hour is creeping on apace. A truly glorious day it has been, warmed by a brilliant sun, the heat of which has been tempered by one of those gentle zephyrs that love to play where all is warmth and sunshine.

But now the day is dying, fading, as it were, gradually away. Time, which the science of man can never stay, stalks slowly on his path. It is he who declares that the spell of life which has lit the day with its brilliance, must pass onward into the darkness of advancing night.

For what is life but a greater day of warmth and sunshine, storm and rain? What is death but the night which brings rest after the toils or pleasures of that day? What is the future life beyond, but a new day breaking into existence, perchance in a world more lovely than our own?

So thinks Gloria de Lara as she leans on her oars and watches the dying glories of this fading day vanish beneath the waves of the western sea. The zephyr which has played so joyously amidst the light and sunshine of earlier hours, has fled to his couch of rest, and now not a breath stirs the glassy waters of Glennig Bay, which, lit by the radiance of the setting sun, blazes all around like a lake of molten gold.

Above its gleaming waters and those of Loch Eilort tower heather-girt mountains in their mantles of purple and of blue. Higher still above these well-clad slopes the grey stone of shaggy crags looks down, and higher yet above these lonely scenes the golden eagle hovers, secure from the destroying hand of man. Not altogether lonely though, if one may judge from a pale, thin line of smoke that suddenly curls upwards through the still air from one of those high grey crags. It catches the eye of Gloria de Lara as she leans upon her oars, and sends a flush of surprise to her thoughtful, dreaming face.

"So soon!" she exclaims, and there is a ring of wonder in her tone; but she settles herself to her oars, and sends the boat along with quick, powerful strokes. She has pointed its head for the open sea, straight, in fact, for the channel that joins the heaving swell of the grey Atlantic with the placid waters of Loch Eilort.

Months have passed away since we were last in Gloria de Lara's company. We left her when the spring of the early year was just budding into life, we rejoin her now on the eve of spring's destroyer's advent—autumn.

How has it fared through these months of light and sunshine with this woman and her cause? A retrospect will show.

We have seen how Léonie, on reaching 'The Hut,' had found it vacated, and had ridden on in the direction of Great Marlow. Truth indeed, she took the same route over which Gloria, Speranza, and Evie Ravensdale had ridden the night before. No sooner had it been decided to quit 'The Hut,' than Gloria had despatched Rita Vernon to London, to apprise Flora Desmond of the change, and then she and her two companions had ridden on in the darkness of night towards Great Marlow. On reaching the outskirts of the town, the three had turned down a narrow lane leading in the direction of Bisham Abbey woods, and Gloria, with a confidence which familiarity with a place always engenders, had led the way. Finally, the lane had opened into green fields with a line of bridle gates leading through them, and these she had carefully followed for a time. At length, however, Gloria had borne away from the beaten track, and directed her horse's head towards a long strip or belt of trees, at the further end of which stood a solitary cottage with a large barn behind it, and some compactly built dog-kennels in the rear. In one of the windows of this lonely dwelling a solitary light was burning, a light which told the fugitive in silent words of the faithful watch that was being kept.

Now this was the cottage of the head keeper of the Bisham Abbey estate, both of whose daughters were troopers in the White Guards' Regiment. The entire family was loyal to Gloria de Lara's cause, and this cottage was one amidst many a dwelling of the people where Gloria knew she had only to knock to gain admittance, only to show herself to obtain a loyal greeting and hospitable and secure shelter from tracking foes. The organisation which had thus contrived to spread a network of secret and devoted friends throughout the length and breadth of the United Kingdom of Great Britain and Ireland was surely no mean and contemptible one, and spoke volumes for the constructive and administrative capacity of Gloria de Lara and Flora Desmond. In every county this network had its headquarters in the Volunteer centres, with which communication was actively kept up by means of a code peculiar to this organisation.

Against these forces of a people's love the Government had brought to bear the forces of the law. All that money and power could procure were at this Government's command. And yet the difficulty of working had become pretty soon apparent, amidst a people whose lips refused to tell, and whose eyes became blinded by a sudden cloud whenever information was sought or demanded. In order to guard against the importation of informers into the Volunteer ranks, Flora Desmond had issued an order to the effect that no more aspirants were to be enrolled, an order which greatly hampered and took by surprise the forces of Scotland Yard, which had counted on informers' assistance to a large degree in obtaining information.

It was at the cottage, therefore, of staunch, true, old Joe Webster, that Gloria had sought her first refuge amongst the people, after her flight from the metropolis. It was from the same cottage that Speranza had bidden her child farewell before setting out on her voyage to the United States, as an accredited delegate to plead the D'Estrangeite cause. It was at this cottage that Flora Desmond had secretly held council with her chief, and had arranged the details of the first public meeting at which Gloria was to appear. And it was at old Joe Webster's cottage, too, that Léonie, in pursuit of the *rôle* which Mr. Trackem had set her to play, had presented herself before Gloria, and representing herself as one who had left home and interests to serve the great cause, had implored Gloria de Lara not to refuse her services, but to let her work for her even in the most menial capacity.

The bright, earnest face of the girl, her dark eyes glowing with genius, her pleading voice and apparent enthusiasm, had struck home to Gloria de Lara's heart, the noble nature of which could not suspect treachery to lurk beneath such evident devotion. Léonie's prayer had been heard by the woman who trusted her, and on whose betrayal and destruction she was bent. The first great meeting had been one of unlimited success for the D'Estrangeite cause, and therefore of proportionate discomfiture and humiliation for the Government. In the crowded Hall of Liberty, the D'Estrangeite members had assembled to protest against the assumption by the Nationals of the conduct of affairs without first making an appeal to the country, and also to call for a free pardon for Flora Desmond, and a fresh trial for Gloria de Lara. Government reporters had attended and taken voluminous notes of the speeches, policemen and detectives had assembled in full force by command of Mr. Mayhew, and established a strict watch. Proceedings, in fact, were in full swing, and it only needed the presence of one being on whom the thoughts of all were centred in that vast throng, to complete the assembly. Suddenly, upon the lowest of the six circular galleries that surrounded the dome of the hall, two forms were seen to appear. No need in pointing them out to inquire who they were. The low cheer which greeted their first appearance, soon swelled into a roar of wild, tumultuous applause and welcome, which flooded the vast building with deafening strain, and told of the enthusiasm and love that awoke it. What other being but Gloria de Lara could have commanded such an ovation? Truth it was she and her trusty companion Flora Desmond, who stood before them, habited in the uniform of the White Guards' Regiment, in which the people knew them both so well.

In full view of the crowded House, in full view of the D'Estrangeite members, in full view of Government reporters, and Mr. Mayhew's police and detective forces, Gloria had addressed the vast throng. Spellbound the people had listened to her words of hope, of encouragement, and of cheer. And when, in conclusion, she had bidden them fight on for the right, and actively resist wrong, the cheers had rung out again and again with deafening roar. Yet even as those cheers began to die away and the people's eyes turn lovingly once more to their great leader, Gloria and her companion had vanished.

And what had Mr. Mayhew's police been about? Why had they not arrested these daring two? How possible? The only means by which the galleries above could be reached, was through some twenty iron doors below. Yet when the police sought an entry, they found these doors securely barred by an invisible hand from within.

Of course a cordon of constables had been quickly drawn around the building, and detectives had watched anxiously day and night. Futile! as it soon became evident, when news reached the Government a few days later that Gloria de Lara had addressed a meeting in the north of England, that the police and troops hastily summoned had attempted to arrest her, but that, securely guarded by the Women's Border Light Horse Volunteers, she had managed to effect an escape, and no trace of her whereabouts had up till then been obtained. Energetic authorities, however, took care to cap this unwelcome intelligence with the information that the police were prosecuting an unremitting search! *Cui bono?*

Meeting upon meeting had followed; concourse after concourse had assembled. Simultaneously they would be heard of in the north, south, east, and west of England, of Scotland, or of Ireland. No public placards or advertisements announced these meetings, and yet they were always well attended. It seemed as though some secret, mysteriously silent fiery cross passed through the districts in which they were held.

But the authorities could not say for certain; they could only surmise. Machinery was at work beneath the surface which they had no power to fathom. The speakers at these meetings were manifold and various. The D'Estrangeite members were particularly active, but after Gloria de Lara and Flora Desmond, the people's favourites were undoubtedly the Duke of Ravensdale, Nigel Estcourt, Lady Manderton, Launcelot Trevor, Archie Douglasdale, and Jack Delamere! Wonder of wonders! What! Colonel Delamere? the swagger Guardsman, the spoilt child of Society, the man whose life had hitherto been one long succession of amusement and pleasure? Is it possible? Quite so. There is no impossibility when Nature steps in to the rescue.

What influence has been at work thus to change the current of Jack Delamere's pleasant but useless existence? What has induced him to take up the cudgels for Gloria de Lara's cause? Ay, what?

Ever since that evening when, in obedience to orders, Jack Delamere had charged the crowd which barred the way between his Blues and the White Guards, ever since that day when he had marked the heroism of those men and women that composed it, ever since he had seen them go down before the horses of his troopers, sacrificing their lives so that their idol's might be spared, Jack Delamere had been a faithful and devoted adherent of the D'Estrangeite cause. Perhaps, too, his love for Flora Desmond may have influenced him. Who knows? The influence of a noble and high-souled woman is surely the greatest incentive a man can have to do right.

Money, too, had poured in from all quarters of the globe, and from all manners and classes of people. The women, who in the palmy days of Hector D'Estrange had responded to his appeal on behalf of the Hall of Liberty, had not been laggard when the author of its being had again called upon them for sympathy and aid. The sinews of war had flowed in rapidly, and none had commanded it more quickly than Speranza de Lara.

Such a state of things had of course become intolerable to the Devonsmere Ministry, which in the early days of the movement had so confidently predicted its speedy collapse, as well as the arrest of Gloria de Lara and Flora Desmond. Every effort to capture these two had, however, proved unavailing, protected as they had been by a people's love.

A people's love! It was a noble gift to have won, a treasure of which they might well be proud, one which they might surely pray ever to deserve. None knew better than Gloria de Lara and Flora Desmond, that without it their fates must long since have been a prison's cell and a felon's doom.

In the eyes of this Government matters had become desperate. The efforts of the police had been paralysed. Conflicts had taken place between the military and the Women's Volunteer Regiments, and strong measures appeared necessary to check the disorders. Gloria de Lara's enemies had pointed to the Volunteer organisation as the root of the mischief, and it had been resolved to destroy it. Parliament had been asked to grant exceptional powers to meet this dangerous combination. Parliament had acquiesced, and forthwith a proclamation had been issued declaring the Women's Volunteer organisation to be illegal, and decreeing the instant disbandment of its regiments. The exceptional powers had furthermore empowered the police to arrest and imprison without trial all women who should be seen wearing the uniform of these regiments; and it had likewise been decreed a felony to shelter or harbour the persons of Gloria de Lara or Lady Flora Desmond, or to take part in any public meeting in which they should participate.

This Coercion Act, the first which had ever been passed for Great Britain and Ireland combined, had rendered the position of Gloria de Lara and Flora Desmond one of extreme peril, while threatening the liberties of thousands of their countrymen. A secret meeting had been called, the situation discussed, and it had been agreed that for the sake of the cause thus threatened these two must leave the country.

But how? That was the question. Every port and sea-going vessel was strictly watched. In this dilemma Archie Douglasdale had submitted a plan.

This plan was that his sister and Gloria de Lara, together with Nigel Estcourt and himself, should retire to one of his properties on the shores of Glennig Bay, where amidst its shaggy woods nestled a little fishing box, remote from the haunts of man. In this lonely retreat, guarded by trusty Ruglen retainers, he had declared his belief that for a time they could rest concealed, while Evie Ravensdale, repairing to London, should from there direct the immediate fitting-out of his yacht, in which, so soon as ready, he should put to sea, and work round to the Sound of Arisaig, where the fugitives could be embarked. And this plan had been approved of and acted upon. Gloria de Lara, Flora Desmond, Nigel Estcourt, and Archie Douglasdale had taken up their quarters in this safe retreat, and Evie Ravensdale had repaired to London. With him had gone Léonie, who had been commissioned to bear back the duke's instructions when all was ready. It was a fatal arrangement this last; but Léonie had played her part well, and had won the confidence of all. Thus it is that we find Gloria de Lara on the last dying day of summer, amidst the scenes described at the opening of this chapter.

Léonie has arrived from London. She has been instructed, she declares, to inform Gloria de Lara that the duke's yacht *Eilean* will proceed to sea and cruise about in the neighbourhood of Muck Island, so as to avoid the steamer track. The duke himself will make Glennig Bay in a fishing smack, embarking everyone thereon the day after his arrival. This arrival is timed for today, and Evie Ravensdale has sent a private message by Léonie asking Gloria to meet the smack at its entrance to the bay. At least so says Léonie, and Gloria believes her. She has sent the former to the top of a high crag to watch for the advent of the smack, with instructions to light a warning fire on sighting it. We have seen the pale blue line arise, and now Gloria, with quick, rapid strokes, is pulling for the bay's entrance. Her heart is happy, for is not Evie Ravensdale at hand? She never dreams of treachery.

The boat flies through the water, which parts with hissing sound on either side of the bow's keel. Now the splash and upheaving of the craft tells the rower that she has left the bay and entered the open sea. She casts a glance ahead, and sees the smack bearing down towards her, and then she sees the sail lowered and the vessel hove to. Once more she plies her oars, for she has caught sight of a tall figure waving to her, and making signs to bring the boat alongside the smack.

"Ship oars!" she hears a voice exclaiming as she nears it, and she obeys with alacrity.

In another moment a sailor has seized the painter, and two others have sprung into the boat. She looks up expecting to see the face of Evie Ravensdale. One glance, and she knows that she is betrayed.

"Up with the sails! Starboard the helm! Put the boat about, and fetch yon lad off the rocks," is the quick command she hears given as the sailors heave her aloft on to the deck, and two other men push her into the cabin below. Then the hatch is battened down. There is a coarse laugh. Once more has Léonie won.

II

"There is the smoke, Estcourt; Ravensdale must be in sight," exclaims Flora Desmond, as she leans on her empty rifle and scans the peaceful scene far away below.

"So soon?" inquires the young man looking up. "We must have strangely miscalculated the time."

"Well, there's the smoke right enough, Estcourt; and Léonie is far too smart to make a mistake. However, no need to hurry; it is such a glorious evening, and the last for me on these dear old hills, perhaps forever."

She says the last words sadly, and there is a yearning look in her fine eyes as they rove the familiar glens and corries, rugged crags and purple stretches which she and Archie Douglasdale learnt to know by heart in childhood, in their happy hunting excursions together long ago. Far away below. Loch Eilort and Glennig Bay shimmer in the setting sun, whose light is gleaming across the grey waters of the open sea.

These two have been away all day after deer, and Archie Douglasdale is still absent on the same quest. They have not seen him since they parted with him on the Black Crags some seven hours ago.

Lord Estcourt rises and comes to her side. He is a tall, well-made man, with expressive features, and a pair of grey eyes which Society has declared to be magnificent. Plenty of women therein have been willing to fall in love with Nigel Estcourt; no end of scheming and would-be mothers-in-law have instructed their daughters in the virtues, wealth, and charming characteristics of that very nice young fellow, and charged the poor things to exert their utmost to win him. But Nigel Estcourt has never yet been seen to pay court to any woman, and Fashion marvels thereat. But since he was a boy of seventeen he has held love's secret next his heart. It was at Ruglen Manor, long ago, when, as a mere lad, he first saw Flora Ruglen, that Nigel Estcourt first opened the book of love. It was to him that she, his first girl friend, had opened her heart, and it was to her that his boyish soul had responded. Born with a golden spoon in his mouth, with all that the world most covets, it was but natural that Fashion should court him. But Nigel Estcourt was not responsive to its adulation, and snubbed it most unmercifully.

When Flora Ruglen had married Sir Reginald Desmond, young Nigel had sorely grieved; but his friendship for her had not abated, for he loved her just the same. He was still only a boy, of course, and no one would have seriously predicted that this, his first love, would be his last.

Other men had loved Flora Desmond, and love her still. She has had no lack of offers since poor Reggie Desmond died. Over and over again has smart Jack Delamere pressed his suit. He has never loved any woman like he does her, but he presses his suit in vain; for gently, kindly but firmly, Flora Desmond has told him that she will never marry again. She had told Estcourt the same thing when for the first time, now three years ago, he had confessed his love and asked her to marry him. She had told him then that he must put that love from him forever, for the reply which she then gave him would remain unchanged. Yet, with tears in her lovely eyes. Flora had told him also how deeply she valued his friendship, how grateful and honoured she felt by his love, and how she prayed that the strong, firm bond which had held them together so long, since as boy and girl they had first made friends, would endure through life. Perhaps if one thing had not happened, Flora Desmond might have returned young Estcourt's love. Perhaps if the wand of fate had not decreed otherwise, her heart might have gone out to him. It seemed almost natural that she should love him, he who had received her earliest confidences and been her first friend. But one thing had intervened to make this impossible. Flora Desmond loved another.

Some women can love much and often, some can almost adore, and then forget. To Flora this was impossible. Hers was a heart which could not lightly love, which, slow to appreciate, would nevertheless, when once unlocked, love truly, faithfully, and well. And thus it had been with this woman so seemingly love free. For years ago that feeling had flooded her heart, had taken possession of her, never to pass away, when as Lady Flora Desmond, but a year after her marriage, she had seen Evie Ravensdale for the first time.

Who shall describe or fathom the depth of a true and pure love? None have been able to do so yet, none ever will. Flora's love was such as asked for no return, content only to be allowed to love.

And yet, who knows that there may not have shot, now and again, through Flora's heart when, after the death of Reginald Desmond, she and Evie Ravensdale were thrown often into each other's company, a gleam of hope that her love might in time come to be returned? It may have been so; but if so, it vanished finally and forever when the personality of Hector D'Estrange was revealed in Gloria de Lara. Unmistakably on that evening when she had rescued this latter from the prison-van and had handed her into Evie Ravensdale's safe keeping at Montragee House, Flora Desmond had read in the dark and beautiful eyes of the young duke the secret of his heart.

It never entered her mind to cavil at his choice or to resent it. No pang of jealousy had shot through her heart against the woman to whom his love had been clearly given. Only, when she had read his secret, had the feeling rushed over her that the love which she had nursed and cherished for so long, was imperishable and impossible of recall.

Not that she wished or sought to recall it. Flora would have sooner died than part with the first true love of her life; it was to her a treasure that she prized beyond expression, priceless to her in value. He lays his right hand on her shoulder for a moment as he stands by her side, and she feels it tremble.

"It is a day I shall never forget. Flora," he says gently; "I have been very happy. It will be something for your old friend to look back upon, when you are far away."

"What do you mean Estcourt?" she inquires hastily. "But you are coming with us?"

"No," he answers decisively. "I have other work to do. I shall never rest till I have obtained for you the pardon that will extricate you from this outlawed life. I can be of use to you by remaining, I have some influence still in high quarters, and I could do you no good by going to America. Of course I should like to go; you know. Flora, I am never so happy as when I am with you, but I don't mean to think of *Ego* on this occasion."

The tears rise to her eyes.

"I shall miss you, Estcourt, dear old Estcourt," she says softly; and then her hand steals into his, and he feels the grateful pressure in its firm touch.

The blood rushes to the young man's face, for that touch thrills him through and through, though the ring in her voice tells him that affection, and affection only, not love, is there.

"You'll never miss me as I shall you," he answers passionately. "Ah, Flora! you don't know the dull, blank void that comes over me when you are not by; you don't understand the lonely feeling that masters me, the yearning to see your dear face again. Of course. Flora, you cannot understand what I suffer, for I don't believe you know what love means. I have often heard you called 'the cold Lady Flora.' I begin to believe you are rightly named."

　　　　　　　　　　LADY FLORENCE DIXIE

It is her turn to flush now, but she turns her head away that he may not see the hot blood in her cheeks. Evie Ravensdale's face is before her in imagination. She sees the dear, dark, dreamy eyes, the clear-cut features, the beautiful forehead around which the raven curls are clustering; she sees him as plainly as though he stood before her, for is not his presence burnt into her mind with the exactitude of reality? She loves him with all her heart, and power, and soul, and mind. No sacrifice for his sake would seem hard. To die that he might live would be a joy. If Flora Desmond does not know what love means, then who does?

But Estcourt can only judge by what he sees. He knows she has rejected the love of many men. There is no one, save himself, to whom she appears to give a preference, and has she not told him that she can never marry him? Is he not justified in his conclusions, therefore? Perhaps so. Few men have ever been able to read a woman right.

She pulls herself together, however, and turns his remark off with a jest.

"Cold am I, Estcourt? An iceberg, probably! I almost think so, too, for it's actually beginning to feel chilly up here. How blood-red the sun has turned. Mark my words; we are in for a storm this evening, and I doubt any embarkation being possible tomorrow. I know these old shores well."

"If you are chilly, Flora," he says almost bitterly, "we had better make haste down the Crag Vale. It would not do for you to catch cold." Her evident desire to turn the conversation has not escaped him. It hurts him, and he shows it.

She marks the bitter tone of his voice. Flora knows Estcourt so well. A woman can generally read a man pretty correctly if she chooses to; of a certainty if the man loves her.

She faces him suddenly with the glow of the blood-red sun lighting up her handsome face. She is earnest in what she is going to say, and she looks it.

"Estcourt, dear old Estcourt, let there be no misunderstanding between us two, and on the eve of parting. This may be the last opportunity of telling you what I wish to. Don't gibe me as cold and heartless, for it is not true, not true. Do I not know how chivalrously and devotedly you have loved me, and am I not grateful to you for your noble and generous love? Why should I ask the question, because you know it? You know I would not speak untruly, and I tell you that your love is very precious to me, and I value your great friendship more than anybody else's in this world. Were you not my first friend? Am I likely to forget that? But, Estcourt, dear old man, you must not throw your love away on me, for I shall never marry again. I shall always look on you as my first, best, and truest friend, and love you dearly, very dearly as such, but I can never marry again—no, Estcourt, never!"

"Nor I," he answers quietly, with a sad smile. "You are hardly the woman to bid a man marry where he does not love. Flora, I have loved you ever since I first saw you; I shall never love anyone else but you. At least you will do me the justice to believe that I am as unalterable as you are. Let us never bring this subject up again. Let it bide by the Crag Vale Cairn."

He kisses her hand tenderly and respectfully, and then he lets it fall.

"Let's go down now, Flora dear," he says gently. "I wonder why Ravensdale's smack has not turned the point yet. It ought to be round by now if Léonie were right."

"I'll back her to be right," answers Flora, with a slight laugh. "She's not likely to mislead Gloria, who, by-the-bye, I saw turning the point in her coracle quite ten minutes ago. They'll be round in a second, I daresay."

The two scramble down the rough face of the mountain side in silence. The thoughts of both are busy. Suddenly, however, Estcourt brings himself to a halt and calls out to Flora, who is a little ahead of him,

"Flora! who can that be?"

Her eyes follow the direction in which his hand points, and she sees a four-oared boat coming out of Loch Eilort into the Sound of Arisaig at a rapid pace, and heading for Glennig Bay.

"It must be Archie," she calls back. "I suppose he got to the far end of the lake, and has come back by water. The boat is Bruce Ruglen's, and the oarsmen are his four sons. I know it and them well."

He comes running down to where she is standing.

"Flora dear," he says quickly, "use your eyes. The man in the stern is not Douglasdale. It's Evie, as I live! What can Léonie have meant, and why does not Gloria come back? Surely there cannot have been treachery? My God! surely not?"

But Flora never stops to surmise. Her face is deadly pale, and she has turned at his words, and is hurrying with fleet steps down the mountain side, with Estcourt following quickly in the rear. Fast, faster she goes. Flora Desmond is as nimble as a deer. No monstrous, tied-back petticoats encumber her. She is habited in the neat, graceful kilt in the tartan of her brother's clan and her own, which suits to perfection her supple, well-made form. In it she is free to use the physical powers which Nature has given her, and which she has never sought to stunt or to curtail.

She makes straight for the shore, and as she moves along she loads her rifle. Then as she reaches the water's edge she fires it off.

This attracts the inmates of the boat. They look her way, and perceive that she is signalling to them to come in shore. In a moment Evie Ravensdale has turned the boat's nose in her direction, and she sees that he is urging the oarsmen to exert their utmost.

The men endeavour to obey; they bend their backs, and send the boat hissing through the still waters. Foam flakelets fly before the racing keel propelled by irresistible force, and yet to Flora Desmond it appears to come but slowly.

"Back water, men!" she shouts, as the boat nears the shore. "Don't beach her. I want to push her off and jump in."

Estcourt is beside her now, and they are both up to their knees in the water. The men are resting on their oars as the boat glides slowly forward.

But Flora and Estcourt have it by the prow.

"Now, Estcourt, push off!" exclaims the former, as bending chest downwards she arrests its course. The edge of her kilt in front sinks into the water, in another moment her knee is on the boat's edge, and she is standing in the bow with her companion by her side.

"Evie!" she exclaims, in a low excited voice, "how is it you have come this way? Is anything wrong? We expected you in a smack, and Gloria has gone to meet you."

"A smack!" gasps the young duke. "What do you mean?"

But she does not answer him. She has turned, and is addressing the four clansmen.

"Ruglens," she says quickly, "pull to the point for your lives! Pull men, pull; pull with the strength God gave you. God in heaven, pull!"

They answer to her appeal, do these young giants. Do they not know her well? Is she not a Ruglen? Are they not Ruglens too? Have they not as children played with their young chief and his sister, joined in their rambles, mingled with their sports? Well do these Highland laddies understand her quick command, understand it and obey. She has crossed to the stern, where the duke sits staring mutely at her.

"Give me the helm, Evie," she says quietly. "I can steer the shortest cut. Don't look like that, Evie; it may be all a mistake."

But her voice tells him she does not think so.

The boat tears through the water; the clansmen are doing their best. There is not a word spoken. Only the splash of the oars, the dull thud of the twisting rowlocks, the hiss of the boat's keel, break the stillness of Glennig's Bay.

They have reached the point now. Four more gallant strokes from the men whose brows are thickly studded with the bead drops of extraordinary toil, and the boat rises on the first rolling swell of the open sea.

The smack is there; it catches the straining eyes of Evie Ravensdale, as he springs up and gazes across the great grey ocean waste. To her dying day Flora will never forget the terrible groan of agony which bursts from him.

Ay, the smack is there, but they come too late. The brown sail is spread, it is already far away, vanishing into the creeping, dull, dark veil of the advancing night and rising storm.

III

"All shall come right, everything shall be explained; you shall have immediate liberty, if, on behalf of your mother, you will promise me what I ask. I know perfectly well she will do it if you ask her. Now will you?"

The speaker is a middle-aged man, with deep, dark eyes, handsome features, and bold, resolute carriage. Grey hairs peep here and there from out his thick beard, moustache, and whiskers, and there are grey hairs in his once raven hair. He is dressed in a navy-blue serge suit, and wears the buttons of the royal yacht squadron.

To all appearance the person he is addressing is a young man of some twenty-three or twenty-four summers. He is tall, and slight, with a face of extreme beauty. He has rich gold-auburn hair, and his eyes are deep blue in colour. Nothing will compare with them but the sapphire.

He wears a well-fitting shepherd's plaid kilt, stockings to match, and silver mounted brogues. A loose white flannel shirt and waistcoat and jacket complete his attire.

"I will not," is the stern, cold reply which he gives to the speaker's query.

This latter grinds his teeth, but checks the rising anger within him, and speaks once more in a persuasive, almost pleading voice.

"Think again. Consider all that depends on your decision. After all, my request is perfectly honourable. I simply ask that she shall consent to re-marry me."

"Great God! and you call that an honourable request, Lord Westray? You think it a simple matter, that my mother should wed again my father's murderer? I tell you a death of hideous torture would be more preferable to me, than that a fate so awful should befall her. Cease, I pray you, this subject. I have but one answer to your hateful proposal, and that is, no!"

"Have you weighed well in your mind the fate that awaits you, Hector D'Estrange, if you persist in this refusal?" asks Lord Westray threateningly.

"My name is Gloria de Lara, my lord, not Hector D'Estrange, as I think you know full well. The fate that awaits me I fully realise. I am condemned to death for a murder never committed; I am to die that your vile vengeance on my beloved mother may be fully wreaked. Do your worst. I do not fear death; and my mother will bear the blow as bravely and as nobly as she has borne others."

She folds her arms proudly, and there is a world of scorn in her beautiful eyes as she fixes them on the cowardly brute before her. A wild gust of wind shrieks angrily above board as the smack rises and plunges in the trough of a choppy sea. The blood-red sun has vanished, an inky darkness has set in, and the wind is rapidly increasing from a fresh breeze into a regular fierce and nasty gale.

Lord Westray staggers, and almost reels up against her as the smack lurches forward on the crest of a more than usually excitable wave. There is a rush of feet on deck, and men's voices are heard shouting above the noisy wind. She starts back from him in horror; she would not touch him for the world. His very presence in the close, stuffy little cabin seems to stifle her. Gladly would she seek an asylum in the ocean's angry waves, and trust to Fate to enable her to reach the shore, or die.

The cabin door opens, and the skipper peers in.

"Beg pardon, sir," he says, touching his oil-skin cap, "but I must put to sea, sir, I must. We're in for a regular duster. I daren't coast no longer, sir. It's pitch black, and the shore for miles along is almighty dangerous."

"I'll come on deck, Hutchins," answers Lord Westray quickly. He is a good sailor, but the intelligence does not please him. As he turns to leave the cabin Léonie steals in. She is drenched with sea water, and her hair is wringing wet. As she seats herself in a corner of the cabin she glances shyly at Gloria. This latter returns the look with one of mingled pity and contempt. Léonie's eyes drop before that look. For the first time in her life a feeling of shame rushes over her.

"This is a terrible storm," she says in a low voice, as a wave crashes along the deck, part of it finding its way into the cabin. "I heard one of the men say he did not think the boat would weather it."

"God grant it may not!" answers Gloria sternly, and then, as if influenced by a sudden impulse, she continues gently, "Ah! Léonie, child, what could have tempted you to act so basely? What have I ever done to you that you should treat me thus?"

"I did my duty," answers the girl sullenly. "I did what I was ordered to do. It is my trade."

"Your trade, child? Good heavens! what are you, and who ordered you to betray me?"

"My master, Mr. Trackem," answers Léonie, simply. "I belong to his detective gang. I've served him ever since I can remember. I've never failed him yet, and he told me not to fail him this time. I promised I would not, and I have obeyed him."

There is an evident sincerity in her tone, and Gloria, with her power of deep insight into character, reads Léonie's at a glance.

"Have you no mother, no father, my poor Léonie?" she inquires softly, as she comes over to the girl's side, and lays her hand on her curly head.

"Mother, father? No, of course not," answers Léonie, with a slight laugh. "They are both dead. Mr. Trackem always says he's acted father, mother, brother, sister, uncle, aunt, and cousin by me. I don't quite know what he means by that, but that is what he says."

"Poor Léonie, poor wee Léonie. God! what a fate! You are not to blame then, my poor child. Ah! how fully I forgive you," says Gloria, as with a sudden impulse she stoops and kisses the girl who has betrayed her, on the cheek. Only another revelation has come to her from that cesspool of Modern Babylon; only another fearful wrong unknown, unstudied, and unforbidden, brought to light.

Léonie looks up quickly. There is a queer expression in her intelligent eyes.

"Why do you kiss me? Why do you speak so kindly? Why do you forgive me for betraying you?" she inquires rather eagerly.

"Because I believe in God," answers Gloria gently.

"God! Why, Mr. Trackem always laughs at God," interposes Léonie, with a shrug of her shoulders. "He always tells me that God is an invention of the devil, and all clergymen and priests are fallen angels."

"Oh, hush, Léonie; hush, my poor, poor child! This is terrible. Do not talk in that awful way," and the tears start trembling to Gloria's lovely eyes. "Léonie, God is good; He is our friend, He helps those who pray to Him. If we die tonight we shall be brought face to face with Him."

"I don't understand what you mean," answers the girl quietly, "but I do know this. I expected abuse and reproaches from you, but I have received only kindness, forgiveness, and gentle words. You have kissed me, and no one has ever done that before. I am sorry now I betrayed you. Yes, I am; and I will try and save you if I can—unless, unless we are drowned tonight. Do you think we shall be drowned? You can swim, I know, but I can't. Mr. Trackem never taught me how to do that."

"If it comes to swimming I will do my best to help you, Léonie, at least so long as God gives me strength to do so," answers Gloria quietly.

Again Léonie looks up. In her untrained, untutored mind Nature is beginning to assert its sway, and gratitude knocks gently at her heart.

"You would do that for me, would you? You would try to save my life, after what I have done to you? Did God teach you that?" she asks with a quivering voice.

"Yes, Léonie."

"Then I love God, and I love you. May I give you a kiss, just as you kissed me? I want to show you how I love you," cries Léonie, with a half sob. "No one has ever been kind to me like this before."

She rises as she speaks, and takes one of Gloria's hands. This latter is almost startled by the extraordinary likeness which for a brief moment sweeps across the girl's features, a likeness to Bernie Fontenoy.

There is a terrible crash overhead. It sounds like falling timber. Again a rush of feet, and Gloria and Léonie hear the skipper's voice raised in loud command.

"He is ordering out the boat, Léonie. That must have been the mast that went with that crash. I can feel by the movement of the ship that she's helpless. We shall drift on the rocks, and then she'll soon break up," exclaims Gloria, almost eagerly.

"Then we shall be drowned," answers her companion in a quiet, composed voice. "I'm not afraid. I think I should have been if this had happened yesterday, but I am not now."

She stops suddenly as the cabin door creaks open to admit Lord Westray.

He looks flurried and anxious, but his glance at once seeks Gloria.

"The smack is practically a wreck," he says quickly, "and we are going to take to the boat. I will save you if you will promise me what I asked you."

"Go!" cries Gloria sternly. "Now you know that I will die rather than do so. Go, bad man! and may God have mercy on you."

He looks at her furiously. But there is no time for arguing; the skipper is calling to him to hurry.

"So be it," he bursts out, with a coarse laugh. "Your blood be on your own head. I'll leave you. and save the gallows the trouble of hanging you. Come on, girl."

These last words are addressed to Léonie.

"What! go with you, and leave her? I'll drown rather!" exclaims Léonie, with a contemptuous laugh.

"Drown like a rat, then," he says with an oath, as he hangs the door and leaves them. They hear him scrambling up the little companion ladder, they hear his voice shouting to the skipper, but the wind shrieks louder, and the howl of the tempest drowns all other sounds.

Again there is a rush of water along the deck, a hissing and washing sound, as the huge wave which has occasioned it tears madly on its course, part of it bursting open the cabin door, and flooding the floor on which Gloria and Léonie are standing.

"We must get on deck, Léonie; we can't stay here, child. Here, take hold of my hand; we must keep together," exclaims Gloria in a quick, peremptory voice.

They are half-blinded by the thick spray which sweeps in their faces as they stagger up the ladder, clinging like grim death to the rails. It is pitch dark, not the faintest gleam of light gives them the smallest indication of their whereabouts, only the white foam of the towering billows now and again flashes across their aching eyes, blinded by the salt sea-water.

Plenty of wreckage is floating about on the deck, and amongst it a life-belt knocks up against one of Gloria's ankles. With a pleased exclamation she at once secures it, and proceeds to slip it over Léonie's shoulders.

"If this poor wreck founders," she explains as she does so, "this will keep you afloat, child. I am glad I saw it."

"But you," says Léonie quickly; "you have not one."

"Never mind me, child. You forget that I can swim. If we manage to stick together, this belt will be a great help to me, as you will see. And now, Léonie, we can do nothing but cling to these rails and trust in God. Keep a good look out for the waves. When you see one rushing this way don't try and stand up against it, it will only knock you backwards, but bend yourself, hold your breath, and put your head through it. Quick, have a care, child!" She utters these last words in a sharp warning tone as she tightens her grasp on Léonie's hand. A dense dark wall seems to tower above them, a swirl and a rush is all she hears as a monster wave envelops her and Léonie in its folds. It tears the rail, to which her left hand clings, from her grasp. She feels herself lifted up like a straw, and borne forward by the resistless rush and volume of water. With the desperation of death in her clutch, her right hand still grips the still, cold fingers of her young companion, whose grasp has slackened altogether. A floating spar strikes her with some force. She clutches at it, but it sweeps past her, and is gone as the wave carries her ever onwards.

A sudden ebb in the resistless current as if by magic arrests her course. She feels herself dragged back along the line she has come. Then the volume of water abruptly leaves her, and her feet touch the deck again.

Gloria is up in a moment; she knows there is not a minute to spare. In her present position another such a billow would sweep her clear of the smack altogether into the raging sea.

"Jump up, Léonie!" she shouts, but Léonie never stirs. As Gloria tugs at her arm to try and arouse her, she knows by the dead weight of the girl's body that Léonie is either dead or insensible.

With a supreme effort she raises the now helpless girl in her arms, and staggers forward to the cabin with her burden. A wave strikes her as she reaches it, and dashes her once more to the ground. For a second time she is swept like a straw along the deck, and for the second time the ebb arrests her progress, and leaves her in the same position as before.

"Oh God!" she gasps, "how long? This is indeed a living death."

She still grasps the stiff, clammy fingers of the helpless girl, but hope has left her. She only now wishes that death may come, and come quickly.

There is a wild shriek ahead. It rises high above the wind's roar. Then a ghastly, unearthly sound comes out of the blackness of night. Even on death's threshold it awakes to attention the senses of Gloria de Lara. Through the blinding spray she strains the last glance on life which she feels is left to her. High above, like a huge black mountain rising suddenly out of the sea, looms a gigantic apparition. It towers above her like some fearful, unknown spectre. There is a flash of light in the air, a loud shout, a grating sound. Loud o'er all shrieks the tempest whistle, she feels the smack part from her, a mighty current sucks her beneath the waves; down, down it drags her into the bottomless abyss of the ocean's awful crater, as the great ship sweeps forward on its course. Even in this moment of death's agony Gloria's brain is clear. She relaxes her grasp of Léonie, who, with the life-belt around her, has that one straw of hope to cling to. As the waters of the surging Atlantic sweep over her her last cry is to God; her last vision of the life which she is quitting, is the face of Evie Ravensdale.

IV

Peace after the storm! Ay, in so far that the tempest fiend has vanished, leaving behind him only the low moan of the dying gale. High above the heights which look down on Eilean Fianan, Tiorin's ruins, and the lovely woods of Shona's Isle, hover the cloud mists of rising morn, through whose seemingly tissue veil glint and gleam the joyous sparks, fantastic offspring of the new-born sun.

Its light, too, is warming those heights with a rosy glow, and the thick dark woods are pierced with its golden shafts. Like myriad diamonds sparkle the raindrops on the pines, and the dew on the glades and fairy rings, where elfin goblins have held their midnight orgies.

Yet the gale has left its after-birth in the rolling swell, which beats in relentless fury on the rock-girt coast of Shona's Isle, and lashes the sandy stretch of beach between Ardtoe and Ru Druimnich. High tide is rising on those shores, an inland current has set in, and in its grasp are the trophies of the storm-fiend's victory over the handiwork of man.

What are these trophies? Why, here and there a spar, a tossing barrel, a broken oar. There is something floating, too, on the heaving swell with which the waves are making merry, for they carry it to the sandy beach and drag it back again, toss it still further inland, and smother it in their spray.

It is a choice plaything; the salt sea waves are battling for it hard, but the tide and the inland current say them nay, and the sandy beach gives it a rugged welcome. There for a time it may rest.

It! But what may it be? A human body, surely?

Out in the bay the yacht *Eilean* is coasting up and down. Eager eyes are scanning the waste of water, and every sign of wreckage is minutely observed. Ever and anon the voices of the men aloft shout down some new discovery to the anxious watchers on the deck below. There is a look of intense agony in the eyes of the young Duke of Ravensdale as he paces that snow-white deck. His features are drawn and haggard, his cheeks are deathly pale, and the lines of care have seared their mark indelibly across his high and noble brow.

"Wreckage ahoy!" The men on the look-out have spied another victim of the gale which the inland current is drawing to Ardnamurchan's shores. What can it be? It looks like the back of a whale, or a huge porpoise turning over in its course. What can it be?

The *Eilean* steams towards it, and comes close up alongside it. No, it is no whale. Only the remnant of a fishing smack, part of which appears to have been bodily severed from the whole.

The sharp order to man the lifeboat cutter is given. In a few minutes it is riding the heaving swell. All eyes are occupied with this new discovery; even the look-out men have forgotten their duty aloft. Suddenly, however. Flora's Desmond's voice rings out. She has been keeping silent, faithful watch by Evie Ravensdale.

"What's that?" she cries.

In a moment he is straining with an eager, hungry look those wild, despairing eyes. She is pointing away to starboard, and he sees, unmistakably sees, a human head and shoulders rising up and down on the grey ocean's surface. With a low cry he springs forward. Were it not for Flora's restraining clutch he would be overboard and swimming to meet it.

"Wait, Evie!" she says imploringly. "The boat wall fetch it in a moment. Don't go, Evie. Alas, it is not she!"

She has a clear sight has Flora Desmond. She has caught a glimpse of the dead white face thrown back as it rises on the crest of the heaving swell, and she knows that it is not the face of Gloria de Lara. But when the lifeboat cutter retrieves the body, and it is hoisted on to the deck, then indeed Flora cannot restrain a cry of horror as she recognises in the set, rigid face, wide open, staring eyes, and close clenched teeth the unmistakable features of the girl traitoress, the female Judas, Léonie.

"Take her from my sight! Oh God! take her away!" bursts from the pale lips of Evie Ravensdale, as in a moment the sight of the body before him drives from his heart the clinging hope that Gloria is not dead. He knows now that the storm-fiend has claimed her for his victim, that on this earth the dark blue eyes will never look their love again.

As they bear Léonie from his sight an unnatural calmness seizes him. He turns to Flora.

"We must do our duty, Flora. Mine is to see you safe. We will put the helm about, and steer for the great free land. And when we get there Flora, you will see her mother and break it to her, won't you?"

His words are so cold and measured, his face so unmoved, that Flora is half fearful for his reason. She lays her hand gently on his arm.

"Not yet, Evie. We must put back to Shona first. We must not give up the search yet. I mean to examine the whole coast line between this and Ru Druimnich."

"But she is dead, Flora. Don't you know she is dead?" he says coldly.

"Still, Evie, we may find her dear body. Oh no, Evie, we must not give up the search; we must seek on," answers Flora. She dare not buoy him up with the fresh hope that Gloria may be alive. The sight of Léonie has told her this cannot be; yet still she is resolved more than ever to search on for the body of her friend. The boatswain is standing near. She sends him with instructions to the captain, to put the yacht's head about and run for Moidart's Loch, and then she resumes her watch by Evie Ravensdale. Time flies, but he does not notice her; his eyes are staring out over the ocean wave. As they near the Loch, Nigel Estcourt comes up.

"A moment, Flora," he says, motioning her to come apart. "The doctor is trying to bring Léonie round. He says life is not extinct. If he can only succeed, we may be able to extract from her what has happened. Will you go and see her? I will keep Ravensdale company while you go down?"

"You must be very gentle, Estcourt. You must watch him closely, too; I am terribly afraid for his reason. He seems turned to stone since he set eyes on Léonie. It is a bad sign. If tears would come they would relieve him. Ah! God help him. It is terrible."

She sighs deeply as she turns from him. Heavy at heart, yet is Flora's heart heavier still when it thinks of the agony which Evie Ravensdale is suffering. What would she not endure to bring comfort and peace to his tortured soul!

She makes her way down to the cabin where Léonie is lying; the doctor, with the stewardess and her assistant, are busy treating her. He looks up hopefully as Flora enters.

"She has moved; she has struggled for breath," he observes quickly. "Lady Flora, she will live. She seems to me a mere child. I wonder who she is."

But Flora does not answer, only she moves over to the couch, and looks down on the motionless girl.

It is strange, but as she looks she sees the same remarkable resemblance in this girl to Bernie Fontenoy, which Gloria had remarked the previous night. Certainly it is strange, very strange.

There is a long-drawn sigh, and then a struggle for breath. Léonie clutches the air with her hands, and her lips move.

"I am stifling," she gasps; "don't choke me, don't, please don't! Let me breathe, please let me breathe!" The doctor raises her up slightly, and again Léonie sighs. Then she draws a long breath. "I love you," she says softly; "I love you, Gloria. I love God, too. I wish I hadn't betrayed you now. But you have forgiven me, you have been kind to me, you have kissed me. Oh! those waves, those dreadful waves! They will kill you; you have given me the life-belt, and you have not got one. Take it off, Gloria. Put it on yourself and leave me. I don't mind drowning. I would like to drown for you. Let me kiss you first. Let me sleep now; let me die."

Her hitherto fixed and staring eyes shoot with a gleam of returning intelligence. She closes them, and her head falls forward.

"She will sleep now," observes the doctor, as he lays her down and turns her on her side, "and when she awakes she will be all right. A marvellous recovery. She must have wonderful vitality in her. We will leave her now quiet, Lady Flora. The yacht is in motion again. Do we continue the search?"

"Yes, but along the coast. I must go now, doctor. You will let me know later how the patient is, won't you?"

"Certainly," he answers cheerfully.

Flora returns on deck. Léonie's words have puzzled her. They were clearly addressed to Gloria, and yet these disjointed utterances can convey but one interpretation of her fate. Gladly would Flora swallow a grain of hope, but she knows that it would only make the reality harder to bear, a reality which she has faced and accepted already.

"Gloria," she whispers, "if you can hear me now, you will know how true was Flora's friendship. God help me, and I will clear your name of that foul charge laid to your door. Léonie may know something of it, and she will tell me, for on the threshold of death has she not said that she loves you?"

Brave, noble Flora! Self is buried in those generous words. She never pauses to think of the danger in which she stands, or the trouble which she must suffer But Flora is heroic.

The yacht is gliding into Moidart's Loch, and again the lifeboat cutter is manned and lowered. Flora has determined to search the whole shore within the radius of the drifting inland current, which long experience of these coasts has taught her, draws wrecks thereto.

She will conduct the search in this direction herself, while, as is now arranged, Estcourt and Archie Douglasdale will prosecute it along Shona's rocky coast in the large gig. Archie had returned to Glennig Bay, on the evening before, only to find the fishing box deserted, his sister,

Ravensdale, and Estcourt gone. One of his trusty Ruglen retainers awaited him, however, with the information that they had crossed the hills by Kinlockmoidart for Eilean Shona, where the duke's yacht lay anchored. The message which Léonie had been entrusted to convey was to this very effect, the duke having further commissioned her to apprise Gloria of his intended arrival alone, from the Loch Eilort side.

"Evie," says Flora gently, "you will come with me, will you not? I am going to search the sand beaches in the cutter up to Ru Druimnich. Come, Evie."

He turns almost sullenly. God help him! The torture he is suffering is writ in his eyes. "She is dead," is all he says. But he follows Flora, nevertheless, and they enter the cutter together. Then he bows his face in his hands and remains silent.

The search they make is thorough. How could it be else with Flora in command? And gradually the cutter creeps slowly on in the direction of the body on the shore.

It is sighted at length; the look-out man utters his warning cry, and Flora stands suddenly up and stares eagerly ahead.

Yes, there it lies, high and dry on the sandy beach. Undoubtedly a human form.

"Bend to your oars, lads!" she cries. "I'm going to beach her"; and with that she brings the boat's nose sharply for the shore. "Evie," she says again, "rouse yourself, Evie. We shall be in the breakers in a minute. There is a body on the beach."

He looks up quickly. Just a gleam of hope is in his wild eyes, and he is thoroughly on the alert. The boat rushes forward; it rises high on the first breaker, and is hurled towards the shore. True is the hand that holds the tiller and the nerve that guides it. Straight as a dart does Flora keep the cutter's nose, and her voice encourages the oarsmen to their duty, the seething foam half fills the boat, but it gallantly rides the water still, as another breaker bears it onward. Now the keel grates the sandy bottom.

"Ship oars, lads, and out of her!" Flora commands, but she sets the example, too.

She is in the water waist high. In a moment the stalwart sailors have obeyed her. Rough, willing hands grasp the cutter's sides, and with combined force to the seaman's cheery "Pull, boys, together," run her high and dry on to the beach.

But Evie Ravensdale has rushed forward. Hope still surges in his heart. The body is stretched out upon the sand, the figure is lying on its face, the hands are clenched. It is easy, however, to see that the body is not that of a woman; it is plain as plain can be that it is a man.

He sees this at once, and turns away with a bitter, despairing cry. It was a mad, vain hope to have indulged in, and yet in his breaking heart, Evie Ravensdale had prayed to be allowed to look upon her face once more, ay, even though it were in death.

An exclamation from Flora for a moment attracts him. She has followed him and has turned the body over.

"Evie!" she cries, and there is a passionate ring of triumph in her voice, "though Gloria be dead, her pure, fair fame is saved. Though God has taken her, He has dashed to the ground the foul lie with which they sought to doom her. Look, Evie, look! Her noble name is cleared."

With a startled, eager look he comes to her side. He sees at his feet the pallid upturned face of a dead man. This man has dark hair, and a dark thick beard, moustache and whiskers in which grey hairs are stealing fast. This man has dark eyes, but the lustre of life has left them, and his white teeth are clenched together with a horrid grin.

He stares down at the corpse below him. The wild, hungry look in his beautiful eyes is dying now. Triumph and exultation are there.

"Gloria!" he cries, "my darling, you have triumphed. They thought they could kill you with a false and awful lie. There is your answer. Nor shall your great cause die. I swear to win it for you! I swear—I swear it now!"

He turns away with a gasping sob. But Flora has no longer any fear for him. Evie Ravensdale's vow will bid him live, live on for Gloria's sake.

Calmly and quietly she turns to the sailors. "We will carry that body to Dorlin, my lads. Guard it well. There lies the man whom a too confident jury declared to be dead, for whose murder the noblest of women was unjustly condemned. That corpse is Lord Westray!"

V

The blinds are drawn down in the single window of a small bedroom that overlooks a narrow, dull, and dingy street, not far removed from Trafalgar Square. The room, though clean, bears a poverty-stricken look, for in it, in addition to the bed, there are only two chairs, an old table, and a dilapidated sofa with a thin rug covering it. There is a small washhand-stand in this room besides the other articles named, but this is all.

Lying on the bed is a large-eyed, pale, emaciated young man, upon whose face is unmistakably written the sign of death. His thin hands, in which the blue veins show prominently clear, lie listlessly on the coverlet, though now and again the feeble fingers twitch nervously thereat, and a hectic flush covers his pale cheeks. His large hollow eyes have a brilliant, shining look in them, and they appear to be fixed on the door of the room which stands slightly ajar.

There is a sound of the street door downstairs opening, and the movement of several feet. The young man raises himself up and listens eagerly, but the exertion is too much for him, and he sinks back with a heavy sigh. The footsteps he has heard are ascending the staircase, however, and his eyes devour the door more eagerly than before. It opens and admits a young girl, a girl who would decidedly be called pretty were it not for the pinched, careworn look that rules in her regular and well-cut features. She bears a great resemblance to the invalid whom we have been describing. This is not to be wondered at, seeing she is his twin-sister.

"Maggie," he exclaims in a low voice as she enters, "have you brought him?"

"Yes, Eric," she answers at once, as she comes to his bedside, and puts the old faded coverlet at which his fingers have been twitching smooth and tidy.

"Where is he?" again asks the brother in the same low voice.

"Downstairs, Eric. I'll fetch him up. He's brought another gentleman with him. He calls him a magistrate, I think. He said this gentleman must take your deposition, because he couldn't," says Maggie, as she opens the door. The next minute she is running down the somewhat rickety staircase. Two gentlemen are standing in the passage below.

"This way, please, sirs," she says politely, and they follow up behind her to Eric Fortescue's room. The two gentlemen are Colonel Francis Barrett, divisional magistrate, and Evie, Duke of Ravensdale.

Eric Fortescue fixes his eyes on the latter, whom he knows well by sight. He has seen him often before with Hector D'Estrange.

"You wish to see me, my lad?" inquires the duke in a kind, but sad voice. "Your sister tells me you have something particular to say to me?"

"Yes," answers the sick youth, in his low, feeble voice; "and I want you, sir, to take down what I say, and hear me swear it's all true. I want to tell you quick, sir, because I'm dying; I can't last long."

There is a sob over by the window. Maggie is looking out into the miserable street with her forehead pressed against one of its cracked panes.

"Say all you have to say very slowly to this gentleman then, my lad," answers Evie Ravensdale. "He is a magistrate, and will take your deposition, and hear you swear to it."

"I want to tell you, sir, how wicked I have been. But God has forgiven me, for Father Vaughan has heard my confession, and given me absolution. I'm a Catholic, sir, you know. But Father Vaughan told me I ought to tell you what I'm going to, because of the great wrong which other people have suffered by what I've helped to do. So, sir, this is it."

"I'm twenty-three years of age, sir, and I have earned my living since a boy, and since poor mother died, in the service of Mr. Trackem. He's a private detective agent, sir, and something else besides. He always said I was a sharp lad, and that I did things quick for him, so that when I was eighteen he made me his head clerk, and used to tell me all about his affairs and jobs. It was he and I who arranged that attack on Mrs. de Lara, and several days before it I had watched her every night when she came out for her evening stroll, and the night before the attack I got into her sitting-room while she was out, and stole a lot of her note-paper and some of her writing. I was at Mr. D'Estrange's trial, sir, and all what Mrs. de Lara and Miss Vernon and you swore to was quite true, and nearly all what Mr. Trackem said was a lie. Well, sir, after Mr. D'Estrange and you and Miss Vernon rescued Mrs. de Lara, Mr. Trackem and I and Lord Westray held a consultation. His lordship was very much put about, and swore he would be revenged. He offered me and Mr. Trackem a deal of money to help him, and then Mr. Trackem hatched the plan, sir. I can imitate handwriting well, and he made me write two letters copying Mrs. de Lara's handwriting. One was to her maid, saying she was going up to London, and the other to Mr. Trackem, telling him to keep the house in Verdegrease Crescent for her and Lord Westray. And then Lord Westray himself wrote several letters in the vein described by Mr. Trackem at the trial. And then, sir, Mr. Trackem arranged with his lordship all about buying a poor man's body, as soon as one could be found suitable for the purpose. You look startled, sir, but it's not difficult to do a job of that sort in some parts of London, and, in fact, one was soon got. We put Lord Westray's gold ring on one of its little fingers, and hung the chain and locket about its neck, and it was me, sir, that took it down by night and buried it in Mrs. de Lara's grounds where it was found, and close to it I buried the clothes which Lord Westray was wearing the night that Mr. D'Estrange fired at him. By this time Lord Westray had gone abroad, but it was all arranged that in two years' time or so Mr. D'Estrange was to be accused of the murder. When that time had elapsed, anonymous letters were sent to the present Lord Westray, telling him all about the murder, and then Mr. Trackem went and told his lordship what he knew. Everything happened as we wanted it to. The matter was placed in Mr. Trackem's hands; he communicated with the police, and he employed me and a dog of his called Nero, a half-bred bloodhound, to hunt the grounds of Mrs. de Lara's place at night in search of the body and clothes. I had previously given Nero a lesson or two as to their whereabouts, so he soon traced them in the presence of the police. This is all I know, sir. On my dying oath I swear that Mr. D'Estrange did not murder Lord Westray. The wound received was slight, and soon healed up. This is my confession, sir. I know I did wrong, but I was a poor boy, and I was sorely tempted by the money offered me. I loved a girl, sir. She was called Léonie, and she was in Mr. Trackem's service. I wanted to marry her, and I didn't dare ask her till I got money. But God has punished me. I shall never see Léonie again; she's gone away, I don't know where, and now I'm dying. If it had not been for dear sister Maggie I should have been dead by now, for Lord Westray never paid me the money he promised to; least if he gave it to Mr. Trackem I never got it. Not that I want it now. I would not touch it for all the world, indeed I would not. And now, sir, I want to ask you to forgive me as I know God has, and I want you to ask Mrs. de Lara and Mr. D'Estrange to forgive me too. I think if they saw me as you do now, sir, they would pity and forgive me."

The young man pauses, and listens eagerly for a reply. The hectic flush has deepened in his cheeks, and his eyes gleam with the fire that heralds death more brilliantly than ever.

"My poor lad, I do forgive you, as I hope to be forgiven myself," says Evie Ravensdale softly. Terrible and horrible as is the plot which this dying youth has disclosed to him, yet in the presence of that death which he can see approaching fast, he feels that he must forgive.

"And Mrs. de Lara, Mr. D'Estrange?" persists Eric Fortescue anxiously.

"Mr. D'Estrange is dead," is all that Evie Ravensdale can trust himself to reply.

Eric Fortescue starts up in his bed, and stares wildly at the duke.

"Not hanged, sir? Oh God! not hanged, sir? I thought he escaped, sir?"

A hollow racking cough seizes him. The blood dyes his lips as he falls back helplessly as before. In a moment Maggie is by his side with her left arm tenderly round him, and supporting him in a sitting position, as she wipes the blood from his lips with an old handkerchief.

"Have you anything, my girl, to moisten his lips with?" inquires the duke, horrified at the sight before him.

"No, sir," she answers in a low, hopeless voice. "He had his last orange yesterday, and I have not a penny left except enough for the rent. I daren't use that. They would turn us out if that was not paid punctual."

Evie Ravensdale shudders; words would not paint his feelings.

"Here, Maggie," he says, "here is some money. Run, my girl, and buy what you think he will fancy, and we will stay with him until you return. At least, colonel, I won't ask you to. I know your time is precious. Will you swear this lad, and let him sign that deposition, and then I won't keep you? But I want to stay myself and see him comfortable before I leave."

With a happy smile lighting up her face Maggie Fortescue hurries from the room, and then Eric swears to and signs the deposition. The signature is tremblingly and weakly penned, still there it is, a living witness to the truth of Speranza and Gloria de Lara's innocence.

These formalities completed, Colonel Barrett takes his departure with the precious document in his safe keeping. Its contents will ring through the world before another sun is down. No sooner has he gone, than Eric Fortescue turns his eyes once more on the duke.

"I'm glad he's gone, sir," he says slowly, and speaking with difficulty, "because I want to tell you one more thing very particular, sir. It will be my last words, I think, for I feel I'm sinking. It's about Léonie, sir. I want to tell you who she is, sir. Mr. Trackem told me, sir, long ago. Her mother was Nell Stanley. Of course you know who I mean, sir—the big beauty whom your father, sir, took away from Lord Beauladown. It was she they fought that duel over. Well, Léonie is Nell Stanley's child, and her father was the late Duke of Ravensdale. He treated her mother very bad, poor thing, and forsook her altogether after she got disfigured with the small-pox. She came to live in Verdegrease Crescent, and earned her living on the streets. But she did not live long, and died at Mr. Trackem's house when Léonie was three years old. Mr. Trackem was beginning detective business then. Léonie was so pretty and so smart, that he kept her and trained her to the work, and that's how I came to know her, sir. And I did love her, and it was my love which tempted me to do all the wicked things I did. But God has punished me, sir. I am dying. I shall never see Léonie anymore. Still I should be happy if I knew you would care for her, sir."

He says the last words in a whisper. He has used all the strength that he possesses to make this last statement. Poor Eric Fortescue! *It is his last.*

Maggie's footstep is on the stairs; she is coming up so quickly. She has bought some grapes amongst other things with the duke's gift.

"Look, Eric dear!" she exclaims, as she hurries in, and holds up a big bunch of fine black grapes for him to view. "Look what I've got you!"

But Eric's eyes are closed, and the hectic flush has given way to a deathly pallor. He has made his last effort on this earth.

She sets the things down on the rickety table with a low cry, and comes over to the bedside.

"Eric," she pleads, "look at Maggie, Eric, poor Maggie; she's brought you such nice things."

He opens his big eyes, the brilliant gleam in them has died out; there is a dead, heavy, vacant look in them.

"I'm going, Maggie," she hears him mutter; "tell Father Vaughan I *did* tell all. There's mother, Maggie; how pretty she looks. She's in a garden full of flowers and fruits and pretty things. The sun is so bright and the air so pure. And there's Léonie—dear, pretty little Léonie. Don't hold me, Maggie; I must go to her, I must—"

And Maggie, bending over her twin-brother, hears his voice grow still, feels on her cheek the last breath of life that goes forth with these words, for Eric Fortescue is dead.

Poor Maggie! She is weak, and ill, and suffering. For weeks she has worked hard to support her brother, and watched by his bedside in her spare hours. She has stinted herself of food to buy him little delicacies. But of late, work has been hard to get, and during the last week she has obtained but scant employment, barely sufficient to buy bread with. At this moment food has not passed her lips for thirty-six hours, and the last bite she had, was a few crusts soaked in water, the remnants of some bread from the crumb of which she had made her brother a little bread and milk. Poor Maggie! It is as well. He wants no bread and milk now.

But she does not cry or sob when she knows it is all over. She merely closes the dull, staring, lustreless eyes, smooths the worn coverlet once more, joins his hands as if in prayer, and drawing a small crucifix from her chest, kisses it, and places it between his thin white fingers. Then she turns to Evie Ravensdale.

"He is dead, your Grace," she says meekly; "it is God's will. I will never forget your kindness in forgiving him. Poor Eric! he was a good lad if he had not been led astray. Can I fetch you a cab, your Grace?"

Her voice is quiet, almost matter-of-fact, and yet Maggie Fortescue is alone in the world, hungry, tired, weary, and penniless.

"No, Maggie," he says gently, "certainly not. I am going away now, but I will send someone to help you. And when you have buried your poor brother, you must come to this address and let me know. I have several things to ask you, and you must let me help you to earn a comfortable living."

"God bless your Grace!" she answers in a low voice. Then, as Evie Ravensdale turns to go, she holds out some silver to him, saying as she does so:

"It's the change, your Grace, out of what you gave me to get those things for Eric."

"Keep it, keep it, Maggie," he says huskily; and then he turns and leaves the poor scantily furnished room in which he has learned so much, and in which he has established, absolutely and completely, the innocence of the woman whose lost image is ever before his eyes.

VI

And while Erie Fortescue unburdens his soul of the heavy sin that has stained it, and bears it, purified and triumphant, through the portals of a new life, there is confusion and rage in the heart of Mr. Trackem as he sits at his business table hastily examining papers and committing them to the safe keeping of a large fire, which consumes each consignment as it is thrown in.

Mr. Trackem's usually confident and satisfied expression, has given place to one of anxiety and fear. That he is disturbed is evident.

"Curse the fellow!" he keeps muttering to himself; and then a gleam of baffled rage shoots from his cunning eyes.

There comes a knock at the door, a peculiar knock. He is evidently acquainted with it, for he looks up eagerly and calls out, "Come in."

A woman enters obedient to the summons. She is a woman with a plump, artificial-looking figure, her hair is yellow, and her eyes, eyelashes, and eyebrows are dark. An unmistakable sign of powder and rouge affords to her cheeks an appearance of pinkness, which all women who decorate themselves in this manner verily believe looks natural and becoming. Alas! if they could only see themselves as others see them! She is overdressed is this woman, with plenty of rings on her fingers and jewellery about her, and her whole air unmistakably stamps her for what she is.

"Well?" inquires Mr. Trackem in an impatient voice, as she comes in. "How you dawdle, Victoire! Were they there?"

"Yes," she replies at once. "I saw the duke, and a strange gentleman, and the girl Maggie, all go into the house."

"Did you follow and hear what Eric said?" again asks Mr. Trackem. He never stops the work upon which he is engaged, in spite of his anxiety to hear what she has to say.

"How could I?" she answers peevishly. "I'm not a fairy who can become invisible at will. I saw them go in, that's all, and then I hurried back here."

"Curse him!" is all Mr. Trackem vouchsafes in reply, but he works away harder than ever.

Hanging over the back of a chair close to his table is a great-coat, and on the seat lies a pot hat, pair of gloves, and walking-stick. On the ground below the chair stands a small black business bag. Into this bag

Mr. Trackem ever and anon commits a paper from out the heap that he is destroying.

There is a long pause. Then Victoire speaks.

"What are you going to do? I suppose you won't be safe here now?" she inquires.

"Safe!" he laughs angrily, "rather not. I suppose they'll have the bloodhounds on me before an hour's out. No, Victoire, I must cut it."

"And what's to become of me?" she asks, somewhat aghast. "You'll leave me some money, Trackem, and let me know where you are going to?"

"Money! I've deuced little left of that now; and as for telling you where I'm going to, I'm not such a fool. Why, you'd blurt it out any moment," and Mr. Trackem laughs sneeringly.

"But what's to become of me?" she again inquires.

"Damned if I know!" he replies impatiently. "I don't suppose you'll have much trouble in making a living along with someone else, same way as you've made it here. You don't suppose I can saddle myself with you now, and drag you about wherever I go? What a fool you are, Victoire!"

"Then you are going to throw me up?" she asks in a low voice.

"Haven't I told you I can't drag you about all over the place?" he answers savagely.

"But you'll leave me a little money, won't you?" she says, with a half sob. "I haven't got a farthing, Trackem."

"Then you must go and make it, my girl," he replies coarsely. "You'll have no difficulty in doing that, and I've no money to give you. You know perfectly well that I've nigh ruined myself with lending all the money that I did to that Lord Westray, and now he's dead I can't get it back. Curse him! I wish I'd never seen him, or had anything to do with that Mrs. de Lara and her daughter. They've beat us fair and square, Victoire, even though the daughter be dead. Fair and square."

"I hate them both," she bursts out with unreasoning fury. "They are the cause of my misery now. Oh, Trackem! don't forsake me. I might have had a comfortable, respectable home with Charles, but I threw it up to be with you. What did I do it for but because I loved you? I'm a bad one, no doubt; but at least I loved you, and do love you still. Don't forsake me! I'll stop here and put the trackers off the scent, and do all I know how to help you, only promise me you'll let me know where you are by-and-by, and let me join you again."

A brilliant thought strikes Mr. Trackem. He has not the slightest intention of doing as she asks, but it will be just as well, he thinks, to lead her to believe that he will. And meantime she may be useful in assisting his escape.

"Well, Victoire," he says in a more conciliatory voice, "you're a good girl and a faithful one. Look here, here's five pounds, and I'll send you more soon. Stay here as long as you can, and keep the bloodhounds at bay. If the staff get uneasy, you can hoodwink them. When you change your address put it in the *Times*. And now, my girl, give us a kiss. I must be off. Every moment makes it more risky."

He has finished burning his compromising papers, has taken up his hat, stick, and gloves, thrown his coat over one arm, and picked up the business bag. He is quite ready to go.

She throws her arms round his neck. Fallen, degraded, wicked as is Victoire Hester, yet she loves this vile, scheming, and contemptible wretch, for whose sake she has steeped her soul in the inky dye of sin, and turned from the path of honour and of truth.

"There now, there now, that's enough, old girl," he says hastily, and as she unclasps her hands from about his neck, he steps quickly towards the door and opens it.

"Remember, Victoire, you baulk the trackers," he says significantly, and then he passes out from her presence, and is gone.

She hears the front door open and shut again, and springs to the window. She can just catch sight of him as he passes along the Crescent. It is her last glimpse, and in spite of his promise to the contrary, she feels that it is. But Victoire Hester for the moment forgets herself. In the presence of the danger which threatens the man she loves, she becomes calm. All trace of his hasty departure must be quickly obliterated. She feels that this is imperatively necessary. Quickly she sets to work, tidies up his table, sets the room neat, and with her own hands collects the burnt paper and carries it off. Then she opens the windows to let out the smell which the burning paper has emitted, heaps more coals on the fire, and moves into Mr. Trackem's bedroom to arrange his things. In less than an hour all is ship-shape and tidy as usual. There is not a sign of hasty departure.

A few hours later there comes a ring at the front door. Victoire has given instructions that she will see anyone that calls. She has often before undertaken this duty in Mr. Trackem's absence, and the servant sees nothing strange in the order. He therefore admits the new-comers, and shows them into Mr. Trackem's business room. These two new-comers are men. They are dressed in dark clothes, and they both seat themselves to await his coming.

"Run him in pretty sharp, eh?" observes one of them with, a smile, as the door closes on the servant.

"Haven't got him yet, Bush," retorts the other quietly. Inspector Truffle is not of so sanguine a temperament as is Inspector Bush.

"As good as though," replies Inspector Bush confidently, but he stops abruptly as he hears steps approaching. Again the door of Mr. Trackem's business room opens. Victoire enters. There is blank disappointment on Inspector Bush's face. Victoire sees it as she fixes her dark eyes full upon him.

"Good-afternoon, gentlemen," she says, quietly; "you wished to see Mr. Trackem? I am sorry to say he is away, but I expect him back the day after tomorrow. His head clerk is ill too, but I can do anything for you in Mr. Trackem's place. I always attend to his affairs in his absence."

She smiles good-naturedly on the blank, nonplussed detectives. She seems to give her attention especially to Inspector Bush. Inspector Truffle rises to the occasion.

"Thank you, madam," he says briskly, "but I fear the business we have come about can only be transacted with Mr. Trackem. The fact is, madam, we came to settle an account that we owe him, and which would require Mr. Trackem's signature to be of any use as a receipt. And the worst of it is, we are going away, and shall not be able to call again."

He fixes a piercing glance upon her as he speaks, but Victoire is equal to the occasion. She does not believe a word of Inspector Truffle's statement, and divines perfectly well what his business is.

She assumes a disappointed air as she exclaims,

"It is a great pity. But what is to be done? I do not think I can possibly get Mr. Trackem back before the day after tomorrow. However, I will telegraph to him, and will send you his reply. Will you favour me with your address?"

Here is a poser. Victoire sees it, and inwardly chuckles. But again Inspector Truffle attempts to uphold the fair fame of detective smartness.

"Certainly, madam," he replies, as he takes out his card-case and hands her a card therefrom, upon which she reads the address of a well-known firm of solicitors.

She assumes a most deferential manner.

"I think Mr. Trackem will make every effort to be here by tomorrow.

I will telegraph at once, and unless you hear to the contrary, will you kindly call on Mr. Trackem at the same hour tomorrow, if you please, gentlemen?"

Mr. Truffle is triumphant.

"We will," he answers. "Well, thank you, madam. Good-afternoon to you."

"Good-afternoon, gentlemen," she replies with admirably feigned regret ringing in her voice.

Inspectors Truffle and Bush betake themselves to the comfortable hansom that awaits them. As it rattles along, the former breaks silence.

"We managed that capitally," he says with a chuckle. "Quite took her in. The chink of money soon made her open her ears. Bet you it brings Mr. Trackem home pretty quick."

"Yes," answers Inspector Bush. "I didn't like the look of the woman when she first came in, but she took the bait readily enough. Poor things, those sort of women. No match for the likes of us, eh?"

Inspector Truffle has had more experience than Inspector Bush, and doesn't agree there. But he thinks, as he drives along, that anyhow *this one* is quite taken in.

Is she, though? You'll find out your mistake, inspector, when you call tomorrow with Inspector Bush *at the same hour!*

VII

The lights are low and softly subdued in Evie Ravensdale's private study or sanctum in Montragee House, the blinds and curtains are drawn, the fire casts its flickering shadows on the ceiling and walls as ever and anon the little gas-jets from the coals shoot forth their vivid blaze, relapsing immediately after into smoke and gloom. The sounds of mimic warfare which they produce are the only ones which break the stillness prevailing, unless it be the low breathing of the dog Nero, which is stretched upon the hearthrug.

He would hardly, however, lie there so quietly and contentedly, if he were the only occupant of the room, for a dog's chief characteristic is love of company, loneliness being his pet aversion.

Nor is he alone, as we shall see if we glance at the big armchair drawn up in front of the fire, and looking again, perceive that it is occupied.

The figure which sits there, is in truth very still and silent. It is laying back with its knees crossed and its arms resting on each side of the chair. Its head is slightly bent forward, and its dreamy eyes glitter in the firelight, which they are roving as if in search of an object prized but lost.

What does Evie Ravensdale see in that flickering firelight which appears suddenly to arrest his gaze? It must be some cherished object indeed, judging by the happy smile which for a few brief moments lights up the otherwise sad face, on which melancholy has stamped its mournful features. That which he sees is but a passing vision however, for the smile quickly dies away, and leaves the dark eyes searching again amidst the glowing coals, for the picture that has come and vanished. Above the fireplace, shrouded on either side by heavy curtains of old-gold plush, hangs the oil painting which represents his first meeting with Hector D'Estrange. It is only when alone that Evie Ravensdale draws those curtains aside, and then none can see the emotion which the picture arouses in him. For the memories which it awakens, albeit noble and tender, are painful, recalling, as they do, the image of her whom in life he has most cherished and now lost.

He is sitting there alone, but his mind is busy and his brain hard at work. The sudden revulsion of feeling throughout the country, aroused by the discovery of the drowned body of Lord Westray and the tragic fate of Gloria de Lara, coupled with the published declarations of Léonie

LADY FLORENCE DIXIE

Stanley, and later on the startling dying depositions of Eric Fortescue, have all combined to create this reaction in favour of the D'Estrangeite party. The Devonsmere Government, weak in composition and intellect, at once succumbed, and Lord Pandulph Chertsey, the free lance of the National party, stepped into the Duke of Devonsmere's shoes. But Lord Pandulph was too clever and practical to attempt to govern the fiery steed of public opinion with mimic reins of power. He appealed to that tribunal which alone has the right to nominate its rulers, the people, and demanded of the country its mandate. And now the country, without demur or hesitation, has spoken out in no uncertain tone. The light of a pure and noble life has penetrated the darkness of opposition and prejudice, and has fulfilled the prophecy which in childhood Gloria de Lara predicted. The cause of right and justice has triumphed, and the reign of selfishness, greed, and monopoly has passed away.

By a glorious majority D'Estrangeism has won. The Progressists are nowhere, and the Nationals have been returned mutilated in numbers. The D'Estrangeites, recruited by sixty additional seats, declare the country's will, and Evie Ravensdale, at the command of his sovereign, has formed a Ministry, known under the name of the Second D'Estrangeite Cabinet.

These changes have been rapid. Little more than a month has passed away since the death of Gloria de Lara resounded through the world, and already the vision which her childhood's genius conjured up as she spoke to the waves of the blue Adriatic, and predicted victory, is on the eve of realisation. For even as it had been her first act of power to bring in a bill for the complete emancipation of women, so is it Evie Ravensdale's intention to do likewise.

But the position is different. When Hector D'Estrange submitted his bill to the Commons, he knew that for many reasons it was doomed, the first and foremost being that the country had not spoken, or pronounced unmistakably for or against the change. On this occasion there can be no misunderstanding however, for the Parliament returned gives the D'Estrangeites a majority over the other parties in the House combined, and in plain words declares the will of the people. But there is just this difference again. Whereas the first bill was introduced to the Commons, the second, in virtue of Evie Ravensdale's rank, must make its *début* in the Lords. Will this latter assembly accept it? It remains to be seen. Yet surely in the face of the country's mandate, the peers will submit to the people's wishes!

No wonder then that the brain of the young Premier is busy and hard at work. In three hours from now, he will be submitting the bill to his peers, and appealing to them in the name of justice and right, in the name of fairness and honesty, in the name of the great dead, to breathe upon it the breath of life. Surely the victory which the child Gloria foretold, which the young genius foresaw, is now at length to be won. Ah! surely yes.

"My darling," he whispers softly, as the vision, which for a few brief moments has shone in the gleaming coals, passes away in the changing light thereof, "my darling, would to God that you were here, would to God that I had the counsel of your clear brain, the courage of your strong heart to support me! Yet hear me, Gloria, and help me to keep my vow. Have I not sworn to dedicate my life to the great work which your noble genius conceived and sought to accomplish? And with God's help I will be the faithful servant of your great cause. So help me God!"

He rises as he speaks, and fixes his gaze on the painting above him. It almost seems to him as though the figure of Hector D'Estrange portrayed therein, stands there in living life. He can hardly realise, as he looks at the beautiful face, that the spirit which made Gloria so noble in life, does not animate it now. In the subdued light and the flickering gleam of the fire, the features look living and real; to Evie Ravensdale they bring high resolves and noble inspirations, which only the influence of that which is great and lofty, can awaken.

Estcourt is late in the House, too late to hear the whole of the Premier's speech; he has been delayed by business of pressing moment. About five o'clock in the afternoon, a telegram had been put into his bands, the contents of which had dazed and struck him well-nigh speechless. He could not summon courage to credit its contents. Recovering however, from his surprise, his first impulse had been to seek his chief and lay the telegram before him. Second thoughts had decided him, however, on not doing so, and he had elected instead to send off a long telegram himself. This telegram bore reference entirely to the one which he had received, and was addressed to a friend in South America. During the remainder of the day Estcourt has been anxiously and feverishly awaiting the reply. So important does be regard this reply, that he continues to await it, and in the House of Lords, crowded by every active member belonging to it, he alone is absent. It is natural, therefore, that his absence should have caused both surprise and comment, especially as he is a prominent member of the Second D'Estrangeite Ministry.

He has come in now, however, and his colleagues eye him curiously. They cannot help noticing the suppressed look of excitement in his face, and the eager, restless expression in his eyes. Estcourt's ordinary manner is so quiet and calm that these unusual symptoms are all the more noticeable and surprising. But the duke is still speaking; attention is soon again riveted on what he is saying, and Estcourt is enabled, at any rate, to hear the latter part of a speech whose persuasive eloquence and oratorical power, amaze the House, Evie Ravensdale never before having been regarded but as a common-place speaker, and orator of mediocre talent.

"On this solemn occasion," he is saying as Estcourt comes in, "I beseech of your lordships to cast aside the cloak of old prejudices and selfish monopoly, and obey the unmistakable will of the country, which has appointed a House of Commons pledged to carry this great act of human justice and reparation. I appeal to you to show on this occasion a true courage worthy of men, and abolish forever from the Statute Book those disabilities under which women are deprived of rights to which they are entitled by reason of their common humanity with man. The stale arguments of past days can no longer be advanced in opposition to this bill. The false and brutal pretexts which formerly were adopted to reason away the human rights of women, can no longer be resorted to. Woman has triumphantly established the fact that her mental capacities are equal to man's—ay, and her physical powers of strength and endurance as well, where she has been given fair chances and fair play. There remains but one argument against the removal of her disabilities and the triumphant assertion of the principles of this bill; that one argument is selfishness. Men are unwilling, in many instances, to allow women whom they have held in subjection so long, to assume a position of equality with themselves. These men object to remove the halo with which they have self-crowned themselves; they object, in fact, to share with women the good things of this earth. There is but one definition of this attitude of opposition, and that is selfishness, my lords, pure and unadulterated selfishness. But the time has come when this selfishness is too glaring and apparent to pass from sight, when it must be faced, fought with, and conquered. On its defeat depends—not the welfare of man only, put the welfare and advance of the world. We have sought to rule against the laws of Nature too long, we have sought, by artificial means, to keep the world going, and we have failed. What has the rule of man accomplished? The vain gratification of a few, the misery of millions and hundreds of millions. War has been invented to glorify men, to uphold dynasties loathed, in many instances, by the people; vice and immorality rage for the gratification of the ruler man; philanthropy exists to patch up the sores and abscesses brought about in Society by his excesses; the starving, the criminal, and the miserable, are supported by taxes wrung from the people. Religion spreads abroad its thousands of arms, each one asserting its sole right to be, but the fact remains: war is spreading, crime increasing, immorality assuming giant proportions, misery, disease, and wrongdoing growing mightier day by day, while the forces that could and would stay these horrors, still wear the badge of slavery.

"I appeal to your lordships to face these facts, and act upon them generously and courageously. From our midst a great and commanding figure has but lately passed away,—one who began in childhood an heroic and courageous resistance to wrong, and who maintained that resistance through her all too short career. Gloria de Lara, in the person of Hector D'Estrange, triumphantly established the fact of woman's equality with man, and undeniably asserted the right of her sex to share with him in the government of the world.

"And I ask your lordships to consider in a generous manner the motives which first prompted the great heart of Gloria de Lara to do battle for her sex, and which ultimately strengthened its resolve to maintain the contest to the last. Was it not a dawning comprehension of the terrible wrong under which her mother had become an outcast in this world, shunned and despised by Society at large? Did not Gloria de Lara recognise that in woman's unnatural position lay the root of the evil? Then, as she grew up, and personally made herself acquainted with the woes afflicting Society, did she not struggle to remedy this position, recognising therein the key to human suffering? I bear testimony to her life of patient, unwearying research amidst the suffering and slaving classes. This it was that gave her such a grasp of her subject, when in the House of Commons she sought to unveil to the members thereof the horrors that existed. The dream of her life was, to be spared in order to carry great social measures of reform, but she recognised the fact that to do this effectually, woman must first be placed on the level of equality with man. For this she struggled, for this she fought on against overwhelming odds. I need not dwell on the false and brutal charge which was brought against her, which forced her to disclose her sex, which condemned her to die, and which—when rescued by her own Women Guards—made her an outcast and a wanderer, and a felon in the eyes of the law. The falsity of this detestable lie has been abundantly proved in the discovery of the dead body of the man who ruined and blasted her mother's life, who brought about her own pathetic and irredeemable death. In her name I appeal for justice, and I confidently believe that I shall not appeal in vain. I desire that the division shortly to be taken shall seal the fate of the measure on behalf of victory or defeat. You have the voice of the country ringing in your ears, but high above that voice should sound the loud appeal, which a great and noble example sends forth, the appeal of the glorious dead."

He sits down amidst a storm of applause, unusual in this august and dignified assembly. He hardly hears it; he takes no note of the varied scene around him. Evie Ravensdale sees before him the face of but one being, that being Gloria de Lara. Is not her spirit near encouraging, upholding, and leading him on to victory?

But he is awakened from his dream at the call of duty. The division is being taken at last, and all wait in breathless expectation for the result.

"The Content's have it!" By a majority of 107 the peers obey the country's mandate, and acknowledge the people's will as law. Gloria has triumphed. That which she predicted is realised, the vow which she made is accomplished. Ah! in this moment of victory, who would not wish her here, instead of in the cold arms of death?

Of death? Silence is being called for, and Lord Estcourt is endeavouring to make himself heard. He is successful at last.

"I wish to explain to the House," he begins, "why I was not in my place when my noble friend began his speech. My excuse will be acceptable to this House, I feel sure. The fact is, I received a telegram containing startling intelligence, so startling that I conceived it to be a hoax. I took steps to ascertain the truth, and am satisfied of the authenticity of the first intelligence. I have to announce to your lordships the glorious news that Gloria de Lara is not dead. By God's almighty goodness she is alive—alive to witness the triumph of her cause. Truly indeed you may exclaim with me in accepting this wonderful intelligence, it is God's will—it is the hand of God."

VIII

"Gloria De Lara lives!" The words have rung far and wide o'er land and distant sea. They have entered the homes of the great, the cottages of the poor, they have brought joy to millions of weary hearts, who know that while that great name breathes the breath of life, reform cannot die.

Yes, Gloria lives, lives! But how? Have we not seen her in the clutch of Death?

We left her therein. We left her being borne down by the resistless, sucking whirlpool of the sinking smack as the massive trading steamer, which had cut clean through the frail barque, bore on its course. As she parted her hold of Léonie, Gloria had clutched the sinking wreck with that strong and tenacious grip which the drowning alone can command. The lighter and severed portion of the wreck had been swept forward by an enormous wave, which carried with it likewise the body of Léonie, supported on the crest of the sea by the life-belt, which Gloria had tied around her.

But the bright, flashing light which had danced in Gloria's eyes ere she was borne downwards, had searched from stem to stern the helpless, storm-tossed craft, and the anxious gaze of the man on the look out had been able to detect those two frail human forms. As the shout of "Boat ahoy!" had rung out through the shrieking storm, the steamer had crashed through her frail antagonist in the manner already described. But the skipper of *The Maid of Glad Tidings*, as such the steamer was named, was brave and humane. In spite of the storm he had skilfully brought his vessel to the rescue. The electric light had swept the sea in search of the unlucky boat, and after a time a portion of her had been sighted, a helpless and dismantled wreck. Yet to that wreck a human form was clinging.

A brave crew had manned the lifeboat, and with the true pluck of British seamen, had fought against terrible odds to rescue that one lone, helpless creature. They succeeded; and amidst that black night and howling storm, another deed of heroism had silently written its tale upon the scrolls of British fame. And as Captain Ruglen's gaze had first fallen on the rescued victim of the storm, he had started. He was a big, powerful man, with a tender, kindly heart. When, therefore, he bent over the silent figure and raised it in his arms, bearing it below to his own cabin, his men only saw in this act another evidence of the skipper's kindly disposition. Yet in that brief glance, Gloria de Lara had been recognised; for what devoted adherent of her cause who had ever looked upon her face could forget it? Certes, not Captain Ruglen. A member of Ruglen clan, he was also an out-and-out D'Estrangeite; nor was this the first time that he had been in the company of Hector D'Estrange. But he knew that the once successful and powerful idol of Society was now a hunted and doomed felon, with a large reward out for her apprehension. He knew that many of his crew were not D'Estrangeites, and that it might go hard with him and her if she were recognised. Thus had he borne her to his cabin, determined there to protect and shield her, and carry her to the far-away free shores of the Spanish main, whither *The Maid of Glad Tidings* was bound.

Reaching it, Gloria's first act had been to wire to Speranza de Lara in North America, and to Estcourt in England. As yet she had heard no tidings of the wonderful events which had led up to the triumph of her cause.

But those tidings sped back to her along the electric wire. They came in the shape of a loving message of welcome from the man she loved. From Evie Ravensdale she learnt how victory had crowned her efforts; from him came the tidings of great joy that her vow had been accomplished.

ONCE MORE THE VAST CROWD of London surges in the streets,—a happy, joyous, good-humoured crowd nevertheless. Every house is gay with bunting and flags, and triumphal arches are in every street through which the procession will pass along.

What procession?

Why, is not this the day upon which Gloria de Lara is to reach our shores, and is she not to be welcomed back and publicly honoured in the great Hall of Liberty, where, when last she stood, she was a condemned and hunted felon?

The yacht *Eilean* has gone to meet her. It has joined the *Colossus*, in which Gloria has made her passage from South America at the mouth of the Thames. The party on board the *Eilean* consists solely of Speranza de Lara, Flora Desmond, and her child, a fine girl of seven years, together with Evie Ravensdale, Estcourt, Léonie, and Rita Vernon. All, with the exception of Speranza, wear the white gold-braided uniform of the White Guards' Regiment of the Women Volunteers, an organisation which a Royal Proclamation has called back to life.

The *Colossus* has yielded up its precious charge. As the cutter bears Gloria de Lara away from the great war monster's side towards the white, graceful *Eilean* that awaits her, the cannon belch forth their parting salute and welcome in one breath. There, standing on the deck ready to grasp her hand in a deep and loving tenderness, with heart-felt gratitude for her wonderful deliverance, stand the two beings whom she loves most in the world, Speranza de Lara and Evie Ravensdale. What human words could describe that meeting, for they thought her dead, and behold she is there in living life?

Tilbury Docks are reached; the roar of distant cannon announce her arrival. There she stands on the yacht's bridge with Evie Ravensdale by her side. As the crowd sways to and fro to catch a glimpse of her, the people see that she wears the White Guards' Uniform. The regiment is there to meet and welcome her. As she leaves the yacht, its band strikes up the beautiful march "Triumphant," the same which had welcomed her to the Hall of Liberty, when, as Hector D'Estrange, she had performed the opening ceremony. The milk-white steed which she had ridden on that occasion now awaits her in its trappings of white-and-gold. Never has horse been so groomed and petted as this one.

In sight of the crowd she bids her mother a courteous and tender farewell, for Speranza has elected to drive straight to Montragee House, there to await her child's return. A brilliant mounted throng await the former's coming; many well-known faces are there, amongst which Gloria catches sight of those of Lady Manderton and Launcelot Trevor.

Now she has mounted her milk-white charger Saladin, and with Evie Ravensdale and Nigel Estcourt on her right, and Flora Desmond and Archie Douglasdale on her left, is riding slowly forward. In close attendance behind are Rita Vernon and Léonie Stanley. The latter's eyes are busy in the crowd, and seem to search the ranks forward as they ride along. The brilliant throng of mounted friends close in, the cheering of the crowd is deafening; it will be one long loud roar until the Hall of Liberty is reached.

The way is kept by the Women's Volunteer Regiments, and the order is perfect. As Gloria and Flora ride along, they catch glimpses of old, tried, true, and trusty friends among the ranks—friends who in time of trouble stood by them, and laboured lovingly to make easier the rugged path which they were then treading.

It is a soul-inspiring sight. Many of the people have brought flowers with them, and as the procession approaches they cast them loosely in the air, out of which they descend in a shower of many colours to carpet the way, along which Gloria must pass, with their bright and variegated bloom. The strains of the White Guards' band, the glitter of their white-and-gold uniforms, the loud cheering of the enthusiastic crowds as the brilliant cavalcade moves along, is a sight which the onlooker is not likely to forget. It thrills the hearts of that vast woman world, assembled to do honour to the one who has worked for and who has won their emancipation.

One long triumphal march. One uninterrupted scene of unchecked enthusiasm is the welcome accorded her from the Docks to the Hall of Liberty. The sun is shining on the gilded statues and million panes which crown that wondrous structure, as she approaches the building which her genius conceived and raised,—approaches it, no longer as the hunted felon upon whose head the price of gold is set, but as a free woman, a victorious general who has conquered the demon armies of Monopoly and Selfishness, and thrown open to the people the free gates of happiness and reform. Now through the giant portals she rides once more. Great God! what a burst of welcome, and what a scene! From floor to ceiling the monster building is crammed. Every available space has been occupied; there is not a foot of standing room.

She has uncovered, and they see her face as she rides round the circular ride towards the huge platform,—the same face of exquisite beauty which they remember and know so well. As she dismounts, she is received by the chairman of the committee appointed to carry out the day's proceedings, and to present the people's address of welcome, to which thousands of representative names from every county have been attached.

On the platform are gathered every member of the Ministry and every D'Estrangeite Member of Parliament. Truly a royal welcome by staunch and faithful friends; for as Gloria dismounts and steps upon the platform she is greeted with a loud long cheer by these men of generous mould, who have fought so nobly on behalf of her holy cause. All honour be to them forever!

Sir Arthur Hazlerigg, Lord Mayor of London, presents and reads the address of welcome, and as he concludes it, Gloria de Lara stands forward to reply. An intense silence falls. All are eager to hear again a voice which they had believed to be forever stilled in death.

"My friends," she begins, and though the voice has all the clear, ringing sweetness of yore, there is undoubtedly a tremor in it, "it would require a special language, one of which we have yet no knowledge, to convey to you the emotions which this scene of magnificent welcome awakens within me. From the bottom of my heart I thank you for it, as well as all those true and gallant friends who have created this glorious day; for next to God it is the people who have created it. In this welcome which you give to me, the humble and all too unworthy representative of a magnificent cause, the great principle of human freedom is at length recognised, that freedom inherited at birth, and only wrung from individuals by oppression and wrong. Human freedom means the right to take part in the creation of laws for the better government and perfection of man; it means that man and woman are born equal, are created to work hand in hand for the greater happiness of mankind. Hitherto this principle of mighty truth has not been recognised, with the awful results shown forth in man's ever-increasing degradation. By the acknowledgment of this principle you have laid the train which, when fired, will put an end to immorality and social wrongs, which will make evil unpleasant to perform, and which will degrade the performer to the position of a leper, the shunned and outcast of Society, loathed and despised by his fellow-men. By the acknowledgment of this principle, a day of darkness has sunk to rise no more, and one of brightness, and promise, and fair hope has arisen to cheer us along the glorious path of reform. Much there is to be done, mountains of prejudice, and selfishness, and greed yet to be faced and conquered; but the army which the acknowledgment of human freedom has raised, is an army which will fight victoriously to the end; for it is an army in which men and women will do battle side by side and shoulder to shoulder, undeterred by class jealousies or the odious assumption of superiority by one sex over another. My friends, as I stand today in this Hall of Liberty and look upon this magnificent scene, memories rise up before me of a stirring and eventful past. I see before me now, a picture which in childhood I loved to imagine, a glorious reality which in the past haunted my waking dreams. On many incidents of that past I would prefer not to dwell, arousing, as they must, the bitterness of human nature. Rather is the province of the conqueror, of the victorious to forgive and forget, to look forward to the future, and strive for the possibilities which that future may contain. We are starting along a new path in life, a path open to all, not monopolised by the few, a path which, as time goes on, shall show traces of victory on all sides. I ask the great army of my countrymen to endeavour to win those victories as speedily as possible, so that in the future, the day may dawn when there shall be no misery, no wickedness, no crime. In that army, women now find a place; let them triumphantly prove their right to be there. They have yet an uphill road to climb, but I have confidence that they will compass it, and now that the gates of freedom are thrown open to them, take part in all the great deeds of the world. Upon them the eyes of this world will be fixed; upon them depends the ultimate freedom of the human race. I have no fear as to the result; I do not for one moment dread the trial. I believe, moreover, that the presence and natural companionship of woman will upraise and influence man's character for good, banishing from his daily life those coarser habits which self-indulgence and lack of moral influence have allowed to creep therein, and that Society, in its remodelled state, will thus be enabled to deal with the evils which infest it. My friends, I need detain you no longer. On my arrival in this country I was informed that my old constituency had re-elected me as its member. I rejoice to hear that I have several women fellow-members in the Legislature to whom men, generous and noble-hearted men, have relinquished places. To tell you that the remainder of my life, which God has so mercifully spared to me, will be employed in working for the people, in devoting every energy I possess to their advancement, is the sum of my declaration here today. Rest assured that for them, no one will struggle harder than Gloria de Lara."

A simple speech, a quiet, honest declaration. Though she stands there, the cynosure of all eyes, there is no vanity or conceit in those few simple words. Gloria's aim is unveiled. It is the upraising and triumph of humanity. She lives but to work on its behalf.

She is on the point of stepping back amidst a perfect hurricane of cheers, when Evie Ravensdale comes to her side.

"One moment, Gloria; stay where you are," he whispers. "I have something to say."

He raises his hand to ask for silence, and the people accord it to him.

"My friends," he exclaims, "for with Gloria de Lara may I not call you my friends? I have a pleasing task to perform in that which I am going to say. As Gloria de Lara has told you, the law of this country has at length acknowledged the principle of human freedom, and woman's right to equal man is finally recognised. When the country spoke out so unmistakably on behalf of human freedom, my sovereign bade me assume the reins of power. I accepted them, not unwillingly; for the only object I had in life was to carry out the great reforms which the genius of Gloria de Lara had conceived, and of which she had made me the confident. At that time I believed, with all others, that she was dead. But, my friends, she is alive. And now I tell you that she only has a right to assume the reins confided to me, she alone has the right to carry those great reforms. The person who conceived them alone has that right, and I, her deputy, relinquish it to her. I tell you that Gloria de Lara must be your Prime Minister, while I will take my part as a humble worker with the people. With the full approval of my colleagues and every D'Estrangeite member, I intend forthwith to tender my resignation, and to advise my sovereign to send for Gloria de Lara."

There can be no mistaking the genuine ring of approval in the mighty cheer that bursts forth from the thousands of throats in that densely packed building. Truly the child's heartfelt prayer has been answered in this splendid tribute paid to her unselfish labours, from the days of childhood far into those of womanhood.

IX

Wealth and magnificence rear their forms in and around the precincts of St. Stephen's. They do not, however, monopolise the entire space, for here and there the squalid streets of poverty abide, with all their *wealth* and *magnificence* of suffering, crime, and sin. One of these streets is just across the river, and the clock in the big tower of the Houses of Parliament can peep and peer therein, even from its misty height.

Staring from a dust-begrimed window on the second floor of a dirty-looking dwelling situated in the street named, stands a woman, whose rough, untidy hair is tied back in a knot, and whose coarse, seared features show signs of former enamelling, now disused. Poor wretch! there is hunger and misery in her eyes, and despair as well. Some would say insanity gleams there.

She is listening to the cannons' roar as they belch forth their welcome to Gloria de Lara. Their booming sound is maddening to the hungry, lonely, despairing woman, who stands there with not a friend in the world.

Yes, he has forsaken her, got away scot-free himself, but left her to wait for and look for him in vain. Victoire Hester has parted with her jewellery and tawdry finery for a mere song, the five-pound note which Mr. Trackem gave her is expended, and she has not a farthing left in the world. Tomorrow she must find three shillings for the rent of her miserable, unhealthy room, and she has not got it, nor has a morsel of food touched her lips this day. She is broken-hearted. Worse than that, she is jealous, angry, bitter. It maddens her to think of Gloria at the pinnacle of success, and she who sought to assist in her ruin, at the bottom of the abyss of abject misery.

What is left to her in the world? Nothing. Her character is gone. She cannot find work, and if she could, she would not undertake it. She has no heart to do anything, for in her coarse, hard way, she loved Trackem, loved him only to lose him.

"Whose fault but hers?" she mutters angrily as the cannon boom once more. "Why should she be happy, while I die here like a dog? Not that I want to live, I mean to die; but she sha'n't live to be happy, that she sha'n't! I'll send her first, and then I'll go myself. Ha, ha!"

Surely insanity rings in that voice. Poor Victoire! You do not know how lovingly Gloria would forgive you, if she only knew the state you were in, how eagerly she would seek to raise you from that fallen state, and set you on the straight path once more. But all this you do not know.

She goes over to a tumble-down-looking chest of drawers that has seen better days, and pulls open one of the drawers. Out of this she takes a six-chambered bull-dog revolver, examines it carefully, and slips it into her pocket. It used to belong to Mr. Trackem, and she had brought it away with her when she left the house in Verdegrease Crescent, a few hours after the departure of Inspectors Truffle and Bush. She has kept it by her,—it is about the only thing she has not parted with,—vaguely feeling that it may be useful, if Mr. Trackem does not answer her piteous appeals in the agony columns of the *Times;* for Victoire Hester has determined to put an end to herself now that he has forsaken her. The rich and well clothed may condemn her, but who could, who diving into the arid desert of that lonely, hopeless heart, beheld the mortal wound inflicted by despair?

The revolver safe, she next unearths an old woollen shawl, which she flings over her head and pins under her chin. Then she is ready, and she gropes her way down the dark staircase into the street.

She is hungry, weary, and weak, but she walks briskly along, looking straight ahead of her. People are hurrying across Westminster Bridge eager to get a good place in the line along which Gloria de Lara will pass on her way from the Hall of Liberty to Montragee House. Victoire Hester is intent on securing a good place too.

And she is successful. She takes her stand in Whitehall, not a stone's throw from the Duke of Ravensdale's mansion. She will have a long time to wait, but she steels herself to endure it.

Denser and denser grows the throng, but Victoire Hester, though pushed and hustled about, nevertheless maintains her position in the front rank. She feels she must hold that at any cost; it is necessary for her purpose. There is a tremor in the crowd, as if an electric current had passed through it. Now the boom of cannon resounds once more. These warning-notes tell the people that the ceremony is over in the Hall of Liberty, and that Gloria de Lara is leaving it for Montragee House.

A hum runs along the serried walls of human forms; the electric current is apparently again at work. From afar strains of martial music come floating to the people's ears, arousing them to the pitch of expectancy and excitement. There is a dull continuous roar too; it never seems to cease, as it rises and falls like the waves of a turbulent sea, breaking upon the wild shores of a rock-bound coast. Yet as it comes nearer, the roar assumes a human sound; it is that of thousands and tens of thousands of voices cheering lustily. Victoire Hester's trembling hand gropes in her pocket for the revolver. She knows now that Gloria de Lara is approaching, and that the moment which will close her own life is at hand. Yes, surely insanity is writ in those eyes as they stare hungrily forward. How terribly they gleam!

No one notices her, however. Every eye is bent upon the approaching procession. There comes the band of the White Guards,—how soul-stirring its music!—and there, too, is the milk-white charger Saladin, with arching neck and proud carriage; for does he not bear a precious charge indeed, in the person of Gloria de Lara?

The sun gleams down upon her gilded helmet, and lights with a living blaze the gold braiding upon her uniform. How beautiful she looks as she rides along with the glance of eager thousands upon her! How she loves the people! How they return that love! Surely none in that wildly enthusiastic crowd would seek to harm her?

Yes, *one* would though, and we know who. The madness in Victoire Hester's brain is increased by the scene before her. More than ever she questions the right of this woman to be happy, to be the idol of thousands, whilst she is doomed to be friendless and miserable.

Will no one stay her hand? Will no one arrest and strike down the engine of death which she is steadily raising and bringing to bear full on Gloria's breast? Ah! can no one in this moment of wild excitement see the danger that threatens the idol of the people? See! Victoire's finger is on the trigger! God! can no one see and stay it?

Yes, one can see it, though she cannot stay it—one whose glance has faithfully swept the crowd ahead of Gloria all the way along. Only a pair of dark grey faithful eyes, with a wondrous wealth of lashes shading their intelligent depths, only a girl in years, yet with the light of genius stamped on the beautiful forehead above them. She sees and recognises Victoire Hester in spite of her changed aspect and the mad look in her eyes. Léonie Stanley sees the revolver raised and the assassin's finger on the trigger. Deep into her horse's flanks she drives her spurs. He springs furiously forward, brushes roughly against Saladin and his rider, and covers like a shield the person of Gloria de Lara.

Only just in time though! The revolver's note rings forth, speeding from its lips the messenger of death; yet another note, and it claims two victims for its own. One is a wild, pale, haggard woman stretched out upon the street, from whose temple blood is flowing, the other a young officer of the White Guards' Regiment, who has fallen forward on the grey neck of her horse, and whose blood is staining his dappled well-groomed coat. Dear little Léonie, she has not lived in vain; she has proved her love and gratitude at last; she has shown how ill-fitting was the cloak of Judas, in which the wicked had striven to clothe her. She has lived to prove her gratitude, and is faithful unto death.

X

1999. It is a lovely scene on which that balloon looks down,—a scene of peaceful villages and well-tilled fields, a scene of busy towns and happy working people, a scene of peace and prosperity, comfort and contentment, which only a righteous Government could produce and maintain.

The balloon is passing over London, a London vastly changed from the London of 1900. Somehow it wears a countrified aspect, for every street has its double row of shady trees, and gardens and parks abound at every turn. This London, unlike its predecessor, is not smoke-begrimed, nor can it boast of dirty courts and filthy alleys like the London of 1900. Every house, great and small, bears the aspect of cleanliness and comfort, for poverty and misery are things no longer known.

A stranger in the balloon looks down with interest upon this scene. His gaze, wandering across the mighty city, is arrested by two gleaming gilded statues crowning a monster edifice, upon whose cap of glittering panes the sun is shining brightly.

"Is that the Hall of Liberty?" he inquires of his guide.

"Yes," answers the person addressed, "the same as was raised a century ago by the great Duchess of Ravensdale, of noble memory."

"Is she buried there?" asks the stranger dreamily.

"Buried there! Ah, no!" replies the man almost indignantly. "I thought all the world knew where Gloria of Ravensdale sleeps. There is a beautiful grave overlooking the Atlantic Ocean, on the shores of Glennig Bay. It is there where Gloria sleeps, by the side of her husband Evelyn, the good Duke of Ravensdale. It was her wish, and her wish with the nation was law. Every year the grave is resorted to by thousands, who lay upon it their tributes of lovely flowers."

"Is anyone else buried there?" again the stranger asks.

"Yes, sir, a great woman. Lady Flora Desmond. She survived Gloria of Ravensdale for many years, and carried on her noble works of reform. She was Prime Minister for twenty years, and her last request was to be buried at the feet of the Duke and Duchess of Ravensdale."

"The Ravensdales owned immense wealth, and parted with it all, so history says," murmurs the stranger.

"Ay, sir, they gave it all to the poor. At least, they spent it on the poor, and by their noble example induced others to do likewise," answers the man. "There is no poverty in this country now, sir. As we pass across it you will see evidence of peace and contentment, and plenty everywhere. We owe it all to the glorious reforms of Gloria of Ravensdale."

"That is a very lovely garden not far from Westminster Bridge which you lately pointed out to me," continued the stranger. "What a glorious wealth of flowers!"

"Ah! that sir is where Léonie Stanley saved Gloria de Lara from assassination by a maniac. But she lost her life in doing so. She was accorded a public funeral, and by the wish of the nation buried where she fell. The garden was laid out afterwards. It is the nation's pride to keep it beautiful. Léonie's heroic deed will forever live in the hearts of a grateful people."

"And where is the great Lord Estcourt buried?"

"In the National Burial Ground, where only those whom the nation loves to honour are laid."

"Yonder splendid building is the Imperial Parliament, is it not?" pursues the stranger.

"Yes, sir. That is where the representatives of our Federated Empire watch over its welfare. To Gloria of Ravensdale we owe the triumph of Imperial Federation. She lived long enough to see England, Ireland, Scotland, and Wales peacefully attending to their private affairs in their Local Parliaments, while sending delegates to represent them in the Imperial Assembly. Ah, sir! that Imperial Assembly is a wonderful sight. Therein we see gathered together representative men and women from all parts of our glorious Empire, working hand in hand to spread its influence amongst the nations of the world, with all of whom we are at peace."

The balloon is rapidly drifting northwards. As the shades of evening begin to creep on apace it moves along Scotland's western coasts. The aeronaut in charge of it guides it above the graves of Evie and Gloria Ravensdale, and Lady Flora Desmond. As the sun goes down across the western sea, it bathes, with a farewell flood of glory, the last resting-place on this earth of the great dead. The balloon descends, guided by a skilful hand. It soon reaches the ground, and in a short time the stranger stands by these graves. Three simple marble hearts lie above them, on which are engraved in golden letters the names of those who sleep below. And at the head of the graves a marble cross is standing with a few simple words thereon. The stranger goes over to the cross, and reads:—

Sacred to the Memory of
GLORIA DE LARA, DUCHESS OF RAVENSDALE,
The mighty Champion of Women's Freedom
and the Saviour of her People.
As also to that of Evelyn, the good Duke of Ravensdale,
and the beloved and revered Lady Flora Desmond.
Their names are engraved in the hearts of millions now and for
all time. Amen.

Surely Gloria Lad triumphed? What greater reward did she hope
for than the welfare and love of the people?

Maremna's Dream

*A soft wind sweeps across Maremna's form, She starts, and springs
from off her heath'ry couch.
It was a dream, and yet not all a dream;
For scenes which in her wand'rings she's beheld
Have throng'd that vision. She has seen again
That which has cross'd her in the paths of men,
That which has taught her life's reality.
Yet deep within, Maremna's soul is stirr'd
By that bright vision of a fight well won,
A gleam of hope that yet these things shall be,
That freedom shall not ever droop and pine,
But strike a blow for glorious liberty.
A waking vision to Maremna's soul,
Yet none the less inspiring, for the gleam
Which first awoke within her mightier half
Has glow'd and burnt into a fervent flame,
Which none but God can ever extinguish.
A blood-red sunset!
Bathed in its glow Maremna stands alone.
Alone where oft in childhood she has play'd.
The vision is before her bright and clear—
Lo! it awakes her from a living trance,
Bids her arise and buckle on her mail.
Far off she hears the busy din of war,
And knows that duty calls her to the fray.*

In that brief hour Maremna's vow is made.
Low sinks the sun, and gloom o'erspreads the earth,
As down the rugged mountain side she wends
Her way. Maremna's high resolve is ta'en—
Faithful till Death to be, unto her vow.

The End

A Note About the Author

Lady Florence Dixie (1855–1905) was a Scottish feminist, novelist, and war correspondent. Born in Dumfries, Scotland, she was the daughter of Archibald Douglas, Marquess of Queensberry, and his wife Caroline Margaret Clayton. As a girl, Florence was inseparable from her twin brother James and spent much of her youth swimming, hunting, and riding with her brothers. Following their father's death from a possible suicide in 1858, the family moved to France with Caroline in the midst of a custody dispute with the Douglas family. Several years later, having retained custody of her children, Caroline returned to England, where Florence was first educated at home by a governess and then at a convent school. Soon, tragedy struck once more—having completed the first ascent of the Matterhorn, her older brother Francis fell to his death while descending, leaving the family distraught and causing sensational headlines in newspapers around the globe. In 1875, Florence married Sir Alexander Beaumont Churchill Dixie, with whom she would raise two sons. Two years later, she published her first novel, *Abel Avenged: a Dramatic Tragedy* (1877), launching a career in literature. Important early works include *Across Patagonia* (1880), a travel narrative, and *In the Land of Misfortune* (1882), the result of her work as a correspondent during the First Boer and Anglo-Zulu Wars. In 1890, Dixie published her utopian novel *Gloriana; Or, the Revolution of 1900*, the culmination of a lifetime devoted to feminist ideals.

A Note from the Publisher

Spanning many genres, from non-fiction essays to literature classics to children's books and lyric poetry, Mint Edition books showcase the master works of our time in a modern new package. The text is freshly typeset, is clean and easy to read, and features a new note about the author in each volume. Many books also include exclusive new introductory material. Every book boasts a striking new cover, which makes it as appropriate for collecting as it is for gift giving. Mint Edition books are only printed when a reader orders them, so natural resources are not wasted. We're proud that our books are never manufactured in excess and exist only in the exact quantity they need to be read and enjoyed.

bookfinity™

Discover more of your favorite classics with Bookfinity™.

- Track your reading with custom book lists.
- Get great book recommendations for your personalized Reader Type.
- Add reviews for your favorite books.
- AND MUCH MORE!

Visit **bookfinity.com** and take the fun Reader Type quiz to get started.

Enjoy our classic and modern companion pairings!

Printed in the USA
CPSIA information can be obtained
at www.ICGtesting.com
JSHW022330140824
68134JS00019B/1402

9 781513 299921